G000155358

Tofu Landing

02974065

Tofu Landing

EVAN MALONEY

QUARTET BOOKS

First published in 2010 by
Quartet Books Limited
A member of the Namara Group
27 Goodge Street, London WIT 2LD

Copyright © Evan Maloney 2010

The right of Evan Maloney to be identified
as the author of this work has been asserted
by him in accordance with the
Copyright, Designs and Patents Act, 1988

All rights reserved.
No part of this book may be reproduced in
any form or by any means without prior
written permission from the publisher

A catalogue record for this book
is available from the British Library

ISBN 978 0 7043 7164 4

Typeset by Antony Gray
Printed and bound in Great Britain by
T J International Ltd, Padstow, Cornwall

BRIGHTON & HOVE COUNCIL	
Bertrams	05/03/2010
	£10.00
BM	01000908

For Mum, Dad and James

Acknowledgements

Thanks to my wife Eliza and both our families for their continued support. Also to the Wardlaw and Moriarty families, and to the many people who have read my work and supported me as a writer for many years: Hugh Martin, Emma Franz, Ian McLean, Caspar Deman, Karen Mann, Sarah Lewis, Cameron Hayes, Katie Beale, Jenny Evans, Lucy Baker, Sara Niner, Mark Slattery, Gary Hall, Kath Black, Ivan Hanna, Ivor Indyk, Simon Black, Emelia Hanbury, Juliet Francis, Yumiko Tanaka, Edward Porembny, Chris Kennett, Luke Vaughan, David Higgins, Ainsley, Jo, Pat, Margaret, Mark, all my Buddhist friends. To Annette Fraser for her proof-reading, Miguel Gaudencio for his photography and friendship, to Chimene, David and Naim at Quartet, to my former SIS students for their patience, and finally, to all the 'Splatters'.

‘I have done that,’ says my memory. ‘I cannot have done that’ – says my pride, and remains adamant. At last – memory yields.

NIETZSCHE

1

Declan was unconvinced but he went to the place in Turin Street to meet Bridget the next day. The building was a former council block, eighteen storeys of brick the colour of dark chocolate. It loomed above the surrounding low-rise apartments and terraced houses like a redwood trunk in a field of stinkweed. The elevator smelt like a cesspool, and Declan tried to hold his breath as he ascended to the seventeenth floor.

'What do you think of the Chocolate Block?' Bridget asked when she opened the front door to her apartment. 'It's cool, huh? Total retro experience.' She was wearing tight black and white striped leggings with a fur-lined jacket, and the composite effect made her look like the love child of a zebra and a fox. Her brown hair was dyed bottle blonde and pulled back from her face in a savage looking ponytail. She was not extravagantly beautiful, but she exuded a dynamic sexual energy that immediately prompted an image in Declan's mind of the two of them having sex on the sofa. He could feel Bridget's long fingernails tearing into his back as she screamed like a horror-movie extra about to die.

The first thing Vivian showed Declan was the view over the city from the balcony on the top floor. Declan could not remember the last time he had seen a decent London horizon. In London the skyline was usually just a strip of grey directly above the streets.

'This floor is called Heaven,' Bridget said. 'The bottom floor, where your bedroom is, we call that Purgatory.'

How wildly imaginative, Declan thought.

They walked back down the stairs to the kitchen and Bridget finished preparing a dinner of stuffed roast aubergines filled with basil and ricotta, followed by steamed sultana and treacle pudding. She showed Declan one of the wines she had bought to go with the meal.

'What do you think? Pinot Grigio goes with ricotta, no?'

'I've got no idea,' Declan answered. 'What's the occasion?'

'Dinner. I can't stand plain food, and I'm the only person in this flat who can be bothered to cook properly. Can you cook?'

'I do a pretty good coconut-milk curry.'

Bridget smiled approvingly, put the aubergines in the oven and took Declan into the living room, which extended from the kitchen. It was one of those desultory living spaces characteristic of London share accommodation. The sofa was orange, the wall paint was green, and a yellow bookshelf stood in one corner of the room. On one side of the sofa lay several table-height piles of magazines; mostly female celebrity fashion fare like *Marie Claire*, *Elle*, and *Vogue*, as well as art and music magazines. The bookshelves were littered with old receipts, underground tickets, and prescription-drug packets. On the wall hung a large Rothko print, a Pamela Anderson Baywatch-era poster, and another poster of the Rods lead singer Tristan Russell sweating under stage lights during some Hade's basement gig.

'So, what do you do, Declan?' Bridget asked. It was the generic opener to London conversation, and Declan tried to deflect the question.

'Nice Rothko,' he remarked. He saw Bridget's green eyes shine with instant respect which, like instant coffee, was never as good as the real thing. 'When you look at his paintings, it's hard to believe the guy slashed his wrists,' he continued.

Bridget was genuinely surprised. 'Rothko killed himself?'

'I think the paintings were meant to hide the suffering. The illusion fooled everyone, didn't it?'

'They're so peaceful, so tranquil,' Bridget allowed herself a moment of introspection and then smiled perkily. 'Kate tells me you have brain damage?'

Declan coughed surprise. 'Oh, yes, but … it's mostly grown over now, like an … um … an ancient tomb.'

'What happened?'

'I got … it was … four years ago.'

Bridget looked like she wanted to chisel her way into Declan's cerebral cortex with an ice-pick.

'And you write film reviews, *apparently*?'

'Yeah. Just landed in it recently, actually, friend of a friend working for *Metro* offered me the job.'

Bridget did not seem to know what he was talking about.

'*Metro*, you know it. The free paper you get on the Underground stations?'

'Urgh, I don't do the tube. Do you not find it hard to write with the, you know, the brain thing?'

'My cerebellum was permanently damaged. It affects balance and coordination.'

'Oh.' Bridget nudged Declan with a wink, 'You don't look like a Spaz. Kate said your *emotions* were affected, or something?'

'Kate didn't know me before.'

'But your emotions *were* affected?'

'Maybe. I don't think about it.'

Declan did think about it. All the time. As a young man he had been a turgid, boiling mass of passion and ambition. After the brain injury he lost his direction, his intellect was intact but he no longer felt much passion for his life. Most mornings he struggled with the simple ambition of getting out of bed. The doctors had told him this was not unusual.

'I lose my balance and slur my words,' Declan said, 'when I'm tired, or when I'm drunk.'

Bridget grunted. 'Don't worry, we're all emotionally retarded here.'

'And I … um … I can't read books like I used to. I can't paint any more either; my arm gets tired.'

'You used to be an artist?'

'In my twenties, yeah, kind of, but I … I had to give it up.'

'Hmm. How long have you been in living in London?'

'A couple of years.'

Bridget smirked.

'Fucking tough, isn't it? It chews up the weak and spits them out in six months. You just can't stop. You just have to put your head down and charge all the time.'

'I write art reviews sometimes.'

'Really?' Bridget shifted her body forward and held her throat in one hand.

'Not much, cos, you know, most art's crap these days, isn't it? Why bang on about it?'

'So why do you bang on about it?'

'I've made a few art friends, like Kate. They ask me to write stuff for their shows and I don't have the balls to say no.'

'I'm exhibiting some of my photographs next month at EX Gallery. Maybe you could write something for the catalogue.'

'Love to,' Declan lied. 'I'm not trained in art theory or anything. I just like to look at pictures, you know?'

Bridget shook her head. 'Absolutely, I think to look at art and to feel it is so much more important than studying it.'

'Did you study art?'

'Yes. No. Yes. Well, the thing is, I work with Polaroids, snapshots, in the Wolfgang Tillman style. I just love the immediacy of his work. I despise the artifice of prepared studio photography *à la* Mario Testino, they're so commercial, whereas what I do is so real and gritty.' She squeezed each of her fists and both her eyelids as she said the word 'gritty', like Princess Bala in the movie *Antz* when she visits the workers' bar.

Bridget continued to talk about her exhibition while Declan's mind turned over the past until he noticed a change in her tone, and realised she was offering him the room.

'The rent's a hundred and fifty a week, the deposit is four hundred. When do you want to move in?'

Declan did not reply immediately. On a practical level, he would not be able to afford a hundred and fifty pounds a week unless he started eating baked beans for dinner every night. On a personal level, he did not really want to live with Bridget, but he was too embarrassed to say so. Maybe he was too scared of Bridget to say no. Instead, he asked if he shouldn't meet her flatmates. Bridget dismissed the suggestion with a wave of the hand.

'The Posse are all at Glastonbury.'

The Posse? Declan thought, saying nothing.

'Besides,' Bridget continued, 'they trust my judgement. Even if they don't, I own the place and I'm the only one capable of making a rational decision. I'm not just talking about, "What shall we eat for dinner?" ' She lowered her voice conspiratorially and invited Declan into her personal vision of the Posse.

'Juliet is a moron. Don't get me wrong, I love her to bits, but she can't even remember her own birthday and she lies through her teeth. Drake is retarded. Seriously, he's suffered massive neurological damage. Oh ... I don't mean like you, I mean, it's all self-inflicted on Drake's part, he can't string a sentence together, but he *can* and *does* supply us with good drugs. Vivian is just a baby, adorable, but no idea how the world actually works. Claire is a total slut so watch yourself; she'll try to shag you in the first week. Then my boyfriend David, if I can be so bold, is a lazy sack of shit that can't even pay for his own cigarettes.'

2

The next day, as Declan unpacked his belongings, he wondered how Bridget would describe him to The Posse. 'He's a harmless retard. He looks a bit lost in the city. Calls himself an art critic! Just another frustrated wannabe artist.'

And how would he describe Bridget?

Bridget and Drake were the only born and bred Londoners in the Posse and, perhaps unsurprisingly, Bridget was the Alpha female of the house. Given that there was no Alpha male, Bridget was the uncontested Posse leader. She was also the landlord. Her mother had bought the top floor flat when Bridget began her fine art course at the London Metropolitan University. The flat directly below came up for sale soon after she graduated and her father bought that one. Bridget created a hole in the floor/ceiling and dropped some stairs down to the bottom floor so that the two small flats were conjoined into one medium-sized flat. The living-room space in Heaven was converted into the largest bedroom, which Bridget took for herself.

Bridget's parents divorced when she was in primary school and they had subsequently tried to out-spoil their only daughter with gifts in lieu of time. They were both very rich and seemed to enjoy the competition. They were what people liked to call 'well-connected'. Her father, Pierre, ran a PR company in Paris and her mother, Abigail, was a London socialite who lived in an ivy-clad mansion in Kensington. As a child, Bridget's next door neighbour was Christopher Rawlings, who went to Hollywood in his early thirties and directed a superheroes movie. Bridget was a member of the upper classes who chose to reject the establishment in favour of a bohemian life. She loathed her mother's tea party and bridge set with a passion, and if it weren't for the fact that her parents' money came in handy she would have dissociated herself from them completely. She shared her room and her bed with David, a fellow photographer whom she had met at university. David only took photographs of old shoes. The market for photographs of old shoes was not great, as you might imagine, so David lived mostly off Bridget's income, and money from his parents who were wealthy landowners in Sussex. Bridget made her own money shooting consumer products for mail order catalogues: paper clips, cotton buds, dish washing detergent, and tampons were her livelihood. Notwithstanding this commercial work, she still considered herself an artist first and foremost. Her up-and-coming exhibition at EX gallery was her first.

The first thing Declan did when he moved into Turin Street was to cover his bedroom walls with postcards of all the works of art he had bought since moving to London. Most people bought postcards to send messages home to friends and family, but Declan only ever bought them to stick on his walls. He had over one hundred images ranging from the early Renaissance work of Giotto and Bellini to contemporary artists like Cameron Hayes, Patricia Piccinini and Marc Quinn. The images formed a charmed ring of visual beauty that protected him from all the ugly nocturnal thoughts that were hurled up like the limbs of aborted donkeys from his subconscious. The majority of the prints were paintings: Old Masters, Impressionists, Fauvists, Abstract Impressionists, Surrealists, Pop Artists, and more classical living artists like David

Hockney and Lucien Freud. Declan loved installation-art in a gallery, where the size and power of the work challenged and controlled his gallery experience, but when it came to the postcards on his walls he needed to be in control, he did not want to be challenged. All he wanted was simple beauty, and for the most part, simple beauty was what his walls displayed.

Few things could challenge the ugliness of a human thought like the beauty of a work of art. Even the paintings that depicted terrible scenes, like Jacques-Louis David's *Death of Socrates,* did so with an aesthetic that made the most pitiful tragedy appear sublime. That's what Declan loved about the Old Masters; whenever truth lacked beauty it was airbrushed out of the composition and replaced with something more appealing to the eye. Murder, rape, revenge, greed and violence almost always looked fantastic when they were depicted on a Renaissance canvas.

Declan had stuck a postcard of David's *Death of Socrates* on the wall directly above his desk. He liked to contemplate the image while writing his film reviews and sometimes he jotted down notes about the painting itself. Socrates was something of a celebrity to the educated classes of the eighteenth century, and the noble manner with which he accepted his fate at the hands of a resentful Athenian court was considered an ideal of heroic restraint. He was a noble, courageous and beautiful man, in the deepest sense of the word. He chose to die rather than take flight or deny his ideal of truth.

When he was alive, Socrates was universally regarded as one of the ugliest men ever to tread the earth. He was pot bellied with bulging lizard eyes, a snub nose, and a smile that made sunflowers wither under his gaze. The words and ideas he expressed might have been beautiful, they might have glowed like a rainbow, but it was difficult to paint the beauty of a man's contemplations.

David could only present Socrates physically, and the man's monstrous physical features did not easily lend themselves to notions of wisdom or nobility. They did not invite pathos; in fact, they were more likely to inspire ridicule and crude jokes. Indeed, Socrates was ridiculed about his grotesque features in one of Aristophanes' comedies and, apparently, he stood up during the premiere performance so his fellow Athenians could see that he was, in reality, quite as ugly as the comic playwright had painted him on the stage.

David's painting presents itself as a respectful homage to a great man and yet, at the same time, it insults the man by refuting his philosophy. David's *Death of Socrates* is the ultimate example of visual irony. An ugly man who rejected appearances is depicted as an athletic, middle-aged supermodel. It is art as fraud. Socrates believed the real world was a fraud, so art was just a fraud of a fraud. Maybe that was why Declan loved it.

Socrates was not bothered by his repulsive looks because he believed that the world of appearances was a false and misleading world. He believed that we should look beyond this material world to the world of ideas, and why wouldn't he? His ideas were great, but his face had all the symmetry of a chunk of suppurated road-kill rotting on a desert highway. One can only assume that David agreed with Socrates. He knew that the famous philosopher's appearance would prove to be very misleading, and that the more beautiful a philosopher looked, the nobler he would seem to the French court of the eighteenth century, where the men wore wigs and painted their faces. 'Where is the evil in poisoning a philosopher, especially when he's old and ugly?' asked Voltaire in his satirical play about Socrates. David probably asked himself the same question without the satire and he chose to depict Socrates as an ageing Bruce Willis wearing a beard and a loose toga. His hair is the colour of old piss but his body is pumped, with a washboard stomach, toned biceps and a very impressive looking calf muscle artfully exposed on the mattress. The philosopher is stretched across the bed as voluptuously as a middle-aged man could be stretched across a bed. While most of his disciples are swooning in ecstasies of sorrow around him, except for Plato who sits despondently on the foot of the bed, Socrates is calmly pointing up to the heavens as if ET were about to come down and beam him up to the mother ship. Socrates had a habit of pointing skyward in paintings and his index-raising predisposition made Declan wonder if he didn't spend half his life with one finger in the air.

David's Socrates is technically brilliant, and about as subtle as a Hollywood blockbuster. Every possible emotional teat has been milked on to the canvas for all it is worth. If paintings could have soundtracks, and in Declan's mind they often did, then the soundtrack for *Death of Socrates* would be reminiscent of the soundtracks for movies like *Independence Day* or *Pearl Harbor.*

Declan lay in bed and imagined himself as Socrates, the chalice of poison in his hand, the students imploring him to reconsider if he would drink the poison. Of course he wouldn't. He would never take his own life. If he had been in Socrates' position he would have chosen exile, he would have just moved on. He had moved to London two years earlier because it had an appeal that even the greyest skies could not darken. It was a place where anyone could lose themselves, a place where anyone could remain anonymous. If you arrived in London knowing nobody then you had the power of an actor improvising on a stage, you could choose how much to reveal about your character to an audience, how much to hide, and how much to invent. London was full of actors like this.

Declan was just nodding off to sleep when Bridget knocked on his door.

'Do you want to take a look at my photographs?'

'Sure,' Declan lied.

One wall of Bridget's bedroom was covered with party photographs like stills from Coca Cola commercials, all young smiling people high on drugs. A large pile of Polaroids lay scattered across Bridget's double bed, some contained recognisable close-up portraits, many betrayed the shapes of female nudes (they looked like a paedophile's furtive snaps of naked children, except these children were mature women), other Polaroids were still-life shots of household objects like cocktail glasses, pill bottles, alarm clocks and broken windows; the rest of the images were all blurred colours, hazy lines and indistinct forms. Whatever aesthetic some images might have had was insignificant and purely random. In terms of the framing and the awareness of light and every other compositional detail, there was no single artistic intention evident in any of the photographs. A wombat could have taken better snapshots if only its paws were more nimble. But if they were hung on a respected gallery wall, Declan mused, if they were accompanied by some convoluted quasi-intellectual rhetoric and pushed by a clever self-promoter, then sure, people might start to suspect that they were brilliant. That suspicion was all an artist needed to create the illusion, because nobody really *knew* anything about art any more. It was almost all sound and fury.

Declan said none of this, of course. Instead, he said, 'Wow, they're very abstract.'

'You don't like them,' Bridget gasped.

'No, no, they're nice,' Declan lied. 'They're unusual.'

Bridget exhaled loudly. 'Yes, yes, they're experimental. You see, the light, the colour, everything is thrown into the pot.'

Declan nodded his head. 'Are you going to select the best ones and blow them up?'

'No, no, no, nothing artificial, no tampering with the images. I want purity of form. The power of these images can only be conveyed in a group collective.'

'They're quite small.'

'Yes, I'm going to stick them all over the walls, no frames, no mountings, just hundreds of tiny Polaroids spread across the wall space. I want to capture the chaos of this bloody city, this sprawl, this mass of people who flash past us every day, never meeting our gaze, never really *seeing* us, the bodies, the porn, that isolation. You see? I've juxtaposed things so the figurative work and the nudes take on an inanimate quality.'

Declan nodded again. He did not wonder that EX Gallery was interested in exhibiting Bridget's work. He had been to exhibitions at the trendy Hoxton gallery and, like many other contemporary galleries, it was designed for people with big ears and small eyes who knew nothing much about art except the sale price. Four one-hundred inch video screens had been embedded in the gallery walls and most artists whose work was exhibited appeared on the screens. They were positioned above or around the works, and spoke about the relevance of their art; the themes, the obsessions, the motifs, while people walked around the gallery. The last exhibition Declan had seen there featured several large amorphous lumps of clay, just great big lumps of clay that appeared to have been dumped on the floor from a wheelbarrow or a crate. The artist appeared on the screens and declared, 'It takes a lot of courage to stand in front of my works and say, 'Yes, I did that!' because they are so anti-aesthetic.'

Bridget waited for Declan to say something. Declan waited for Bridget to make the first move.

'It's such a relief to have this outlet,' she said, letting out her breath, 'this regulating valve of artistic expression. I photograph consumer products for catalogues all day, but when I come home I can just … ,' Bridget indicated the pile of Polaroids on the bed, ' … be myself.'

'Right.'

A photograph of an African child was stuck to the wall above Bridget's desk. Declan asked if it was one of the Polaroids.

'That's Okonkwo,' Bridget explained. 'He's my son in Africa.'

'You have a son in Africa?'

'I sponsor him. It's just ten pounds a month and let me tell you, it frees you of a considerable amount of guilt.'

'I'm a member of Greenpeace,' Declan said.

'Excellent, isn't it?'

'I don't know. I still feel pretty guilty.'

Bridget ploughed on, 'All the money we waste putting chemicals up our nose and these people can't even feed themselves. One in six people in the world does not have access to clean water. All the money spent on illegal drugs in one day in the West could buy three square meals and a set of clothing for every starving person in Africa.'

Whether this was factually accurate or not, Bridget did have a point; the way people lived did not make much sense. In a post-nuclear society very little made sense if you were determined to view things through a lens of pure logic. Adults were working longer and longer hours to make more and more money, which they used to buy up entire toy stores for their children in an effort to assuage the guilt. People now caught planes to work instead of finding a job in their own neighbourhood.

Bridget continued with her dubious set of facts.

'In the UK ninety-three million electrical appliances are thrown into the bin every year: mobile phones, radios, CD players, printers, computers, they are sent off to countries like Nigeria, where Okonkwo lives. Did you know Nigeria receives four-hundred thousand unwanted computers every month from Europe?'

'You rifling on about the poor again?' David entered the room with a bottle of wine and introduced himself with the cheerful confidence that is one positive legacy of a Public School education. 'Hello there, you must be the new fellow, right? Declan? Don't listen to this one; six months ago she was saying the world would descend into chaos because of the millennium bug. We're a few months into the twenty-first century now and nothing's happened.' David had short, thick hair and the body of a rugby player who had retired ten years ago. Bridget bristled and pouted like a cod fish, unhappy that her intimate dialectic with Declan had been interrupted.

'What are you doing, David?' she said testily.

'I'm having a glass of wine.' David rolled himself a cigarette. He winked slyly and offered Declan the pouch. Declan did not usually smoke but David's gesture seemed like an invitation to friendship. He took the pouch, rolled himself a cigarette and lit it from David's smoke while Bridget screamed.

'I'm having a private conversation. Can you not bloody well knock?'

'It's my bedroom too,' David smiled to Declan again.

Declan drew back on the cigarette and tried not to cough. 'We can discuss this tomorrow,' he told Bridget.

In the quietness of his own room Declan lay in bed and wondered what he was doing. He was not a superstitious man but he trusted his instincts, even if he was stubborn and lacked the courage to act on them. The minute he had met Bridget his instincts had told him that this was not going to be a good place for him to live. But there he was, inhabiting a room that he did not want to inhabit, living with people he did not want to live with, wishing he were somewhere else as if he had not had any choice in the matter. Despite his misgivings, he was smart enough and old enough to know that, somewhere beneath his conscious thoughts, this was his choice and he was exactly where he wanted to be.

A loud thud echoed from the room above. A woman sobbed and then screamed, 'Fuck you!'

It was Bridget, speaking in a tone of voice that indicated she had drunk at least a bottle of wine. 'You attack everything!'

'I don't attack everything,' David answered.

'I'm going to be *somebody!* I'm making it happen! Tristan Russell's coming to my opening. *Tristan Russell!*'

'Fantastic, you'll be famous because a junkie went to your show.'

'I'll be *successful* because I *want* it! I've got ambition-ambition-ambition!'

'Listen to yourself! You sound like a fucking sales advertisement!'

'I aspire to something!'

'A fucking sales advertisement?'

'You photograph old shoes, *Day–vid.*'

'It's a metaphor,' David said, suddenly calm. He did not sound defensive. He spoke with the kind of lofty imperialism Moses might have had on the Mount. 'It's an artistic statement.'

'You're jealous, that's why you attack me.'

'I'm proud of you, Bridge; I just think your photographs are shit. They're not artistic, they're fake.'

Bridget released a staccato of laughter that cracked and bounced like billiard balls on a wooden floor. 'What do you know about shit? You don't even buy your own toilet paper!'

A pause, and then Bridget started to howl in powerful, sobbing gushes. After several minutes David spoke soothingly, in a low murmur. Then complete silence. Then Bridget began to moan softly. The moans grew louder, developing into grunts and growls until she started to wail and moan.

'Oh yes, David. Fuck me, fuck me! Oh, oh, oooh fuck me!'

David punctuated Bridget's gasping directives with deep guttural moans. It was like listening to two people stabbing each other to death. Finally, after more than a sitcom episode worth of howling and grunting, David moaned like a bull injected with gallons of pure heroin and the night was silent.

3

Declan met Bridget in the kitchen the next morning and he found it difficult to look her in the eye. She punched a coffee filter into the percolator with excessive force.

'House meeting at six tonight, Declan.'

'Tonight? I thought everyone was at Glastonbury.'

'The Posse's coming back early,' Bridget said, and left the kitchen while the water gently came to the boil.

Juliet, Vivien, Drake and Juliet's boyfriend Jake, were coming back from the festival early, because Claire had taken some bad acid and almost died. She was now in hospital. Juliet had called Claire's parents in Manchester some time before an ambulance officer arrived and established that Claire was, in fact, still breathing. The Posse had taken a cocktail of drugs: ecstasy tablets, cocaine and marijuana, all washed down with whisky and beer, but only Claire had taken acid and several hours into the trip she passed out. The haze of euphoria vanished abruptly as everybody who was still conscious was forced to deal with Claire's overdose. Unfortunately, everyone mistook her temporary lack of consciousness for something more permanent and Juliet was hysterical when she phoned Claire's parents.

'You … we … have to come sheeez *dead!*' Juliet howled down the phone. 'Claire's *dead!* Sheeez *deeeaaad*!'

When the ambulance officer informed the Posse of Claire's less than fatal condition, Juliet switched her mobile phone off and she, Vivian and Drake decided it was time to return to Heaven.

At six o'clock the Posse was seated around the dining table in Purgatory. The lagging affects of the drugs that they had consumed over the weekend, combined with the terror of Claire's near-death experience, had drained them of all emotion. They looked like Vietnam veterans deep in the shit for six months and just out on R&R. They were spooning a dessert of crème brulèe into their mouths like automatons. Drake, who was taking his time on his main course of crab cakes with red pepper mayonnaise, licked his lips and made a kind of approving grunt. Declan was beginning to think Bridget was an artist pursuing the wrong career; she should have been a chef.

'Claire won't be back,' Bridget explained as she filled everyone's glasses with more Chardonnay. 'We need another new tenant. Everyone, this is Declan. He's an art critic.'

Juliet, Vivian and Drake all said hello in dull, hollowed-out voices. Juliet's boyfriend Jake smiled without saying anything. Declan felt a twinge of regret as he remembered Bridget's warning about Claire, 'She'll try to shag you in the first week.'

'Are you s–sure Claire's not coming back?' he asked, trying to hide his disappointment.

Bridget nodded her head and dropped a sly smile.

'Thought you were in there didn't you Dec!' she said, with an outrageous delight that would be difficult to exaggerate. 'I warned Dec about Claire's appetites!' Bridget laughed forcefully but the rest of the Posse barely reacted.

As soon as Juliet finished her dessert she reached into her handbag and spread three handfuls of coloured pills across the table. Drake and Vivian joined her searching through the pills with the expertise of fruit pickers looking for ripe cherries, or chimps picking lice from their partner's armpit.

'How do you know Claire won't be back?' Vivian asked, dropping a Mogadon and taking a swig from an Evian bottle. Her phone rang and without waiting for an answer to her question, she left the room to take the call. Drake eyed her carefully as she left.

'I wan' a Brazilian girl or somethin',' Drake grumbled. 'What can't speak English. We' never 'ave ta … speak … ta … ' He looked around the table helplessly and his voice faded to nothing. Bridget was right; the guy had lost a few cells.

Drake Preston was Vivian's ex-boyfriend and an ex-model. He was still a relatively attractive man to look at, apart from the finger length scar on his right cheek, but conversation was his enemy and as soon as he opened his mouth his physical beauty was qualified. Fifteen years of heavy drug use had given him a chemically-induced personality lobotomy and he existed in a lonely world of snap and paranoia. The scar on his right cheek had put an abrupt end to his modelling career when he was twenty-seven. He got the scar after cutting cocaine with plain flour and selling the lumpy white substance to some teenage boys. The teenage boys found him in a Soho nightclub and chased him into the toilets where he tried, unsuccessfully, to blame the mistake on his supplier.

'Wah 'bout you Dave?' Drake asked, hoping to get some support from the other resident male.

'Just make sure you get someone with a job,' David shrugged.

'You don't have a job you lazy fuck-turd!' Bridget screamed, and David lowered his head and rolled himself a cigarette with a languid charm. Bridget glared at him for a moment and picked her nose. She picked her nose without even trying to hide the fact that she was picking her nose, she put her finger right up one nostril and rotated it three times. When she brought it out she looked at it like an entomologist examining ant larva .

'Anyone got a problem with me choosing?' Bridget demanded, wiping her finger on her jeans. Her chin jutted out, waiting. Nobody spoke for a while.

'I'd rather a girl,' Juliet said, swallowing two pills that she'd isolated on the table. 'I don't want a guy I fancy moving in.'

Obviously Declan wasn't Juliet's type, but as soon as this deduction was illuminated in his mind it was followed by a powerful image of Juliet riding him on the table. He sighed patiently and allowed this image its moment in the spotlight, there was no point fighting it. The sex was gentle and slow, Juliet's body tasted like sweet custard and as Declan returned to the real world he could feel the erection in his pants.

'You fancy *me* don't you?' Jake asked Juliet.

'I don't live with you,' Juliet smiled, and then frowned. 'Do I?' She looked around the table uncertainly, her eyes scrambling from one person to the next. 'Does Jake live with me?'

'You're such a fairy, Juliet,' David said gently, circling one finger around his ears.

'Head in the clouds like a– a– a … ' said Drake, clearly pleased someone else was the focus of derision.

'How do you do your job?' Bridget asked.

'She's got great tits,' David answered pleasantly. 'That's all a saleswoman needs.' Juliet laughed along with the rest of the Posse. Perhaps she was too tired to be offended.

Juliet was thirty-two years old and possessed an alluring beauty that was usually attributed to her Greek mother; her father was born in Margate. She lived in Heaven and had blue sky and clouds painted all over her bedroom walls and ceiling. She really did live in the clouds and walking into her room was a bit like stepping into the internal cube of a Magritte painting. She studied art history at university but now worked as a project manager at

Phebron, a multi-national pharmaceutical company that made more than a thousand pounds profit per second. Juliet organised medical symposiums that were primarily an excuse to promote Phebron's new drugs. When she first started at Phebron there were almost as many pharmaceutical sales reps as there were GPs practising in the UK. Many doctors had stopped making appointments with their drug suppliers – ten minutes spent with a rep was a patient lost and that was money lost, and money lost was not good. Juliet had always been able to secure her requisite number of monthly doctors' appointments. Doctors liked her; they liked to look at her, to hear her laughter, to feel her reassuring hand on their forearm.

Juliet's boyfriend, Jake, was seventeen years old and still at school studying for his A levels. Jake could only stay in Heaven on Friday and Saturday nights during the school term but over the summer holidays he stayed more frequently.

The Posse was still laughing at Juliet when Vivian rushed back into the room looking like she'd just won the lottery.

'*Tristan is moving in with me!*' she screamed, jumping up and down on the spot. Juliet and Bridget screamed, and the girls all joined arms in a threesome of excitement while Drake kissed his teeth and glared at his feet.

'Nah way!' Drake screamed. 'I'm not stayin' 'ere wif thaht … thaht … thaht … It's 'im or me.'

'You won't leave us, Drake,' David said calmly.

'Oh yeah? And why not?'

'Because if you do, we will kill you.'

Drake looked as if he had been slapped in the face with a train. He searched David's eyes hoping to find a twinkle that might inform him that the words were said in jest, but David was giving nothing away.

'That's no way to speak to … ,' Drake grumbled. 'Speak to me like … Fucking toffee nosed … posh … public school … '

'Think for a moment, Drake,' Vivian grunted. 'You sell drugs and Triz buys them, lots of them.'

Vivian Birchwood was only nineteen years old but she often complained about having a teenager in the house when Jake was visiting. She had come to London when she was sixteen as part of 'Jail Bait', a girl band created by a man who managed glamour models and dealt in weed. Before that she had lived in Grimsby, a sea-port in North-East Lincolnshire that she described as 'the Chav-Vegas of Lincolnshite'. Her parents worked for the local council and from a young age all she ever dreamed of was being admired by millions of people she didn't know. 'Jail Bait' appeared on television twice and, at their manager's behest, each member slept with a dozen men in the music industry but they failed to attract a record contract, although one of the girls did contract herpes after sleeping with a Virile Records executive. They finally disbanded after their manager was sentenced to two years jail for digital penetration of a minor. As it transpired, one of the band members was only fifteen. Vivian now worked as a promoter at the Shoreditch nightclub, a trendy establishment where models and indie band members hung out and got high together. She also worked part-time for Drake, selling his drugs to the beautiful people on the dance floor. She never woke up until midday and she always had black bags under her eyes, but she was still young enough to get away with the constant party.

Vivian was heading to Hoxton Square after the Posse meeting to see the Rods play a Glastonbury Festival come-down gig. She had a backstage pass courtesy of Tristan Russell, lead singer of the Rods, and the object of much more than mere affection. The Rods were a new indie rock band whose debut album had made the national charts without the band losing any street-cred, thanks largely to the sheer force of Tristan's drug habit and sexual appetite. Hundreds of thousands of people took illegal drugs every week in London and these people tended to support Tristan on principle alone. Even if he represented an extreme form of substance abuse that caused feelings of disquiet, they did not want to be accused of hypocrisy or appear to be sympathising with the sentiments of tabloid journalists and wholesome day-time television presenters. Tristan offered his supporters some appealing contradictions as well. He was a vegetarian. He had a reputation for arriving at out of the way places with his guitar and playing free shows. The previous Christmas he had visited a soup kitchen in Dulwich and surprised the homeless people with a selection of Bob Dylan classics. Six days later he was offered ten thousand pounds to play a private New Year's Eve concert for tongue-studded socialite Zara Montgomery but he never turned up and, instead, played for free to the inmates of Wandsworth Prison.

Two days before the Glastonbury Festival Vivian had brought Tristan to Heaven for the night. Drake had remained in the living room snorting coke and listening to their drug-fuelled sex session upstairs until he could not take it any more. At five in the morning he stormed up to Vivian's bedroom and begged her to get back with him. She refused, but Tristan bought three grams of coke and offered Drake a few lines in return.

'How long have you known Tristan?' David asked, finishing off his crème brulèe.

Vivian sniffed the air and ignored the question. 'If he's going to move in we don't need another person.'

'OK,' Bridget said, 'that's settled.' The three girls all looked at each other knowingly.

'Tristan Russell,' they chimed.

'His fans,' Declan asked, trying not to sound too concerned. 'The girls. Are they … are they … um … How old are they, generally speaking, exactly?'

'You mean the groupies?' Bridget smirked. 'Fifteen to eighteen are they?'

Vivian nodded. 'Scrags most of them.'

'Right,' Declan nodded. 'Are there that many of them?'

'Bloody thousands,' Juliet said. 'Why? You want some action?'

'You dirty snake,' Bridget smirked. Everyone laughed.

'No it's … I've got … I've got a … '

Declan smiled but his hands were shaking and his heart pounded in his chest.

4

The Saturday after Declan had moved into Purgatory he went to a screening of a new, digitally re-mastered French film about human beings that turned into minotaur-like creatures and raped aristocratic women. He caught the bus home at ten o'clock and the first thing he saw when he got off was a large piece of green cardboard stuck to the bus stop with the words 'Posse Housewarming this Way', written in fluorescent red crayon. A bit further along the road was another sign, 'That's Right, Keep Coming'. Another sign at the corner of Turin Road said, 'Getting Warmer', and a fourth sign was stuck to a tree several doors away from the Chocolate Block, 'You're almost there'.

The word 'DISCO!!' was painted across a wooden door which had been laid horizontally against the front wall of the high-rise apartments.

Declan took the elevator to Purgatory and walked through the front door just as David was falling down the stairs like a cartoon character in a Warner Brothers' film. He rolled over acrobatically four or five times on the way down and face-planted on the floor near the front door.

'Diving David? You all right?' Declan asked.

A man wearing a T-shirt with the words 'Selfish Cunt' printed across the front stood at the top of the stairs laughing viciously. David leaped onto his feet like a freshly animated mannequin and laughed with the profound confidence of freshly snorted cocaine.

'Dec! Did you? … How mad was *that*?' he kissed Declan on the mouth and head butted the wall. 'I'm invincible!'

'Aren't we all?'

David spoke avidly, as if he were trying to eat his teeth along with each word that came out of his mouth. Declan indicated David's forehead, said he was bleeding and David nodded excitedly.

'I know, I know, I know, I know – and I can't feel a thing!' He threw his arm around Declan and directed him into the apartment, chattering as they moved down the hallway to the living room. 'He's here, he's here, and he's here! Tristan Russell is at our housewarming! Can you believe it man? Tristan Russell! We could have sold tickets! The guy is so cool, he's so sweet, you must meet him.'

The house was full of people exhibiting various stages and forms of intoxication. Different rooms had been designated for the different drugs being consumed. David and Bridget's room was for coke, Drake's was for ecstasy, Vivian's room was reserved for joint smoking, although people were doing lines, popping pills and smoking joints everywhere except Juliet's room, which had been padlocked and bolted.

Vivian walked past crying Tristan's name and rubbing her nose violently. Drake was following her, trying to grab hold of her arm and pleading with her like an addict for a hit.

'Forget about him, Viv. Come to me room. Come on, Viv. Viv? Viv, come to me room. Forget about Russell. Viv? Viv? Viv?'

But Vivian did not need any more drugs from Drake, she was already over the rainbow and the monkeys were flying around her, and she turned and sneered down her nose from on high in lofty heels.

'Just fuck off, Drake.'

Drake was so used to this kind of abuse that it had no noticeable affect and he continued to beg.

'Nah, come on, Viv, just come to me room is all I'm sayin'. Come on, Viv.'

A young DJ from the Shoreditch club was playing tunes on a pair of tables set up in one corner of the living room. People were dancing and screaming loudly into each other's ears. Declan saw Pete and Kate dancing together like loose pistons in the machinery. They glanced down and observed their bodies' movements or closed their eyes to get closer to the music or out of their bodies, as the base beats hammered their hearts. Pete was a lawyer for a city firm and he and Declan had lived together for six months when Declan first moved to London. Kate, Pete's girlfriend, was an artist and her friendship with Bridget had put Declan in his new 'home'. When Pete recognised Declan his face glowed. Kate looked over and smiled too, and as Declan walked towards them they waved in his direction while dancing to the music.

'Ma–a–a–te!' Pete screamed and put his arm around his friend. He was by nature a quiet man, but put some pills into him and he became so loved-up people assumed he was gay. Maybe he was gay and didn't realise it. He was certainly touching Declan with great affection. Kate was touching him too, which was kind of nice, and she planted a wet kiss on his cheek, popped a pill into his mouth, squeezed his arse and winked.

'Jesus, Kate, you know I don't do drugs.'

'I know, that's what you always say when you do them.'

It was true, for a man who always said 'no' to drugs Declan took a lot of drugs. He rarely bought drugs, he never actively went searching for them, but people offered them to him wherever he went and he always said 'no' and took them anyway. It never occurred to him to go somewhere else.

'Did you tell Kate about my brain damage?' Declan asked Pete once Kate had drifted back into the dancing group. He had to repeat the question three times before Pete heard it properly. Pete pulled a face that lacked commitment to any definitive answer.

'I might have,' he said. 'Don't try to be coy, you tell everyone about it anyway.'

Bridget was dancing near the Rothko print. When she saw Declan she rushed over and took his photograph before he could turn away.

'Declan! Did you hear? Tristan Russell was here. *Tristan Russell* was at our party!' She did a thrilling shimmy with her eyes like a go-go dancer and squeezed Declan's hand tightly. 'He disappeared an hour ago and nobody can find him. You have to come outside and meet this other guy, Jeremy. He's looking for a film reviewer.'

They passed through the kitchen and Declan heard Tristan Russell's name whispered in hushed, reverent tones several times. Bridget took photographs of everyone she walked past. A black man was pouring a packet of flour onto the kitchen bench and when he had moulded a small mountain out of the flour he screamed, '*You fuck wit' me, you fuckin' wit da best!*' and buried his face into Powder Mountain while the people around him laughed and clapped their hands. When he pulled his head out of the flour he looked like a Samuel L. Jackson doll suffering melt-down, cackling so loudly that he could not reprise his Tony Montana lines beyond the first address: *'You fuck wit' … you fuck wit' … you fuck wit'.'*

Juliet was standing by the balcony door mumbling to herself. She saw Declan and Bridget and smiled with a dazed, momentary burst of recognition that made her stagger and put one hand against the door to stop herself from falling. Her voice was as wobbly as her legs.

'He was here, man! Oh my God, man!' She fell forward and kissed Declan, one hand holding on to his neck, she then pulled her head back, smiled and walked back into the flat.

Bridget took three photographs on the Purgatory balcony and introduced Declan to Jeremy Larkin, the presenter of a new television programme called *The Massive*, which screened on Sunday mornings on a relatively unknown cable channel called IVN. Jeremy was ensconced on a sun lounger, wearing dark sunglasses at night and a trilby hat. He took Declan's hand, shook it slowly and his lips twitched. He held the hand much longer than necessary.

'Bridget's told me all about *you*!' he said, pressing Declan's hand to emphasise the word 'you'. 'How'd you like to present our movie review segment?'

'Sure,' Declan said, 'that would be awesome.'

Bridget squealed and drew one arm around her new flatmate, placed a pill in his mouth and screamed. 'He won't be nervous at all, Jeremy, he's as cool as a cucumber.'

'It's live television,' Jeremy explained gently, squeezing Declan's hand again. 'So exciting. We shoot Sundays at ten. Come on in and show us what you've got next week.' He asked for Declan's mobile number and Declan mumbled an apology.

'I … I don't have a mobile phone,' he said, 'I don't like them.'

'You need some kind of visual trademark,' Bridget said quickly, 'a piece of clothing, something on your face?'

'What about a pentagram on my forehead?'

'I'm serious, Dec,' Bridget said.

'She's right,' Jeremy added. 'You need to think of yourself as a product now.'

'Exactly,' Bridget said. 'Try to think of something that makes you stand out in the market, a personal logo that says "Dec".'

Declan went inside, danced to the music and quickly found himself dancing around a woman wearing an electric blue wig. She was tall and blonde under the blue, and her floral caftan was definitely out of season. She put the wig on Declan's head and kissed his lips. Her hands caressed his cheeks and he felt like a beautiful young boy. When the song finished they went to Declan's room, sat down on the bed and talked about themselves, about art and life, and as the drugs surged through Declan's system he could feel the memory of old passions returning. He imagined he had found the girl he was going to marry. *This is the one,* he told himself, *she's beautiful, she loves art, she has a sense of humour and she's wearing an electric blue wig.* It seemed like his destiny had arrived. The conversation was frantic, intense, excited – the linguistic equivalent of drugged mice scampering around a maze during a medical experiment.

'I always liked the blue ones,' Declan hummed, 'the blue ones, yes, yes, yes, they were personal, profound, honest and then he changed didn't he, he changed, objectified. I always thought it was the first, the original, the blue stuff that was really him, not the later stuff that was all … when it all went kind of intellectual and … '

'KAZING!' the woman screamed. 'You know KAZING! It all went kazing didn't it yes, yes, yes … !'

They talked on and on in circles of utter nonsense. At some point Juliet burst through the door laughing. She stopped, looked at the woman in the blue wig, then at Declan, and her eyes seemed to focus on some internal disorientation. She staggered back and put one hand against the wall, looking around the room.

'This, this isn't my room,' she whispered sadly. 'Sorry.'

When Juliet left the woman in the blue wig sneered.

'Keep the sharp knives away from that one.' She stood up and closed the door to the room, 'locking' it with a newspaper wedged between the door and the carpet. She returned to the bed and took her caftan off, revealing a matching white lace bra and G-string, a solid solarium tan and a tattoo with the words 'Billy Oh' sketched around her belly button. She gave Declan another pill and he ran his hands up and down her body. His eyes gazed with dazed appreciation over the magnificent contours of her waist, breasts and hips. She rested her head on one hand and raised one eye brow sardonically.

'Shall we?' she asked.

'Yes, yes, yes just … my God it's amazing the female form it's just, it's perfect.'

Who needed sex when you had drugs this good? The woman with 'Billy Oh' tattooed on her belly did, and after Declan's hand had wandered over her body for half an hour, she finally stood up and slipped back into her caftan.

'What are you, *le sexual retarde*?' she asked, pronouncing the words with a French accent, but without any animosity.

'Where are you going?'

'I'm going to find my boyfriend. If he's still here, maybe I can get laid.'

5

Declan lay awake after the woman with the blue wig had left to find her boyfriend. How had he made such a mistake? He had been convinced that the blue-wigged woman was going to be his future wife, but all she had wanted was some quick sexual release. Maybe the drugs had played misty with his mind.

He went to the bathroom, squeezed some hand cream into the palm of one hand and walked back to his bedroom to masturbate. A quick orgasm when he was on drugs usually made it easier to sleep.

In fact he didn't sleep at all. It felt like his brain had turned into an iron bar and some force of God was slowly, painfully tying it up into knots. He wondered if he would ever recover this time. At midday he got up and realised the fingers and palm of his left hand had turned bright orange. *Why does this sort of thing always happen when I'm coming down?* He focused on the hand but nothing changed. He was not hallucinating. It was definitely a different colour. It was as if his entire palm and the webs of his fingers had gone golden orange overnight.

At first he thought it was some drug-related skin reaction. Then he remembered masturbating, so he went to the bathroom and checked the bottles of cream. One was for fake-tan. He peered into his boxer shorts and there was a beautiful suntanned cock.

Declan stumbled out to the living room, knocking the walls, tripping over the bodies strewn on the floor and feeling that paradoxical post-party combination of exhaustion laced with a throbbing, anxious energy that refused to retire. He knew that within another ten hours his mood would crash and the reality of his life would start to appear in his mind like some portrait of Dorian Gray. Several smashed bottles lay scattered across the living-room floor and someone had stolen a number of roadwork signs. A white, triangular sign framed in red and depicting a male figure leaning a shovel into a pile of dirt was resting against the fridge. A half-burned foam cushion lay in the kitchen sink, and about three kilos of flour had spread a white patina across most of the kitchen surfaces.

Tristan Russell was sitting on the living-room sofa smoking a heated foil of heroin while looking at himself in the wall mirror, a display of multi-tasking that was entirely admirable. He turned his head this way and that in order to observe his eagle's-nest-beehive hairdo from different angles. Apart from the lack of sweat, his face looked much the same as it did in the poster that was stuck to the living-room wall. He was thin, almost fragile looking, with pasty white skin and thick, long, dark hair coiffed into a wild beehive. He looked like a zombie even in the bright morning light, elegantly dressed in a brown three-piece suit cut from some kind of exotic material that resembled the skin of a kiwi fruit. He looked up at Declan with timid, black eyes and smiled politely as he put the heroin foil down.

'Hello there, you must be Declan. The dark man of mystery. The man without a past.'

The soft warmth of his voice was disarming. He spoke like an ethereal Essex thug, the harsh accent gently intoned. Looking at him and hearing him speak for the first time Declan found it both alarming and understandable that the man had carved out such a Class-A reputation as a Byronic Lothario. He could have *been* Byron except for the gritty accent. He clearly had not slept for several days and he looked like a dead body exhumed from the grave and injected with just enough life to be conscious of its surroundings. Declan could not imagine Tristan having the stamina to boil an egg, let alone have sex for five minutes. He was beautiful without being handsome and in terms of the pure physicality of his presence, he could have been any Johnny-come-lately, apart from his fangs, which were large and well pronounced thanks to some equally impressive gums. When he smiled it looked like he was about to eat a wolf.

The most surprising thing about Tristan's physical appearance was his size. He was comically small. He was barely taller than an adolescent girl and Declan had to suppress a smile when this comparison came to mind.

The true power of Tristan's being *qua* being was derived from the media persona he had created for himself, and that had been created for him. He had the raw potency of celebrity and being near him was a bit like being on drugs. OK, yes, Declan *was* on drugs, but the very air around them seemed rife with fame and scandal, and for the first time in a long time Declan felt excited about being alive.

What class of twat am I? he wondered.

He had never met anyone as famous as Tristan before and was surprised to feel his heart pounding in his chest. Did this mean he was blushing? If he wasn't already blushing the idea that he might be blushing had probably made him blush, and he stood in front of Tristan feeling like a young groupie. *Be natural*, he told himself, but as soon as *be natural* becomes a conscious imperative in your mind you can never *be* natural, you can only ever, at the most, *act* natural. Perhaps the most successful people in the world were those who could maintain an act of naturalness in a world composed of pretence. Declan's nerves directed one hand towards his neck to scratch at a non-existent itch. Half way to this goal he realised that any scratching would betray his nerves. He brought his hand down to his side again but there was nothing for it to do except dangle, so he tried to put it in his pocket until he realised that he had no pockets in the trousers he was wearing. There he was, standing before a man that he had judged a pathetic fool and pitied, yes pitied, wondering what to do with his hands.

'How's it going?' Declan said.

'What happened to your hand?' Tristan asked.

Declan put his golden hand behind his back, mumbled a non-answer and changed the subject. He said he liked the poster of Tristan on the wall. Tristan began to sing lightly, with half-closed eyes.

'I'm a pin-up boy looking for a pin / cold metal dreaming, against my skin / I'm running from fame / 'Cos I don't really care / what people I don't know think of my hair.'

'Do you like that song?' he asked when he had finished.

'I don't know it.'

'You have to *know* a song to like it?'

'You have to hear it.'

'You just heard it.'

'Is it yours?' Declan asked, trying to move the conversation away from his taste in music.

'You're not a Rods fan then?' Tristan tried to sound curious but not disappointed.

'My interest in music never really recovered from the death of vinyl records. I could never quite forgive an industry that tried to make me buy the same records twice.'

Tristan laughed. 'So, you're a Romantic.'

'I'm worse, I'm sentimental. I collect all my train tickets in shoe boxes, and take them out on rainy days and cry over all those lost journeys.'

'Really?'

'No.'

Tristan mumbled something to himself and took another hit from the foil of heroin. He then offered it to Declan.

'I'm good,' Declan said, just like a character in a movie. Tristan looked at him, puzzled.

'You *really* don't know that song?'

Declan shook his head. 'Sorry.'

'This is fabulous,' Tristan smiled vaguely. 'I love it. I really love it. Why don't I meet more people like you? People who don't kiss my arse just because I've been called the greatest poet since Byron.'

'Someone called you the greatest poet since Byron?'

'Critic, *NME*, you know, they call it the bible of cool. I call it the bible of school.'

Tristan simulated masturbation to indicate what he thought of school. He took a hit of heroin, lit a cigarette and pointed to the foil. 'Unfortunately the media chooses to focus on this and on my sexual ... voracity, rather than my music. They're crass and vulgar. They have no style. They call me an addict.'

'You *are* smoking heroin in the morning.'

'Addiction,' Tristan said, drawing philosophically on the cigarette before exhaling, 'is just a metaphor.'

Declan nodded his head and waited for Tristan to break into song again, but he didn't. Instead his head lolled about like some knob attached to a well oiled ball bearing. He closed his eyes and slowly began to lean forward, tipping further and further over until the momentum returned him to his senses and he straightened up. He continued speaking in the same soft voice. 'What we're talking about here is a habit. We are all creatures of habit, after all. Some of us go to the gym, some of us eat chocolate, some drink alcohol, some read books, some watch birds, and some take socially taboo substances. What are your habits?'

Declan had to think of an answer. 'I'm in the habit of fucking my life up.'

'Is that my phone?' Tristan asked suddenly. The only sounds Declan heard were the faint chirping of birds and the hum of motors on the main street below.

'I don't hear anything.'

'Who?' Tristan asked, and Declan looked around to see if he were the only person in the room talking to Tristan.

Tristan continued his dialogue with the phantom in his mind. His voice descended down a dark cave. 'Oh, Vivian, yeah right.' Declan had to lean forward to catch the next speech, muttered with reverential piety. 'The ineluctable … modality … of the … visible. She's very beautiful. So very young, so pure and … no productiveness of the highest kind, no remarkable discovery, and no great thought which bears fruit and has results, is in the power of anyone. Man must consider them as unexpected gifts from above, as pure children of God.'

Declan had no idea what Tristan was talking about but it sounded impressive, if not original. Tristan laughed lightly and lit another cigarette while the first burnt in the ashtray. 'Purity is the fruit of all knowledge,' he said, coughing and hacking up some phlegm and spitting it into an empty beer bottle. 'Vivian says you review art?'

'In a blue moon.'

Tristan pointed up to the Rothko print behind him.

'Review that.'

'It's three bands of colour washed onto the canvas.'

'But what does it mean?'

'How do you feel looking at it? That's all it means.'

'I feel calm, but confused.'

'There you go.' Declan lit a cigarette and savoured the feel of the smoke passing like silk down his throat. 'Maybe that's the smack. I always thought Rothko's paintings were about horizons.'

'Horizons?'

'Elemental horizons.' Declan moved over to the print and pointed to the top edge of each of the three colour fields in turn. 'Is this the horizon? Or is this the horizon? Or this? It all depends on your point of view, doesn't it? It could be dark land at the bottom, blue sky in the middle, dark cloud up the top; or land, water, sky; or land, water, mountains; or land, desert, water. You see, the horizon can't be placed. And what are horizons anyway? They look like the end of something but they don't exist in any absolute sense, do they? They're not the end of anything; they're just the limits of your vision at a particular time. You'd have to be like a … a … a … fully grown tree, never moving from the one spot, for your horizon to stay the same all the time.'

Tristan took a hit of heroin and grimaced for a moment then relaxed and regarded the Rothko with a new curiosity. 'Non-endings,' he said quietly. 'Horizons, eh?'

There was a knock on the front door. Declan answered it and a large man with tattoos on his wrists glared down at him.

'Triz 'ere?' he demanded. Before Declan could reply, the man shouted down the hallway. 'Triz? Yer there?'

'Fuck off Nathan!' Tristan shouted from the living room. 'This is not an appropriate time.'

' 'Ee's got a recordin' stud'yo booked,' Nathan explained. 'Can I come in?'

'How did you know he was here?'

'That's me job.'

'Don't let that fucker in!' Tristan screamed. 'Slam the door in his face.'

This was clearly not an option. Nathan looked like he had eaten bullets for breakfast, his mouth was a concertina of missing teeth and his foot was already firmly across the door's threshold. Declan had once read that a properly directed punch in the nose could drill the nose cartilage up into the brain and kill a man. He was trying to imagine what it would feel like to have his nose cartilage drilled into his brain as Nathan smiled and eased past him down the hall and entered the living room.

'Come on, Triz,' he said, 'you can' fuck 'em abowt again.'

Declan stood behind Nathan and smiled an apology. 'Look at the guy,' he shook his head. 'Slam the door in his face, you think?'

Tristan looked up with soft pleading eyes and tried unsuccessfully to tie his shoelaces. Nathan knelt and proceeded to tie each lace for him, and Tristan smiled like a young boy who had just wet his pants in class.

'I just wet my pants,' he said.

Nathan swore and turned to Declan. 'Have you got a spare pair a jeans?'

Declan went to his room and brought out a pair of purple trousers.

'Purple hey?' Tristan noted, and closed one eye as if spying through a keyhole. 'When I am an old woman I shall wear purple,' he whispered.

'And spend my pension on brandy and … and something else,' Declan answered. It was the only other verse of the poem he could half remember but it was enough. Tristan put his hand on Declan's shoulder as Nathan helped him into his pants.

'I'll try not to piss in them,' he promised. 'This man does not know my music Nathan. He does not know who Tristan Russell is.'

Nathan looked at Declan as if he were a cop. 'Bullshit.'

'I'm not very musical,' Declan explained.

'Come on buster,' Tristan said. 'You're coming with us.'

'How are we … we're not driving are we?' Declan asked, but Tristan had already left the apartment.

6

The recording studio was filled with guitars, young girls, smoke, seedy-looking men and a handful of musicians. Declan sat as far away from the young girls as he could and kept his eye on them. After the first few songs he relaxed a little.

A shirtless man lay unconscious on the floor and someone had written 'Fucked Up' in red lipstick on his chest. A man in a duffle coat was arguing with his own reflection in a wall mirror.

'Look at you,' he shouted. 'You're pathetic.'

A girl who looked about fifteen years old was smoking crack from a pipe and when she saw Declan she smiled and offered him some.

'Who are you here with?' Declan asked, taking a hit from the pipe.

'I'm Tristan's PA,' she said excitedly. Declan asked her how she got the job and she gave him a puzzled look. 'I don't really know.' Her name was Liz and she had been working for Tristan since she met him backstage at a concert in Camden the previous week.

Tristan disappeared into a back room with some Rastafarian men and emerged fifteen minutes later to record a song, 'Byron's Rod'.

Byron's rod was a feather filled with ink. Tristan sang. His voice was a halting composition of squawking, croaking passion. He sounded like a junkie desperate for a hit, which was probably not a coincidence. The girls watched him with hawkish eyes, smiling unconsciously and holding their bellies like pregnant women.

They were all beautiful, all young, all in love with an idea that had brought them here. As Declan looked at them he thought that it was just within the realm of possibility that he could be the same age as their fathers.

Vivian arrived in tears and the band members waited, drumming their fingers on surfaces or snorting coke, while Tristan took Vivian into a room and consoled her. He emerged fifteen minutes later with a sly smile. He slung his guitar over his shoulder again and began to play. Vivian watched him with the possessive glare of a lioness, her gaze swooped across the coterie of young girls and she sneered at them collectively. She saw Declan and sat beside him, slipping one hand through his arm. She smiled sadly.

'What are you doing here, Dec?'

Declan pointed to his purple trousers. 'Your man there is wearing my pants. Did you come with Bridget?'

Vivian shook her head and chewed a finger nail and smiled. 'She tried to fuck Tristan last night, that's why he ran off. You know Bridget, she's adorable, I love her to bits, but she's so shallow. All she cares about is being somebody. She'll hitch a ride to the top on anyone's back, and Tristan is not just anyone's back.'

They listened to the song. Vivian tried to hum the tune but it was a new song and she had no idea where it was going. Neither did Tristan, it seemed. He would get halfway through the second verse and stop, confused, while the rest of the band swore and cursed him.

'Do you like this song?' Vivian asked.

'Yeah,' Declan lied. 'He's amazing.'

Tears welled in Vivian's eyes. She tried to smile and when she realised she couldn't she tried to hide her face with one hand.

'He's changed my life,' she said sweetly. 'I used to . . . fall in love, you know?'

'Right.'

'But that's the problem, you fall *in* love, you fall *out* of love.'

'Right.'

'Now I'm older I know, oh, I don't know.'

'Yeah.'

'I just love, which is not like being *in* love.'

Declan was no longer listening.

'What am I going to do?' Vivian asked. 'He'll break my heart. I keep telling myself, play it cool, play it cool, you know? I don't want to push him away, but it's hard, it's so hard to love someone and set them free,' she wiped the tears from her eyes. Her mobile rang and she was suddenly chirpy.

'Vivian speaking? Yes, that's right, yes I am. Yes, we're going to Velvet later this evening, about eleven o'clock. I'll make sure, goodbye.'

Vivian hung up the phone. 'Photographer for *Metro*,' she explained. 'It's good publicity, get your photo in the papers and you soon get an agent. Get an agent and you're famous!'

Vivian looked down for a moment, puzzled.

'What happened to your hand?' she asked.

When the recording session ended nobody could rouse the man with lipstick on his chest. One of the groupies tipped a glass of water over him. Liz, the young girl who had said she was Tristan's PA, slapped the man on either cheek, gently at first, but then hard enough to make Vivian wince. Another girl staggered over to the man's body and kicked him in the kidneys. Tristan grunted something about wasting all his drugs on other people, knelt down and injected the man with enough coke to wake a rhino from a coma, but the man remained comatose on the floor.

The other members of the Rods, having waited three hours for their lead singer to arrive, said they were not going to wait for some drug-soaked hanger-on to wake up. Nobody seemed to know who the man was; he must have arrived with someone, but whoever that someone was, he or she was now too embarrassed to reveal the acquaintance.

'Fuck the geezer,' said the drummer. ' 'Ee's not wiv us,' and he walked toward the exit with the rest of the Rods.

'Wek op mon!' said one of the Rastafarians. When the man did not wake up the Rasta shrugged and he and his friends followed the band. The group of young girls did not follow, and the drummer turned and glared at them collectively.

'Girls?' he said.

The girls all looked at one another uncertainly. Declan was starting to panic.

'What about Tristan?' asked one of the girls.

'Go on,' Tristan urged them, as Vivian hooked one arm through his. 'I'm going to have a bit of a kip anyway.' The girls filed out after the band like a gaggle of ducklings. Nathan said the unconscious man could not be left in the recording studio.

'He'll wake up and steal everything that's not nailed down.' So Declan picked the man up and carried him outside and propped him up by a garbage bin.

'Should we leave him a jacket?' Vivian asked. 'It's getting dark.'

'Fuck him,' Tristan said. 'He shouldn't get so fucked up that he can't look after himself.'

Nathan lowered his voice to irony. 'Do you want me to drive you guys home?'

They arrived back at the Chocolate Block just after dusk. Inside the apartment David was smoking on the sofa while Bridget and

Juliet cleaned the kitchen. Juliet looked up and put the Jif cleaning detergent in the fridge just as Declan entered.

'Juliet!' Bridget screamed as Juliet closed the fridge. 'You don't put the *Jif* in the fridge!'

Juliet smiled her best 'whoops' smile, and took the Jif out of the fridge, placing it in the cupboard under the sink. David shook his head and laughed Juliet's name a couple of times like a gangster in a movie just before he takes out a concealed gun and shoots everyone in the room.

'Everybody, you know Tristan,' Vivian said, and the Posse looked up and smiled hello.

'Hi,' Tristan said softly. Of course nobody spoke. They seemed indifferent to Tristan's presence. The famous singer lit a smoke, his eyes flickered. Declan wondered if he knew this nonchalance was just an act. How calm they were now, compared with last night's feverish excitement about having a celebrity at the party.

'Tristan's going to hang with me,' Vivian said, and everybody nodded acceptance.

Declan put the kettle on, spooned some instant coffee into a cup and took the milk from the fridge. Juliet cleaned the bench beside him.

'Did you enjoy last night, Dec?' she asked when the water began to boil.

'Sure, it was mad.'

'Who was the girl?' she raised her voice to bring everyone into the conversation. 'You know, the hot babe in the blue wig? She and Dec spent a few hours together in his room.'

A volley of whistles and cat-calls followed, everyone wanted to know the details.

'Did you wear a condom?'

'Was she a screamer?'

'Nothing happened,' Declan said. 'I spent three hours rubbing her arm like a genie bottle. She called me *le sexual retarde* and left to find her boyfriend.'

Everybody laughed except Juliet.

'Anyone want to watch a movie in my room?' she asked.

'Why in your room?' David asked.

'Because that's where my laptop is.'

'Yeah?' David dropped his voice to the moronic tone. 'It's a laptop; you can't bring it down here and plug it in.'

'Oh,' said Juliet, biting her pinkie finger and looking ashamed. Everyone laughed again while Juliet observed Declan closely. 'What happened to your hand?' she asked.

Declan did not answer. He had not even heard the question. His brain had hazed over and the darkness came and he shuddered as his breathing laboured in short bursts. He tried to leave the room but lost his balance with the first step, and he fell to the floor before his hand could reach the side of the table.

7

The Massive television studio was a glassed-off section of the Trocadero shopping centre near Piccadilly Circus. The studio space looked like the bowels of some technological beast with cables criss-crossing the floor. Cameras, lights, microphones and booms were planted in every possible space on all three sides of the set, which consisted of only a pale green sofa on a small stage, with a bar area and two stools on one side. People shopping in the centre peered through the glass windows like visitors to a human zoo. They expected to see someone famous and usually walked away disappointed or confused, as if to say, *How come I don't know those people if they're so famous?*

Jeremy slipped a piece of paper into Declan's shirt pocket a couple of minutes before they shot the first live 'Movie Maestro' segment.

'The editor for *Fluid* magazine,' Jeremy said, tapping Declan's chest with the palm of his hand and pulling a *you should be impressed* face. 'They need a film reviewer. I told him you were brilliant.'

Declan took Jeremy's piece of paper from his pocket and scrutinised it like a caveman discovering an iPod.

'But I haven't even started this job.'

'So what? You live with Tristan Russell!' Jeremy cooed. 'Love the new moustache by the way.'

Declan had grown a thin Clark Gable moustache like a personal logo on his upper lip. He was going to wear a hat or silly tie but

Bridget didn't approve. He suggested the moustache and she said it might work.

'Did you manage to see any of the films this week?' Jeremy asked.

Declan nodded and shook his head at the same time. 'Yes, no, I mean, I saw two of them, and I read a few American reviews on *Rotten Tomatoes* for two of the others, but I've got a big fat zero on *Jurassic Park III.* I couldn't even get a press pack. Maybe we should skip it.'

Jeremy waved one hand in the air. 'Just make it up, I mean, you know what the plot will be; lots of dinosaurs chasing people.'

'How many stars should I give it?'

'Give it three to match the title.'

The cameramen took up their positions and Declan sat next to Jeremy on a stool. A girl carrying a clipboard came up and said, 'Nice moustache, David.'

'It's Declan.'

'You call your moustache Declan?' The girl with the clipboard smirked.

'No, no, my name, it's not David, it's Declan.'

'Oh,' she indicated her upper lip. 'You look like a bit of a paedophile.'

'You wish!' Jeremy squealed as the girl with the clipboard hurried away.

'Ten seconds to cameras,' another girl carrying a clipboard said.

The studio was filled with girls carrying clipboards. Declan had no idea what they all did but they were always busy. A young man started counting down from eight and when he got to 'three', he counted silently with his fingers, just like Declan had seen people do in television shows about television shows. When the man's last finger disappeared into his fist, Jeremy's face lit up like a torch. Declan felt nothing inside and he smiled coolly for the camera as Jeremy spoke.

'Welcome back everyone, and if you're thinking of going to the movies this week here's the man who can tell you what to see, it's our regular movie maestro David. Hi, David, how are you?'

Declan paused, and then said, 'Great.'

'Have you seen any good films this week?'

'Yes I have.'

'Fantastiche, that's German, so tell us about the first film.'

'OK the first film is called *Jurassic Park* and it is about these people ... '

'Just a minute,' Jeremy brought one hand up to the side of his head so he could hear the director through his earpiece. 'Isn't this *Jurassic Park ... III*?'

'Oh, yeah, yeah right.'

'So what's this one about?'

'Well, you know, they return to the island, walk around, bump into a dinosaur, there's a lot of screaming, everyone runs away, they stop, get their breaths back, walk a bit more, bump into another dinosaur, run, and so on and so forth. The dinosaurs get bigger, the minority race characters all die, someone comes and rescues all the white survivors, who conclude that tampering with nature is a dangerous thing.'

'Wow,' Jeremy laughed. 'Did you actually go and see the film?'

'Does it matter?' Declan asked dryly and everyone behind camera laughed. Suddenly Jeremy leaned over and licked Declan's ear, he said he wanted to suck his cock. The image was real enough to drain the colour from Declan's face. His subconscious had a habit of creating horror scenarios that seemed designed specifically to destroy him in a particular situation. This was no exception.

'Sounds brilliant. How many stars have you given it? Is it

Nowhere, Somewhere, Nearly There, There or a *Massive*?'

'Well I've … ' Somewhere between Declan's ears he was trying to create a sentence and push Jeremy's tongue out of his face at the same time. 'I'm … it's … a … a three.'

'That's … Nearly There. Hey! And three stars! It matches the title, maestro! OK let's take a look at a clip from the movie.'

The TV monitors started playing the clip from *Dinosaur Invasion III*. Declan told Jeremy his name was Declan and Jeremy squeezed his knee.

'Sorry about that, what am I like? You OK?'

Declan did not answer.

'Jeremy, we've got a problem.' A girl with a clipboard was standing at the foot of the stage. 'You know that premium rate phone number you gave out in the last segment, the one for the competition to win free tickets to Legoland?'

'Yes?'

'You gave out the wrong number?'

'I did?'

'You gave a number for a gay chat line.'

Jeremy paled. He fished out a piece of paper from his pocket. It had two numbers written on it, one on either side. He flipped the paper over several times, comparing the numbers.

'They're really similar, aren't they,' Declan said.

The girl with the clipboard frowned. 'Kids are phoning up and being asked if they want to give or receive.'

The trailer for *Jurassic Park III* ended and Jeremy smiled into the camera and thanked viewers for their interest in the Lego Land competition.

'Unfortunately we've had a technical problem and some calls have not been directed to our phone lines so, once again, the number is … '

When Declan got home that night an impromptu party was in full swing. Tristan and Vivian were kissing on the sofa like a couple of teenagers, while David and Bridget danced to Johnny Cash's 'Wanted Man'. Bridget was taking photographs while she danced. Jake was sitting at the table and watching Juliet crush pills with an ancient looking pestle and mortar. Drake sat beside them twitching and trying to rack up lines of coke, constantly looking at Vivian and Tristan with undisguised horror.

The Posse embraced Declan and congratulated him on the new job.

'You were amazing!' Bridget asked, looking for the entire world as if Declan had just starred in a film with Hugh Grant. 'You were completely cool.'

Declan looked crestfallen. 'They sacked me.'

The energy in the room vanished. Everyone stopped still. A laugh of disbelief burst from Bridget's lungs, but she cut it off when Declan continued to look glum. Finally he smiled, the lie was out and everyone laughed.

'Did you fluff any lines?' David asked.

'Of course he didn't,' said Tristan.

'He was like a Swedish tennis player,' said Bridget.

'I've already been offered another job,' Declan explained, 'reviewing for some magazine.'

The Posse issued a collective scream so loud that Declan laughed at the performance. Bridget ran up and down on the spot to release her excitement. The enthusiasm was largely if not entirely drug-related. Declan knew this, but it felt nice to have a group of people acting so interested in his life; how quickly one builds up friendship structures when drugs are the cement binding them together.

Drake gave Declan a couple of pills and pointed down to a line of coke that was the length of a ploughed field.

'This is for you, champ,' he said, handing Declan a rolled-up fifty-pound note.

'This is all for you,' Juliet said. 'This is your party Dec!'

When the pills started to kick in, the girls danced together. Tristan stood on the spot like a tree blowing in the wind, his arms flaying about as he pivoted from the hips. He looked like a malfunctioning C3P0 having a spasm. Jake sat next to Declan and asked how he was feeling.

'I feel alive, kid.'

'Do you think Juliet loves me?'

It was not often that Declan felt in better psychological shape than another person, but when he saw Jake gazing as a frightened child might, he did feel a certain fleeting superiority. God, it was good not to be seventeen.

'Do you love her?' Declan asked, avoiding the question. Jake nodded his head and swallowed.

'She won't listen to me. She tells me I'm just a kid.'

'Isn't it a bitch when people do that?'

'Ye-uh,' Jake breathed incredulously. 'I mean, I'll be eighteen in September.'

'What do your parents think?'

Jake let the air out of his mouth with a whoosh. 'Like they care, right? They're both too busy working. You know what I think? I think Juliet likes someone else.'

'Who?'

'I don't know, but when she's with me, it's as if she's with someone else, if that makes any sense.'

Juliet came over and kissed Jake on the forehead and rubbed him under the chin. 'What are you boys whispering about?'

'We're not whispering!' Jake yelled.

'And we're *not* boys,' Declan said, with aristocratic emphasis.

Declan didn't wake up until three the next afternoon. He stayed in bed feeling awful for another two hours. At five he made his way to the kitchen, knocking against the walls several times. He made and drank his coffee in the kitchen because he could never have walked back to his bedroom without spilling it on the way. A man in a baseball cap and overalls was packing Claire's belongings to take them back to Manchester, where she was undergoing counselling and psychological treatment.

Bridget and Vivian were cuddling on the sofa in the living room and watching the *Weakest Link*, a new quiz show on BBC2 that was like some kind of promotional video for Darwinian Theory. The ruthless, cut-throat, backstabbing, ridiculing format had made it a daily must-see television programme. At the end of each round the contestants ganged up on the biggest loser, or some other target, and eliminated them with extreme prejudice.

'Hey,' Declan said.

Vivian and Bridget gave him a cursory glance and muttered something inaudible before returning their attention to the programme. 'As a failure you're a great success, aren't you?' said the show's presenter, Anne Robinson. The two girls snorted derision and Anne continued her dismissal: 'You are the weakest link, goodbye.' The loser walked off set with his head lowered. Anne's mouth was set like an old cat's bum, tight with haemorrhoids.

'Wild night last night … ,' Declan ventured.

'Shhh!' Bridget hissed 'We're watching this.'

'I'd like to see Sophie voted off next,' the ex-contestant said. 'I think she needs to be pulled off her high horse.'

Declan stood behind the girls and realised the conversation was over.

That week he wrote reviews for three films and sent them off to Francis Hall, the editor of *Fluid*. He had never read *Fluid* and assumed it was a new style magazine. Francis sent Declan an email of congratulations. He was given a list of five films to review for that month's issue. Declan wrote two hundred words for each film, and e-mailed them to Francis.

Francis: Hi Declan! The reviews are brilliant! I *lurrrv* them! But could they be tweaked a bit for our readership?

Declan: Hi Francis, glad you liked the reviews. How exactly do you want me to 'tweak them'?

Francis: Well, you can't review a film with Mark Wahlberg in it and not mention his hot arse.'

What the hell, Declan thought, so it's not a style magazine. It was one hundred and fifty pounds a month, and all he had to do was tweak. Destiny is not always fatal but it can be much more than a curious cup of tea leaves. How many other people have found themselves suddenly lurching down a career path that would never have occurred to them on any ordinary Sunday in a lifetime?

Declan went to the studio the following Saturday and Trevor asked if he had taken the *Fluid* job. Declan said that he had, and for the entire fifteen minute 'Movie Maestro' segment Trevor rested one hand on Declan's knee under the bar. They finished the fifteen minute spiel and the director cut to an ad break. Declan explained to Trevor that he had not known it was a gay magazine when he took the job.

'Oh, you didn't know?' Trevor drew his lips together.

'No.'

They say that eighty per cent of communication is non-verbal.

Declan was sure he and Trevor understood each other. Trevor was a really nice man, but he was so nice, all the time, to everyone, that the value of his niceness depreciated like a Latin American peso during a communist revolution.

Rationalising the new job as a gay film reviewer was easy. A man did not need to like cock to recognise a good looking actor on the screen, did he? Like most men Declan was homo-sensual, in so far as he was sensitive to the aesthetics of the male form. Perhaps society's understanding of male beauty is more concrete because the ideal has not changed for thousands of years, in terms of physique if not hair style. Greek and Roman sculptors used male models that could have easily found employment with the Ford Agency in New York today, if only they shaved their beards, but one of Titian's female nudes on a catwalk today would be unimaginable.

When Declan took the job as a gay film reviewer he was conscious of the deceit, but he was poor and needed the money. His only concern was that the gay readers would spot his fraudulent voice immediately. They never did, which was comforting and disturbing in equal measure.

People say that power tends to corrupt and absolute power corrupts absolutely. Perhaps this is true. Declan did not know because he had never had any power, but he had been relatively poor, and he knew from experience that poverty was corrupting. Perhaps absolute poverty was even more corrupting than absolute power, because it left a person with few choices. Declan had entered Purgatory thinking he would never be able to afford the rent but now that he was making money he felt a weak sort of optimism. Bridget also introduced him to the editor of a magazine called *Here's Life*.

'I'm not a journalist,' Declan had said.

'You don't have to be,' Bridget laughed.

The magazine claimed to publish gritty real life stories submitted by readers and aimed at a young female demographic. The stories were generally made up by freelancers who then asked friends to sign a contract saying the story was true and that the magazine could publish their name. The magazine had a weekly circulation of more than one million and Declan received eight hundred pounds for an eight hundred word story. The person who signed a contract to say the story was true received three hundred pounds from the magazine. The Posse helped Declan find people to sign the stories he made up, and Drake signed one himself called 'I Used to be a Gangland Killer'. Some nights when they were all high on pills or coke, they would try to come up with stories so outrageous that they would never be accepted by the magazine's editor. Most of these stories were accepted, including 'My Boyfriend Only Eats Dog Food', 'I Masturbate Fifty Times a Day', and 'My Mother Slept With My Boyfriend – and I Don't Care'.

Declan had come to London determined to create a future that buried his past forever. Since arriving, he had barely pointed a finger to direct his own life. He wondered if he would ever make a conscience choice to live the life he wanted. And what sort of life did he want to live?

8

The day Declan's first gay film reviews were published in *Fluid,* he arrived home from a movie screening in Soho Square and the apartment was dark. He turned the light on in the living room and everyone jumped out from behind the sofa.

'Congratulations butt boy!' they yelled, and Bridget started taking photographs. She had bought a copy of the magazine, cut out pictures of naked, gay men and stuck them all over the living-room walls. Juliet read the reviews in a faux-camp voice, 'Is it any good? Who cares? It's got Paul Walker in it,' and everybody laughed and hugged Declan. He was a very convincing gay film reviewer.

Drake gave him a sloppy kiss on the cheek and said, 'I love you like a brother man.' His eyes were moist and he smiled through his tears as he shook his head. Tristan took Declan's hand and tried to focus, but his eyes were beyond the task so he rubbed Declan's cheek and whispered gravely, 'Remember. Remember what I said.'

'I will,' Declan replied. He had no idea what Tristan was talking about. Sitting around the table taking drugs together everyone's bright, smiling faces were glowing with love. *It's love for me,* Declan thought, with something like genuine emotion. *My success has made them happy.*

They all went to the Shoreditch club that night and continued to celebrate. Vivian phoned two news photographers before leaving the flat, and a row of cameramen were waiting at the front door of the club ready to snap her and Tristan as they were ushered through the red ropes.

Inside the club, the Posse was given a large table in the VIP area and Tristan stood up and proposed a toast in Declan's honour.

'I want to say,' he murmured, 'honestly, thank you. Everywhere I go I've got people kissing my poo-hole because of my … reputation.' The girls laughed loudly at the euphemism. 'But you guys, you guys are the first people to treat me like an ordinary wee human being. I've been living among you for a month but it feels like a lifetime, and I don't feel like "Tristan Russell the fantabulous celebrity" with you people. I feel I can be myself, so, thank you for setting me free.'

Everyone clapped and Declan tried to smile but he could feel the tension in his eyes. Vivian and Bridget wiped the tears from their cheeks and Vivian stood and gave Tristan a passionate, throaty kiss.

The girls went off to dance and Declan spoke with Drake about his acting career. Drake screamed something but Declan was not listening. He was looking at Juliet on the dance floor and her body drowned Drake's words completely. Juliet's long fingers moved over her hips with the eroticism of a lover's touch. She held one hand in the air and rang an imaginary bell in time with the music's beat. Her eyes lowered demurely and her black hair throbbed as her body moved. She occasionally swung low to the ground while keeping her back perfectly straight, enacting a seductive booty grind just above the ground as if riding a man or a wild beast, before rising again to her full height.

'Oh fuck me,' Declan whispered unconsciously, but aloud. 'You are so sexy.' He closed his eyes and saw himself scooping

Juliet into his arms and pressing his lips to hers.

'What? Dec? Dec?' Drake punched Declan in the arm. 'Are you talking to me? Because, you know, I … I like you … but … ?'

Juliet opened her eyes, for just a moment, and looked straight at Declan. The air in his mouth stood still and his body was arrested by a thick pulse of desire.

When the song finished the girls came back to the table and Juliet squeezed in beside Declan, her warm thigh pressing against his leg, sending a painful shudder from his belly up to his heart and back down again. He was still unable to breathe properly, and when he gave Juliet a light from his cigarette his hand was shaking.

'Are you cold?' Juliet asked.

'Freezing,' Declan lied.

'Tristan and I have got an announcement,' Vivian said, and everyone looked at her in horror. 'We're going to record a duet!'

Bridget sighed. 'Thank God!' she said, conveying the general sentiment but staring now at Tristan. 'I thought you were pregnant.'

'It's going to be a ballad,' Vivian said. 'Like Kylie and Nick.'

'Love those Aussies,' Tristan said with a wink. 'We just have to try and get a few musicians to play with us. The Rods won't be all, "Smashing, Triz", that's for sure. They resent the fact that I'm more important than them.'

Tristan's relationship with the other Rods had deteriorated to the point that they only communicated to one another through Nathan. Tristan's inability to arrive sober, or even at all to most gigs, had compromised the band's reputation and very few live venues were now booking them. Tristan was equally unreliable when the Rods booked a recording studio. As the chief songwriter in the band, he had written just two and a half songs since moving into Heaven and one of those was the duet with Vivian. None of Tristan's old friends ever came to visit him after he moved into Heaven. Teenage groupies followed him everywhere, of course, and clubbers always lined up to give him free blow or a blow job, but none of his real friends ever came to the flat to either hang out or take drugs. Even Nathan kept away unless his managerial skills were required.

Declan was brought back out of his own thoughts by Bridget, who screamed, 'Oh my God!' across the table.

Tristan was pulling Vivian off the dance floor and marching her back to the table. He threw her into a seat and stood over her, snarling like a thug despite the fact that he was almost two feet shorter than her.

'What's your game then? What's that all about?'

Vivian started to explain that she had only been dancing but Tristan cut her off and brought one index finger under her nose.

'EVER!' he screamed, somewhat cryptically. 'You hear me! Ever, you bitch!' He motioned to smack her with an open palm, but left the hand half-cocked near his shoulders, before turning and walking away.

Declan looked over to David who shrugged his shoulders with bemusement. He mouthed the words 'just dancing' and shrugged once more.

9

Tristan had moved into Heaven in early July and by August the newspapers knew he was living with the Posse. The *Mirror* scooped the names 'Heaven' and 'Purgatory' for the upper and lower floors. The *Evening Standard* called these two floors 'Heaven' and 'Hell', and these two titles were evenly divided up by the papers so Declan was living in either Hell or Purgatory, but never in Heaven. Newspapers ran stories about Tristan's new flatmates but only Bridget and Vivian were mentioned with any degree of accuracy. Bridget was a member of the Brit Art set whose next exhibition was going to be held at EX Gallery in Hoxton. Vivian was a model and performer who worked as a promoter at the trendy Shoreditch club. She was also described as Tristan Russell's latest muse. She was nineteen years old at first, then twenty-one or twenty-two, and then she was nineteen again. Juliet's age varied to a greater extent; she was twenty-three one day, and thirty-two the next. She started off running her own business selling maternity clothing before becoming a pharmacist. On one occasion she was a GP and an events coordinator for the City of London, all on the same day. David was a commercial photographer, but then he lost this employment and became a drug addict. At first Declan was unemployed, like David. In fact Declan might have been David at first, then he became a barman, then a copywriter for a small advertising agency, and finally, inevitably, a gay film reviewer. Luckily none of the papers got his name right, he was Desmond, then Daryl, and his last name was most consistently Twit but there were several Trotters in there as well. 'Daryl Trotter!' Juliet laughed when she read the article.

The day after the party Declan woke at ten. He got up stiffly, wobbled to the door, bounced off the architrave and fell to the floor. Then he picked himself up and walked with one hand sliding along the wall to keep balanced.

Bridget and Vivian were sleeping together on the living-room sofa-bed. They looked like the pair of spooning lovers whose shapes had been moulded from solidified ash at Pompeii. Declan had been to a Pompeii exhibition once when he was ten years old, and seen a mould of a young couple holding each other. It was unforgettable. The lovers had died together thousands of years ago. Now they were locked in an eternal embrace and touring the world like a theatrical event. How much more do people love the past when it can maintain the illusion of appearing concrete?

Declan left the Chocolate Block at midday to attend a movie preview. When he opened the main door onto the street two teenage girls started screaming like Beatles fans from the Sixties.

'*ARGH!*' Declan screamed, louder than the two girls and with far more conviction. His hands came up to protect his face. The girls stopped screaming and looked confused. Declan ran across the street, his heart pounding.

That evening when he arrived home he heard giggling voices in his bedroom. Tristan was lying on his back in Declan's bed with the two teenage girls that had been outside the building that morning.

'*ARGH!*' Declan screamed.

'*ARGH!*' the girls screamed back.

Tristan saw who it was and sighed.

'Jesus, Declan, you scared the monkey off my back. What are you screaming about?'

All three were naked. The girls had extraordinary bodies; thin waists, large breasts, round buttocks all fitted together with no fat, no wrinkles, no blemishes, no signs of aging. They were pure youth and beauty. They could have burst fully formed from the womb of a generically questionable male fantasy, but they were real, and to Declan's mind they represented only mind trauma. The sharks were swimming in his veins as the girls looked up at him and smirked lustfully.

'Why don't you come and get a spanking,' one said. She was stroking Tristan's cock with one hand.

'Yeah,' Tristan laughed. 'Come on, Dec, the girls want to punish you!'

The second girl went down on Tristan and took his whole cock in her mouth. Her tongue came out and started tickling his scrotum. He moaned deeply. It was an impressive performance. Declan had never seen a grown woman get that much cock in her mouth before, let alone a sixteen-year-old girl. Her friend pouted sensually and wriggled an index finger at Declan, but he closed the door without saying anything and ran most of the way to the local pub where he drank six quick pints of Guinness, and threw half of them up in the gutter on the way home.

The bedroom was empty when Declan got back but the penetrating smell of perfume and cheap sex was still in the air. He opened the window and went into the living room where Bridget and Vivian were going through each of the daily newspapers, a habit they had developed since Tristan's arrival.

'Nothing in *The Times*,' Vivian said.

'Tory twats,' snorted Bridget. 'Ah! You're in the *Mirror!*'

Bridget turned the newspaper toward Vivian so she could see the photograph and read the caption.

'Oh that's lovely,' Vivian squealed.

'Your tits look fantastic.' Bridget squeezed Vivian's left breast maternally. 'Your tits are fantastic.'

'It's the dress,' Vivian said modestly. 'I knew that dress would make the papers.'

Declan went up to Heaven and found Juliet sitting on her bed perusing a sheet of medical papers.

'Dim the light,' she commanded as soon as Declan entered. She had one of those adjustable lights with a switch that could be turned one way to reduce the light, and the other way to make it brighter. Declan turned the switch clockwise and the room brightened like a West End musical. Juliet looked up angrily.

'Hey! Hey! I don't like sitting under a spotlight.'

'OK, Blanche DuBois,' Declan said. 'Relax. I'll put the Chinese lantern back over the naked bulb.'

He dimmed the light and walked over to the right-side wall. He squinted to try to see the photographs Juliet had arranged on a cork board. They were all photos of smiling party people holding drinks and cigarettes in their hands, and laughter in their mouths. Declan sat down on the bed beside Juliet.

'Are you wasted?' Juliet asked, 'You're slurring your words.'

'No, no, it's just when I'm tired, the brain damage thing. What you got there?'

'Employment records for pharmacists,' Juliet smiled. She looked Declan up and down several times. 'I go through and look for people who have had three or four employers in as many years.'

'Why?" Declan slurred. 'Does that mean they're fickle?'

'It means they might have a habit. If bosses are suspicious but have no concrete evidence, they don't renew a pharmacist's contract at the end of the year. They say they're cutting down on staff.'

'Right, so what do you do?'

'First, I take some of this.'

Juliet took a pestle and mortar from her bedside table, dropped six pills into the pestle and crushed them into fine white powder with the mortar.

'I feel like a Renaissance artist when I do this,' she smiled.

She emptied the powder onto a square mirror and racked up four lines with the celerity of a sous-chef shaving garlic for a soup stock. She then rolled up a bank note and snorted the first two lines before handing the rolled up note to Declan.

'What is it?'

'Concertal,' Juliet said. 'One of our ADHD drugs for kids; it's a good hit. People don't know it but stimulants are like one big molecular family. Concertal is a psycho-stimulant, it's like cocaine's baby brother.'

'Why don't kids get addicted to it?'

'They do if they exceed the recommended dosage.' Juliet raised her eyebrows and her eyes blinked and flashed like the lights at a drag race. Declan leaned down and cleaned the lines from the mirror.

'Now watch,' Juliet said, and she dialled a number and cleared her throat. When someone answered the phone Juliet spoke in a new, timorous voice that Declan did not recognise. 'Hello Elizabeth Blake speaking, I wanted to speak to someone about my boyfriend. He's a former employee of yours ... Philip Turner? Yes, he ... he's my boyfriend and this is a very sensitive issue but I don't know who else to speak with. In the past few months he, well God, he looks dreadful. I'm ... ' Juliet sobbed into the phone and winked at Declan. She rested one hand on his thigh. 'I ask him if there's something the matter and he says no, but I'm concerned – this is a very sensitive issue. I'm concerned that he might be doing something at work which he shouldn't be doing … Yes, I suppose that is what I'm saying … Was there ever, did you ever think he might be, you know, experimenting … Yes … Yes … Yes … Oh-my-God … Oh-my-God. You really think? … No of course I won't. Thank you. Thank you so much … I won't, thank you.'

Juliet hung up and smiled coyly. 'They thought he was helping himself to the Benzos.'

Juliet dialled another number.

'Hello, is that Mr Turner? Hello, my name is Gertrude Smith, I work for NICE and we need to talk … That's right … I'd rather not say over the phone, but I will say this, it is in your best interest to … '

Juliet jerked back suddenly. 'Hello? Hello? Mr Turner?'

Juliet closed her phone and looked at Declan, stunned. 'I think he just dived through the window of his apartment.'

'What's NICE?' Declan asked, not believing the story.

'National Institute for Health and Clinical Excellence, it's a government watchdog. I can't believe he jumped out the window.'

'I think you're being dramatic. What did he say?'

'He said, "You'll never catch me alive!" There was the sound of smashing glass … and … his voice … screaming and … fading away like … '

Juliet looked mortified for several more seconds then her whole face blinked and a new expression appeared. She winked and smiled, and inspected her list of pharmacists once more. Declan had no idea if she were telling the truth.

'OK, no more Mr Turner, let's have a look here. Mr Darling? Mr Casper Darling,' she dialled the number and winked. 'Want to come with me to meet him?'

'Me?'

'Sure, you can be my boyfriend.'

10

Declan and Juliet met Casper Darling the following night in a Soho bar that had a name like a farmer's vegetable patch. Juliet wore blood-red lipstick, and a low-cut red dress that was a stunning advertisement for her body. She smoked Menthols and sipped a glass of wine, checking her phone for messages every minute or so. Declan watched her languid movements like a schoolboy peeping through the girls' toilet window; her full lips, the angle of her wrist, the two-finger and thumb hold on her glass of wine. Juliet seemed made for celluloid. She flicked her rich black hair over one shoulder and the light rippled through it. A flush of pleasure surged through Declan's belly and he had to open his mouth to let the air out silently from some deep place near his groin. His body was aflame with desire.

'You're a mystery man, aren't you?' Juliet said. She took out a blonde wig and fitted it to her head, adjusting it until every black strand was hidden.

'What do you mean?'

'I've been asking questions. Nobody's got answers. You're the man with no past. Like Mr Bean beamed down to London from outer space and you don't tell anyone anything about … anything.'

'I've got a wife and three young daughters,' Declan explained. 'Kate, Sophie and Emily. Barbara and I divorced a year ago, and I came to London to start over.'

This was not the kind of back story Juliet was expecting. She took a sip of her vodka and winced while searching for something to say. 'Jesus,' was all she could come up with.

Declan waited a bit longer for this reality to settle into Juliet's mind before telling her he was joking. She laughed and sounded relieved.

'What about your family, Juliet?'

Juliet sucked on her teeth. 'What can I say? It's the typical tale of a modern British family. I finished school, I applied to a university as far away from my parents as possible, when I finished my studies I moved to London and now I see Mum and Dad for Christmas and family deaths. And you're going to be famous, Declan,' she concluded. It wasn't a question it was a statement.

'Famous?'

Juliet put her phone on the table, looked up at Declan and delivered a droll smile. 'The TV film review thing.'

'Mmm,' Declan said, shaking his head and letting the vodka slip down his throat. 'Nobody watches the show. I'd say it's got a steady audience in the double figures.'

'Come on, aren't you excited?'

'No,' Declan said.

'But it might be the beginning of a fabulous career. You're a strange creature, aren't you? What aspirations did you have when you were a kid?'

'Honestly? When I was ten I dreamed of living in a great big glass house, with a high fence so kids couldn't throw stones at it. It was two stories high and my wife and I would lie in this king-size bed on the second floor and stare up at the blue sky through the glass roof, and have sex all day.'

'That was your ambition? To fuck in a glass house all day long?'

'That was it. Then I wanted to be an artist, old-school, you know, with paint. But after my brain injury I couldn't … I couldn't … '

'I bet you could.' Juliet looked at Declan steadily. 'Anyway, I'm excited,' she said. Her large brown eyes throbbed with an emotion that was inviting. 'I think you're great.'

Declan gazed down at the gently pulsing flesh of Juliet's cleavage, then realised where he was looking and jerked his head back up to look into her eyes. He could almost believe that she liked him, but Bridget had warned him when he first moved in, *Juliet is a fully-rigged-out twenty-first-century babe. If she were a car she'd been a street racer. She doesn't believe in boyfriends and why would she? She's rich, successful and too stupid, so she sticks to boys that are young, dumb and full of come.*

A tall man dressed in a smart suit entered the bar and looked around. Juliet raised one arm and waved. 'That's him.' Casper was tall with an angular face. He looked suspicious as he approached the table in the back corner of the bar. His eyes were hollow and nervous, and his hands picked at one another in front of his chest like a pair of birds fighting for food. Juliet stood and shook his hand warmly. Her touch seemed to suck some of the suspicion out of his body. He sat down. His eyes wandered unconsciously over her low-cut red dress and lingered around her chest.

'This is my boyfriend, Declan.'

Casper shook Declan's hand, mumbled a greeting and ordered a drink while Juliet checked through the papers she had placed on the table. She spoke in a deep voice, with an authority Declan had never heard before. Her entire manner was as foreign to him as the blonde wig on her head. She sat with her back straight, shoulders square, eyes solemn, occasionally sparkling, in full command of the situation. It was an astonishing metamorphosis.

'Right, Casper. I've been checking your records. You've been frisky haven't you?

'Frisky?'

'You've been moving around quite a bit.' Juliet read from her sheet of paper. 'Highbury, Westmount, Whiteoaks, Eltham, Southall, Finsbury Park ... '

'Who are you?'

'I'm your friend.'

'What do you want?'

Juliet smiled coyly. 'I want to help you.'

'How?'

'I've spoken to a few of your old employers. Let's be frank here, quite a few of them suspected you had a taste for the drugs.' Casper stood to leave and Juliet spoke quickly. 'No, no, no, it's OK, I'm here to help you; I'm your *friend*.'

Casper sat down again and clasped his hands on the table in front of him. 'I don't have any N.I.C.E. friends.'

'I work for a big pharmaceutical,' Juliet said quickly, winking.

'Why didn't you say so?'

'Over the phone? Are you serious? How long have you been you using?'

'I haven't slept in seven months.'

Juliet looked at Casper's anxiety-lined face and smiled. 'Great, you want some help?'

'What you got?'

'I've got the keys to the pantry, dear boy. I can sell you samples at twenty-five per cent, but they're not just for you. I'm not a social worker handing out methadone. You're working at Manning's now? Kentish Town. Good business there. You could easily shift a few thousand a week. Here's what I want you to do. You remove the drug samples from the original marked, sealed containers and put them in standard pharmacy vials with your Manning's label.'

'I punch those samples from the packaging and the pedigree is lost. There's no way of knowing the expiration date.'

'So you don't want to do this?'

'N … no, I'm just saying.'

'Because if you don't want to just say so and I'll walk away.'

'No, I do, I do. Sorry, I do want to do this.'

Just then twenty cops burst out of Declan's imagination and arrested Juliet. Caspar took his police badge out and shook his head mockingly. The idea was so vivid it made the hairs on Declan's scalp rigid and he finished his drink in one gulp.

When the meeting concluded Caspar stayed for two more drinks and when it was time to go, Juliet refused to catch the Underground home with Declan.

'I'm not riding cattle class,' she said. 'It stinks in the summer.'

'I … I don't like taxis,' Declan said.

'Don't worry, I'll pay.'

'No, I mean, I don't like cars.'

In the taxi on the way home Juliet explained her job. Declan focused his whole being on her story and tried to forget the fact that they were flying down the road in a can of metal.

Phebron was the second largest pharmaceutical company operating in the UK, with annual sales of over a billion pounds. The only industry that contributed more to the UK's national GDP was financial services and, as with the operations of financial markets, the pharmaceutical industry's professional activities were an extensive and multifaceted menagerie of corruption. The industry's corrupt practises did not receive anywhere near as much attention as Tristan's Russell's personal, illicit drug consumption, possibly because the drug companies paid a lot more tax; certainly Russell was a more entertaining headline than any pharmaceutical company.

Juliet's job was more in line with promotion management than sales representative. The symposiums she organised were always specifically related to an area of medicine in which Phebron had a new drug to promote. If they had a new drug to combat acne then they underwrote a dermatology conference in which a specialist on acne prevention was the designated keynote speaker. Other dermatological specialists were recruited to give talks on acne prevention. This practise was met with regular expressions of disapproval in both houses of parliament, but Phebron had always escaped legal censure by contending that their symposiums were serious scientific conferences raising the profile of a particular problem or aspect of medical treatment. The symposiums were held in five-star hotels and generally lasted for three days. All travel expenses, accommodation, food and drinks were paid for by Phebron. Up until 1996 Phebron used to throw in free tickets to a West End musical and leave bottles of Moet in each hotel room, but that practice had been dropped after they were accused of bribery.

'It's like working for Satan,' Juliet said. 'It certainly makes what I do a lot easier to rationalise; if you work for Satan it's hard to feel guilty about stealing from him. It's just like following company policy in an admirable and creative way.'

Declan looked at Juliet in wonder. 'It's all an act, isn't it? The ditzy girly shit. You were like Margaret Thatcher back there, only much, much sexier.'

'You've got an eye for volume, Dec.'

'That's one way of putting it. Why do you act stupid?'

'I don't act stupid.'

'You do; vague, forgetful, naive and stupid. That's what the Posse thinks.'

'And you act like a dial-tone. You pretend you have no passion for anything.'

'But you're not stupid at all.' Declan's face formed a question mark. Juliet sighed.

'Time and place, Declan, time and place. I don't need people at home to know anything about me. People think that because I'm good looking with great tits I must be stupid. That has its advantages, you know. I'm far less likely to be suspected by my bosses.'

'But the Posse aren't your bosses, they're your friends.'

'OK.'

'OK? What does that mean?'

'We've all got secrets, Declan, not just you.'

It was true, everyone had secrets. Casper Darling had a secret. The police had arrested him three days before Juliet had first spoken with him on the phone. He had been charged with stealing prescription drugs from the stock room at Manning's, and the case was to go to trial in six weeks. He was looking at a two-year sentence and the end of his professional career, but if he could offer the police information in their wider investigations, he hoped the charges against him might be dropped.

11

The house was empty when Juliet and Declan arrived home. Bridget, David and Drake had gone to the Shoreditch club with Vivian, and Tristan had been missing for a couple of days. Juliet and Declan had a coffee and she tried to dig up some facts about his past, but he evaded all her questions easily.

'Well,' Juliet finally muttered when she realised she was not going to learn anything. She raised her hands above her head and arched her back so her breasts strained against the fabric of her dress, 'I think I might have an early night.'

Declan felt he should have made a suggestion to do something, anything that involved going up to Juliet's room, but he could not think of anything so he nodded his head sadly and said, 'OK.'

Juliet's mouth twitched momentarily, and then she stood up and left.

'Don't let the bed bugs bite!' she said as she ascended the stairway to Heaven.

Declan stayed in the lounge for an hour watching a television programme about the up-and-coming Australian Olympic Games. Shortly after midnight, the door to Purgatory opened and Declan heard Tristan whispering nervously.

'You just wait here.'

Moments later he peered into the living room and eyed Declan with a certain disappointment.

'Anyone else home?' he slurred. Declan shook his head and

Tristan left to bring back whoever was waiting at the front door. He returned with a young girl who looked no more than seventeen years old. Individual teenage girls had no affect on Declan, only when they were in groups, so he smiled and said, 'Hello.'

The girl was carrying a layer of puppy fat, accentuated by the figure-hugging garments she was wearing: a pair of jodhpurs and a Lycra top. Her smile was all metal braces and her pink cheeks were peppered with pimples. Tristan had been drinking. It seemed to agree with him far more than the heroin or crack; his face was flushed and he appeared optimistic in an abstract kind of way. The girl was wasted on ecstasy or something harder; she ground her jaw like a mental patient who had just received electric shock therapy. Her tongue had lost its balance and her eyes were unable to focus.

'Dec, this is … ' Tristan looked at the girl and waited for her to finish the sentence.

'Charlie,' the girl said in a thick, excited voice.

'This is Charlie. Charlie, meet Dec.' As he spoke Tristan indicated Declan's bedroom with his angled head. Declan stood up, said he was feeling tired and had to go to sleep.

'Oh mate,' Tristan purred, 'you don't want to stay up an' have a chat?'

In bed Declan listened through the wall to the conversation between Tristan and the young girl.

'Your girlfriend is beautiful,' Charlie said. 'I've seen her in the papers and stuff.'

'She's not my girlfriend, not really.'

'She's lovely.'

'You're lovely.'

'Not like her.'

'You're unique. You're not quite like anyone else. That's what I love about you.'

The girl laughed shyly. 'What you *love* about me?'

'Love. Yes. Why be stingy with the word? Why be stingy with the emotion? We English are so repressed. I'm not. I'm not afraid to love because I know that real love can never hurt us. Real love wants for nothing, it asks for nothing, it finds joy in whatever shelter is offered, however briefly, from this stormy, stormy life.'

'I love the way you speak with words.'

'I let myself go to love because love is what truly sets us free. Love sets us free while all around us people are bound in chains.'

'You mean like in prison.'

'Morality is a prison. The church is a prison. William Blake wrote a poem about it.'

Declan heard Tristan recite Blake's poem in a sonorous voice:

> 'So I turn'd to the Garden of Love
> That so many sweet flowers bore.
> And I saw it was filled with graves,
> And tombstones where flowers should be;
> And Priests in black gowns were walking their rounds,
> And binding with briars my joys and desires.'

'What does it mean?'

'It means that our joys and desire cannot be tied up, they must be set free. Do you know the phrase *free love*?'

'That's what the hippies did in the Seventies?'

'It was William Blake's phrase, two hundred years before the hippies. He was a prophet of free love.'

'You're like a prophet.'

Tristan began to sing in a bashful voice, an urgent whisper of seduction.

'Only love can set us free / so lay your lovely down beside me / I'll kiss your eyes / your mouth Charlie / I'll kiss your body 'till you see / only love can set us free.'

She paused awkwardly. 'I … I don't know that one,' Charlie confessed.

'Of course you don't. I just made it up, just for you.'

'Oh my God. Oh my *God*.'

'Do you like it?'

'You're amazing. You're the most … ' Charlie let out a soft, languid moan.

'You're so sweet,' Tristan breathed. 'You're so untouched, like a tropical beach on a desert island. Your hair smells of promises, your throat tastes like the dreams I've never touched, each breast feels like the arriving moment of a deep desire.'

'That feels nice.'

'Do you like that?'

'Uh–huh.'

Charlie continued to moan in short, uncertain stabs. The blood drained from Declan's face. He struggled to keep a herd of horrid sexual images from stampeding through his imagination, and was about to bury his head in his pillow when he heard Juliet in the room directly above. The air roared in his ears as he strained to listen. He stood up on the bed so his head was closer to the ceiling, listening. Juliet was moaning gently. Between the moans, Declan could discern the faint hum of a small electric motor. For a moment he thought she must be shaving her legs.

He turned his light on, reached under the bed and found a shoe-box of old love letters that he had packed before moving to London. He pulled up a random letter from Gemma, his first love. They had been seventeen years old when they first started seeing each other. They stayed together for fourteen months without ever having sex. In later years Declan often wondered how he had passed through his eighteenth year without having sex once. He was a reformed Catholic, and that explained a lot of his strange behaviour in the past, but this was one truth that always shocked him. He had not been a virgin at the time, he had enjoyed sex with three different women when he was sixteen but then, at seventeen, he simply waited and waited and waited until the relationship with Gemma capsized. He could still remember the context in which this letter was written. They were in the process of breaking up and Declan was desperately trying to convince Gemma that he loved her. She was not convinced.

You have idealised me out of all proportion, Gemma wrote. *I read the things you say about me and don't see myself. It's like you've invented some other Gemma despite me, and I could never live up to the person you think I am. I would only disappoint you.*

Declan drew in a deep breath as if sucking down all the words. Gemma was right. He had idealised her. He tended to idealise women. It was so easy to do. On a purely aesthetic level women were ideal, they were perfectly beautiful, perfectly formed; there was not a single thing that could be added or subtracted from the female body to improve it. They were goddesses of the flesh. Declan closed his eyes in the darkness and Gemma came to him. She did not kiss him or peel his clothes off and make love to him; she put one arm around him, smiled warmly and rubbed his back with her hand.

'You silly twat,' she said.

12

Tristan entered Declan's room the next morning without knocking and said he needed to take the edge off. He searched through Declan's desk drawers. He looked smaller somehow, his shoulders were not pulled back confidently but slumped forward, and when he found nothing in the drawers he slammed the final drawer closed angrily.

'I feel like shit!' he said, then lowered his voice. 'I can't find anything. I hate being like this. I hate it.'

He pointed to a painting postcard by Artemisia Gentileschi, *Judith Slaying Holofernes.*

'That's lovely, that is.'

'It's a self-portrait,' Declan slurred. 'She was the only female artist who made a name for herself back then. Artemisia Gentileschi – beautiful name, eh?'

'Are you wasted?' Tristan asked. 'What you got?'

'No, it's just, when I'm tired, my speech sounds a bit spaz, that's all.' Declan returned Tristan's attention to the Gentileschi painting. 'The guy getting his head hacked off is the likeness of the guy who raped her when she was a young girl. Art can be a great revenge, no?'

'Her arms look funny. They're too straight.'

'Maybe she wants to keep her distance.'

'Why? Has the guy just farted?'

'Maybe she doesn't want his blood splattering all over her dress. It's a beautiful dress.'

Tristan looked more closely.

'Right, right. I never thought of that. Talk about cold reasoning.' He sighed. 'Yeah, listen, sorry about last night.' He did not sound particularly sorry. 'What goes on the tour stays on the tour, right?'

'As long as you wear a condom.'

'I'm surprised you didn't get a bit of the action the other day. You're not a prude are you?'

'I haven't had sex in ten years.'

Tristan looked like he'd just seen a child murdered.

'I'm joking. I have sex about six hundred times a day,' Declan pointed to his temple with an index finger. 'Up here, I am nothing if not a beast.'

'Tell me about it,' Tristan said. 'My beast escaped the asylum and he's on the loose, baby. You would not believe what these young girls are like.'

'That's probably a good thing for me.'

'Bridget showed me some of your writing,' Tristan said. 'The catalogue for her exhibition next month.'

Tristan was twisting his body as if to avoid looking Declan in the eye, he scratched his arms and his voice was rattled and soft as a rabbit.

You're good with that stuff aren't you?' Tristan continued.

'It's all bollocks.'

'I thought it was terrific.'

'It's just words, ideas about art that don't exist, except in words, and if you need words to create ideas for your art … ' Declan did not finish this sentence because he did not know how to finish it. 'Do you think people had to be told what the Sistine Chapel was all about in order for them to see it as a great work of art?'

'You are a Romantic.' Tristan looked at the postcards of paintings on the bedroom wall. 'Look at all these crusty old paintings. So you really think Bridget's photographs are for shit?'

'I'll tell you what,' Declan answered, 'when art is all about the concept, then language can become more important than the work of art itself. I don't have a problem with conceptual art; there really is some amazing stuff, some glorious installations and videos. Maybe it's the best way to address contemporary audiences. But the "idea image", you know, conceptual art, it opens the door for every Harry and his Dick. If your artistic idea is … just … let's say; some dirty underpants in a box, then you need a special language to convince people that it's actually great art. Concepts don't stand alone so easily, they need to be explained so people can feel impressed by them. But they're explained in a language that can be applied to almost anything. It's not a language that's *only* relevant to *great* concepts. Almost every single, stupid, seemingly meaningless thing has a conceptual value waiting to come out.'

'What do you mean?'

'Well, choose something here in this room.'

Tristan looked about the room for a moment before pointing to an empty beer tankard standing on the windowsill. Declan had used it as an extra large coffee mug, the coffee stains were visible through the glass.

'What about that empty cup of coffee there?'

'How do you want it to be presented as a work of art?' Declan asked, stalling for time. 'A photograph, on a plinth?'

'Yeah, just as it is there, a sculpture or something, dregs and all, on a pedestal.'

'OK, well, I'd start by noting how people often ask whether the glass is half empty or half full. This work is showing that the glass is, in fact, completely empty. It's a work of ultimate pessimism that offers profound reflection on the depletion of natural resources in this era of hyper-consumerism. In the past one hundred years we have almost *emptied the cup*. Note, too, that while the glass has been emptied it hasn't been cleaned, it hasn't been washed, and it hasn't been replaced in the kitchen cupboard. Its contents have been consumed and it has been unceremoniously dumped. Such is the nature of our materialistic society. We consume and move on, consume and move on, leaving the detritus of our voracious appetites in our wake for others to deal with. If one juxtaposes the predetermined purpose of this vessel and its extant utility, one is aware of a psychic conflict; this is not a coffee cup, this is a beer tankard, its proper role and function has been transgressed. It has been employed as a coffee mug because it offers a greater volume of coffee for consumption. It is the *Super-Size Me* of coffee cups, reflecting not just our greed, but also the dislocation between who we actually are and what we have actually become.'

Tristan nodded his head. 'All right, that one was obviously too easy.' He looked around the room for something else to discuss. His pillow had been stripped of its case and was lying naked on the floor.

'What about that pillow?'

'What is a pillow?' Declan asked rhetorically, resting one hand on his chin like a Rodin sculpture and giving himself a moment to think. Tristan smiled at the performance and Declan continued solemnly. 'When we talk about the pillowness of the pillow, what do we mean? What does a pillow represent? It is the soft cushion on which we rest our weary heads at night? It functions as a ... a ... a material soporific that helps us sleep by reducing the discomfort we might otherwise experience when our heads are reclined and our necks bent over. As such it is like a narcotic, not taken orally or injected into the vein, but rested upon to induce slumber.'

Tristan's mouth hung open.

'A pillow is the promoter of dreams,' Declan continued in a sonorous voice. 'It helps us to escape from reality every night. It draws us away from the sensory world of experience and leads us to the numinous world of dreams, or nightmares.'

'You know, all the great poets were inspired by drugs,' Tristan enthused. 'Baudelaire, Coleridge, Byron, Ginsberg, Jim Morrison, you know what he said, by cleansing the *doors* of perception? That's how I find my muse. I travel down those same narcotic vistas as Baudelaire. That is my creative pillow.'

'What distinguishes this pillow from ordinary pillows is its nakedness,' Declan continued. 'It is in a state of undress, it lacks a pillow case. There is something innocent, naïve, and profoundly vulnerable about this pillow. In the absence of its protective case any stain, any blemish, any mark of any kind is likely to be permanent. While a pillow case can be easily removed and washed, the same process would destroy the pillow. As such this pillow represents the innocent, the untouched, the pure and vulnerable psychic spirit that has no skin, no armour, no way of defending itself again the harsh realities of this world.'

Tristan sucked on his tongue thoughtfully.

'That actually sounds … totally … impressive. I'm totally impressed.'

'You see, words can do anything. They can make you believe anything, and most of the time they're just bullshit.'

'So how can you tell when it's just impressive words applied to bullshit art?'

'You don't read the words, you read the work. If the work doesn't speak to you itself, if your mind is silent when you look at it, if your heart is still … well … ' Declan stopped and lit a cigarette. 'They say the best art always reflects the environment in which it is created. So I suppose ugly bullshit art reflects a powerful truth about society today. You know? Language today isn't the string we hang our experience on, it's the string we tie experience up with, so it can't move. It's the string we hang our bullshit on. It's all ugly bullshit words these days, isn't it? That's why I like the dead white guys who painted five hundred years ago. Today people walk around in real life as if they were on a film set, maybe it's always been that way, but at least back then it looked beautiful.'

'It's different with music,' Tristan said. 'Music can't lie like art because there has to be some kind of aesthetic. The sound of music has to be pleasing on some level; it has to be beautiful, even death metal follows established rhythm and melody structures. Do you know a lot of the chords in death metal are the same as the chords in Dylan's "Knocking on Heaving's Door"?'

'Yeah, but these days image is often more important than sound, no?'

'Sure, sure, I don't suppose the Spice Girls would have sold a record if they looked like fat, middle-aged bingo players.'

'They do look like fat, middle-aged bingo players.'

Tristan laughed and rested one hand on Declan's shoulder.

'You see, Dec? You will get where you want to go one day. I know it.'

'And where do I want to go?'

'You want to be on television don't you?'

'No.'

'But that's what you do.'

'That's the job I was offered. I didn't ask for it. I had no desire for it.'

'You don't want to establish yourself on television?'

'I just want to create space between my past and my present. I always wanted to be a painter but after my brain injury … '

'You see? You're like me. You don't sell out.'

'I write gay film reviews.'

Tristan searched the ceiling with a dreadful thrall as if demons were laughing and plucking out his eyes as he spoke.

'No,' he said, and Declan knew that he was not being spoken to. 'In this world there are dreams, and the dreams are what tear us down … ' His chin dropped and he looked at Declan again with a level calm. 'I know what I'm saying. I read your stuff and I know. You'll get respect one day. Me? I'm misunderstood.'

'Come on,' Declan laughed, 'people *worship* you.'

Tristan shook his head. 'Young girls who've never read a book except maybe *Catcher in the Rye*, they worship me. Drug addicts who read *Naked Lunch* and *On the Road* before their brains fried, they worship me. But the people who count, the people whose opinions mean something, they wouldn't waste two seconds on my poetry.'

'Weren't you called the greatest English poet since Byron?'

'Yeah? By some journalist who thought *Don Juan* was a *sonnet.*'

'I see.'

'That journalist gave me three grams of coke and a couple of hookers during the interview. It's my fame, you see? It's destroying me. The fame's what people judge. I'm not considered a serious poet or a respected artist and I never will be. How can anyone take me seriously when I'm always on the front cover of the tabloids? I've been crucified by the press like Jesus Christ.'

'How old was that girl last night?'

Tristan ignored the question. 'If I *weren't* famous I might have had a chance. I might have been recognised as an artist, first and foremost. I might have earned the respect of the people who matter. But fame is a monster and it destroys you. It makes you a monster because it … it takes away your humanity.'

'It makes you a god?'

'A monster,' Tristan repeated.

'Maybe gods are monsters. Absolute power and all that. Zeus was a bit of a prick, wasn't he?'

Tristan lit a cigarette and offered Declan the pack. He sounded like he was delivering a speech at an AA meeting. 'People worship me, but I want respect. I want respect but I don't respect myself.'

'You don't respect yourself?'

'I just told you. I'm a monster. I can't control it. I don't even try to control it. I take drugs so I don't have to control it.' He scratched his arm nervously and looked about Declan's room with doleful eyes, his lips swollen with sober self-pity. 'Even though I'm a monstrosity, they still throw themselves at me and I don't care any more. I used to feel guilty, and then I slowly accepted it. I was against abortion when I was a kid. I thought it was evil, but now I've paid for six. Until you've *tasted* it, you'll never understand. They wait downstairs for me. They drag me into the dirty laundry. They fuck me four at a time, all those mouths, the hands, the tits. No man could resist. How could he? Its heaven and its hell, and they will kill me one day. I know it.' Tristan gave Declan a pleading look. 'Beauty is truth, truth beauty, that's what Byron said.'

Declan considered his next move. When he spoke his voice was droll and the words came out in jest.

'I always thought that … that quote was talking about the truth of scientific hypotheses. You know? Because one of the qualities of a good hypothesis is that it has to be beautiful, it has to be elegant, and it must have symmetry.'

'Science?' Tristan squawked. 'It's about art.' He opened up the desk drawer once again and peered inside. 'You sure you've not got a hit of anything? I'm going nuts and Juliet's still sleeping.' His face suddenly went pale and his voice rumbled softly like a distant storm. 'I know it. I can see it written plain on the wall.'

'What?'

'One day, everything I've done ... ' Tristan put his head in his hands and wept softly. 'I hate myself. I hate my life.'

The hairs on the back of Declan's neck pricked up suddenly, he leapt out of bed and herded Tristan quickly toward the door.

'I'm sorry. I can't listen to this,' he explained. 'I can't.'

'Do you hate me?'

'No. I just can't listen to that kind of thing. Not at the moment. Not ever. Sorry.'

13

' 'Ee gets like that when 'ee 'asn't 'ad any drugs for a while,' Nathan explained the next day when Declan mentioned his conversation with Tristan. 'Self-pitying bullshit it is. 'Ee loves 'imself, 'ee just needs a few drugs to remember 'ow much.'

Nathan had come to wash and dress Tristan and take him to a television studio for an interview, but Tristan's daily ablutions were not going as planned. Vivian had tried to get him into the shower for the best part of an hour, but he was more interested in cleaning his crack pipe and clearing his mind of the reality that had intruded upon his conscious thoughts. By the time Nathan arrived he was wasted. All Nathan could do was rub a wet towel over Tristan's face and spray some deodorant over his body like a Victorian maid covering her lady with perfume.

'He needs a new shirt,' said Vivian maternally. She and Nathan went in search of a shirt and Tristan put an arm on Declan's shoulder.

'Thanks for yesterday,' he said. 'You don't suffer fools, Dec. I was being self-indulgent. I can see that.'

'If I didn't suffer fools I'd have killed myself a long time ago.'

'You'd never kill yourself. You're not the type.'

After Tristan and Nathan had gone, Vivian asked if Declan wanted to watch a porn film.

'Only losers watch porn films alone,' she said. 'You don't want to make me feel like a loser do you?'

They sat down on the sofa and Vivian turned the television on and started the DVD. A young woman was auditioning for a part in a film. The director asked her to take her clothes off, one by one, and then he took his cock out of his trousers and asked her to suck it.

'I fucked a record executive who had a cock like that,' Vivian said. 'My manager said it would get us a record contract.'

'That sucks,' Declan sniffed.

Vivian's mouth was open but there was no emotion in her tone. 'Yeah. He was a fat cunt. What do you think of Tristan?'

'Tristan?' Declan answered, concentrating on the screen. 'I don't really know him.'

'Do you think he loves me?'

'Of course,' Declan lied. (What else was he supposed to say?)

'He sings to me, every night,' Vivian swooned. 'The things he whispers to me when we're making love, you've got no idea.' Vivian smiled to herself. Declan remained silent. 'No one has ever touched me so deeply with their words. He doesn't wear his heart on his sleeve he wears it in his mouth. You can hear it beating every time he opens his lips to speak. That's what he says. He says I've touched him somewhere new, somewhere powerful.'

Vivian's eyes were shining urgently. Declan was unsure if she believed what she was saying, but he knew she wanted to, he also knew she wanted him to help her in whatever way he could.

'You're a beautiful young woman,' Declan said, running one hand paternally through her hair and smiling. 'You're the type of woman that men sing hymns to.'

'He's still a little boy,' Vivian whispered. 'A beautiful little boy. It makes me so angry.'

Declan kept his face neutral and waited for Vivian to continue.

'You know his father's an Anglican priest or something?'

'I had heard that. It's hard to believe.'

'He's some total fire-and-brimstone monster. You know the type; arrogant nutter who thinks he has the one, single truth, obsessed with sin and evil, and so busy pointing his finger in judgement of others he can't see what an arsehole he is.'

'Have you met him?' Declan asked.

'No, but Tristan told me what he's like. When he was seven years old his father sent him to an Anglican church summer camp.'

'What a bastard.'

'Seriously, Dec. There was a young woman there, a church woman, she fiddled with him, sucked his little cock.'

Declan felt a charge of electricity shock through his nervous system. Vivian seemed to be encouraged by this. 'I think that's why he's so … confused. You see, he loved it. He felt guilty afterward, he knew it was wrong. What, with all the stories in the papers about how terrible sexual abuse is, but he couldn't lie to himself. He loved it. He blamed himself. He thought he must be perverted. It confused his moral sense. How could he love something that society said was so terrible?'

'Yeah, but it was twenty years ago, Viv.'

'What do you mean?'

'I mean he has to move on, doesn't he? He can't change what happened when he was a kid. He can't remain rooted to that event like a … a … a tree in the ground.'

'But he doesn't know who he is. He's like fifty different people from one day to the next.'

'Pfftt, we all are.'

'I thought you'd understand,' Vivian pouted. 'I forgot you don't have feelings.'

'Come on, Viv, every kid has shit like that happen to them.'

'You think every young boy gets sexualised by an older woman?'

'Yes! No, I just don't see what the big deal is. A woman gave him a blow job when he was seven, and now he's twenty-nine. At what point do you move on?'

Before Vivian could respond her phone rang. It was a journalist from NME wanting to interview her for a fashion story about her favourite piece of clothing.

However much Vivian's heart was lost she had not lost control of her strategic faculties. She knew that Tristan was like a god incarnate, come down to rescue her from the nightmare of future anonymity. She had failed with Jail Bait, but now with Tristan on her arm she regularly got her face in the gossip columns of magazines and newspapers. She spent up to an hour each day calling publicists and journalists behind Tristan's back to tell them where they were going that night. She stole some of his clothes and sold them on eBay and spent the profits on four designer outfits that hugged her body like sweat. Every day of the week she rang agents and pushed for representation.

'I'm a performer,' she told them. 'I can sing, I can dance and I can act. Tristan Russell and I are going to sing a duet. It's a secret now but I'm giving you the scoop so you can take me on before I go stellar.'

On the one hand she seemed to be controlling the whole relationship and calculating all that she might gain from it. On the other, she was a nineteen-year-old girl, desperately in love with a man she could never have any more than she could have the wind. She knew that Tristan would be gone one day. Only fame was going to save her heart from breaking.

Tristan had a habit of disappearing for a day or two, which made Nathan's job difficult and Vivian's life unbearable. She always convinced herself that he was lying dead in a gutter somewhere with a needle in his arm; a condition which, however appalling, was not as bad as the idea of him lying between three groupies and enjoying their attentions. The first time Tristan went AWOL, Vivian called in sick at the Shoreditch and waited for him to return to Turin Street. She could not sleep. She phoned his mobile every half an hour, as well as phoning anyone who might have known where he was. Nathan stopped taking her calls completely. She drank coffee and chain smoked on the sofa, staring up at the poster of Tristan as if it might metamorphose into the man himself.

After he left with Nathan for the television interview Tristan disappeared. He returned two days later looking like he had been fighting with the Mujahidin in Kabul for a month, without sleep. Only his attire gave the game away; he was wearing a skirt, smudged red lipstick and blue eye-liner. Vivian asked where he had been, as if it were a mystery, and he responded by smashing a cup of hot coffee onto the kitchen wall and roaring like an incubus.

'What are you? My mother?'

'I care! I care!' Vivian tried to hug him but he pushed her away.

'You think I don't know about your eBay scam? Selling my stuff.'

'Triz, Triz, listen that was … I was … it was just crap. I just wanted to look good for you. I needed some new clothes so I could … '

'So you could get your tits in the papers!' Tristan snarled. 'They were *my* things! You stole them!'

'I'm so sorry,' Vivian wept. Tristan composed himself, rubbed her shoulder affectionately and spoke with the same soft, ethereal voice he had used when Declan first met him. 'That's all right, love. You know where Drake is?'

'Drake?' Vivian blinked. 'You want some blow? I got some in my room, come with me, I'll take care of you.'

Tristan's smiled with patronising respect and looked up to Vivian.

'You're a great one, aren't you,' he said, kissing her sweetly on the cheek. 'Come on then, fuck me up.' They walked off hand in hand like Pooh and Piglet in the park.

Tristan was well aware that Vivian was a direct line of access to Drake's supply of drugs. It was a complex matrix of supplies and demands. Vivian used Tristan's fame to promote herself, Tristan used Vivian to get drugs, Vivian used Drake to keep Tristan happy, and Drake used drugs to get the occasional blow job from Vivian.

Declan had already detected something sinister about this overlapping triumvirate of mutual use, and he knew that one day soon things would turn ugly. Of course, he did not know how ugly.

14

By late August the Chocolate Block had become officially cool. The girls carrying clipboards around on the set of *The Massive* wanted to be Declan's friend and invited him to their parties.

'Bring anyone you want to,' they would tell him, meaning, bring Tristan.

Bridget and Vivian started getting their names and pictures in the newspapers more and more regularly. Drake, Juliet and Declan were usually described as 'friends' if ever they managed to get into the frame.

'I don't want my photo in the newspapers,' Juliet told Declan one morning over a coffee breakfast. 'Look at what they're doing? Media whores the two of them. I love them to bits but all they care about is having a name that people know. If Bridget doesn't become famous after this exhibition she'll probably buy a bomb and blow herself up along with a hundred innocent people on the tube.'

Since their meeting with Casper Darling, Juliet and Declan often had breakfast together. Juliet always made the coffee and carried it to the table because Declan was unable to hold two mugs in his hands without spilling coffee all over the floor. The rest of the house was generally asleep when Juliet got up for breakfast, and Declan enjoyed having the time to talk with her alone. When they were alone together she took her mask off. Of course, underneath this mask lay another mask – the mask of the self-contained businesswoman, but it was infinitely preferable to the ether-brained, idiot-girl guise.

Declan was not falling in love with Juliet, he did not think it was that serious, but she was beautiful and intriguing and he liked to spend time with her. OK, maybe he was falling in love with her, whatever that meant, but it was one of those loves that a person chooses out of stubbornness or masochism, or both. Declan was like a male version of Hope Lange's character in *Tootsie*, he was the kind of man who walked into a roomful of women and sought out the one who might cause the most amount of pain.

'What's happening with Casper the chemist?' he asked.

Juliet shrugged. 'He'll call when he's ready. He's just nervous.'

'Why don't you call him back?'

'If I call him back he'll ask me to cut my price to fifteen. I don't want him to think I need him because I don't. I don't need any of them individually. I'd have to lose fifteen of them before I started worrying.'

'Bridget told me that you studied art history?'

'I wanted to be an art critic.' Juliet threw her napkin at Declan. 'That's right, smile. I'll have you know that being an art critic is not that far removed from being a sales rep. Art critics are like doctors in the medical profession and artists are like the drug companies. The critics prescribe certain artists to the public like doctors prescribing drugs, and they are equally rewarded for their service. Do you know Bridget has bribed every critic in London with gifts from her mother? She hates her mother's guts and that woman does everything for her except talk normally. I tell you, kids today are either spoilt rotten or treated like shit.'

'Do you ever want kids, Juliet?'

Juliet gave Declan a loathsome gaze and ignored the question.

'Did you hear,' she answered, 'that Vivian has an agent? Cooper and Whitely. You could get an agent, you know, send them some tapes of your work on *The Massive*.'

'I don't want an agent.'

'You don't want to be on TV?'

'No.'

'So why are you on TV?'

'I was offered the job, I needed the money. I write gay film reviews, Jules, you think I want to be gay?'

'So what do you want?'

'Why does everyone keep asking me that? Why do I have to want anything?'

'It's human nature' Juliet paused and made an 'O' shape with her mouth. 'I think you're just too scared to say what you want, Declan.'

Vivian had already become a recognisable public face. Whenever Declan went shopping with her at the local Tesco, other customers looked at her with suspicion or familiarity. She was regularly photographed holding Tristan up at parties or walking out of a nightclub. Cooper & Whitely were not sure whether to try to market her as a performer or a presenter. After listening to her demo tape, they decided to try for presenting roles.

Bridget was falling behind in the race for recognition. In the weeks leading up to her exhibition at Ex Gallery she cancelled all her commercial photography jobs and went on a publicity drive that would have impressed the marketers of a multinational weapons manufacturer. Bridget was fortunate to have a mother with a contact list that was a publicist's dream. She went through it and ticked all the people she wanted her mother to invite. Tristan Russell's presence would contrast nicely with the stuffiness of Abigail Defond's society set, but Bridget had to promise Abigail that Tristan would not be there.

'I can't very well invite a government minister to a soirée with the country's most celebrated drug addict, can I?' Abigail explained.

'Don't worry, mummy,' Bridget said. 'Tristan doesn't have any money. There's no point in inviting him.'

It's going to be enormous! was Bridget's mantra in the weeks leading up to the opening. She phoned newspapers, magazines, cultural programmes, news services, radio shows and even the London offices of two American news wires. When she talked about her exhibition, she talked about who was going to be there more than the works she would exhibit and this strategy was very effective.

'Everyone will be there. Everyone will cover it. It's going to be such a fantastic clash of class and culture. The hippest young things from East London will be sipping Moet with the stuffiest politicians and society ladies from Kensington.'

Bridget's choice of EX Gallery was the cause of several loud phone arguments between Bridget and Abigail, who believed her society friends would be more comfortable with an exhibition in a Bond Street gallery.

'No fucking way!' Bridget screamed into her phone. 'I've told you, this is my exhibition, not yours, and if you don't want to help me then fuck you, you selfish bitch!'

15

Two weeks before Bridget's exhibition opening Declan went to a dinner party at Pete and Kate's. When Pete opened the door the smile on his face metamorphosed into a look of shock.

'Jesus, Dec, you're wasting away, man. How much weight have you lost?'

'I'm fine, Pete.' Declan entered the living room and Kate looked at him with the same horror.

'Dec, you're so skinny. What's happened?'

During dinner Kate told the guests that Declan was living with Tristan Russell. *No wonder he looks so pasty* their open mouths seemed to say. They all wanted to know what Tristan was like.

'He's actually not what you'd expect at all,' Declan said. Heads leaned forward and everyone waited for him to continue.

After dinner Declan sat on the sofa beside Rebecca, a friend of Kate's who worked in publishing. They shared four lines of coke and Rebecca took photographs with her digital camera. Declan tried not to look at her cleavage, which was on full display every time she leaned over to do a line. She was beautiful but her voice was loud and her eyes restless.

'What's the craziest thing you've seen Russell do?' she asked.

'He wet his pants one morning in the middle of a conversation.'

She laughed lightly and her hand rested on Declan's forearm just long enough for him to think it was intentional.

'But what about you?' she asked. 'What do you do?'

'I write film reviews for a magazine and I also appear … '

'Really?' Rebecca cut Declan off. 'Which magazine? It might be one of ours?'

'It's called *Fluid*, but … '

'*Fluid*?' she stiffened. 'The gay magazine.'

'No, well, yes, it is gay, right, but I'm not … not gay.'

'You write gay film reviews, but you're not gay?'

'No. What can I say? Robin Williams plays gay sometimes and he's married with kids.'

Rebecca nodded her head but she did not look convinced. 'Most gay men are married with kids.'

'I'm not married or gay … with kids. I can prove I'm not gay, actually,' Declan offered.

'Can you?' Rebecca smiled. 'Maybe you're bisexual.'

'If I was, I'd invite your boyfriend along.'

'What makes you think I've got a boyfriend?'

'Do you?'

'Yes.'

'Good.'

'But you didn't know.' Rebecca stopped. 'Why good?'

'Less complicated,' Declan lied, and the lie gave him a fleeting sense of freedom. He sucked bitterly on an Oscar Wilde quote: *wickedness is just an invention of good people to account for the curious attractiveness of others.* It had once been one of his favourite quotes but now it seemed hollow.

By midnight Pete was confident enough to ask to speak to Declan in private. They went into the bedroom and Pete closed the door and turned on Declan.

'Mate, talk to me. What's going on?' he asked.

'What do you mean?'

Pete brought one hand up like a claw and pointed all his fingers at Declan's face.

'All these drugs, aren't they bad for your brain?'

'Come on, Pete, how many lines of coke have you had tonight?'

'I haven't got brain damage, Dec, you have! You need to take care of yourself. You're living in denial.'

'I'm living in denial?'

'Yes, you can't live like this any more.' Having nothing to add to that point Declan waited for Pete to continue. 'What do you say we go away together for a week before summer finishes. We'll go to Italy again and look at the art.'

'You hate art.'

'Ah, I get sick of all those friggin' Madonnas with Child. Couldn't they think of anything else to paint?'

'Family was important back then,' Declan shrugged, 'motherhood was sacred. Besides, artists had no choice; the Church had all the money. And speaking of money, I can't afford a trip to Italy right now.'

Pete sucked his teeth. 'Money-shmoney, it's my shout. You need some time out, recharge the batteries, get connected. We can go for a run together every morning, get some fitness back into the old legs, check out all the Madonnas in the arvo, glass a plonk in the evening.'

'I'll think about it,' Declan said, 'right now I want to try and shag Kate's friend.'

'She's got a boyfriend.'

'I know.'

They returned to the living room and after two more lines of coke Declan convinced Rebecca to leave with him.

Back at Purgatory he tried to direct her straight to the bedroom but she wanted to sit and talk for a while in the living room. Declan made a couple of drinks. Juliet and Jake were upstairs and whenever a noise sounded from Juliet's room Rebecca looked up to the ceiling, waited, and then looked at Declan and smiled. Jake came down to the kitchen and, as he descended the stairs and his body slowly revealed itself, Rebecca stopped breathing and stared. She smiled resentfully when she saw it was a young boy and looked at Declan and whispered, 'Who's that?'

'The boyfriend of a flatmate.'

'Bit young, isn't he?'

After sitting and talking for an hour Rebecca finally agreed to go into the bedroom. She took off her dress and offered each breast before giving Declan a blow job and positioning herself on her hands and knees on the bed. It was a perfunctory sexual experience and when it was over Rebecca asked Declan if he minded her sleeping on the sofa in the living room.

'I don't have a spare duvet,' Declan said.

'That's fine,' she said, and slipped one of his T-shirts on and left.

16

When Declan woke the next morning Rebecca had already gone. He lay in bed looking at the painting of Socrates pointing to Heaven. His mind felt blocked like a storm drain at a music festival, but he could feel the memory of the warm pressure of Rebecca's bottom cheeks imprinted on his thighs. He let out a sigh and got up and pointed himself toward the kitchen, knocking against the walls all the way, like a frightened bull in a narrow tunnel making his way out to the *corrida*.

Drake came out of the bathroom smoking a joint and slapped Declan on the shoulder. He only showered for special occasions and Declan asked him what was going on.

'Ma–a–ate you never guess who I met last night at Shoreditch? Castin' agent works with *Ralph Sweeney*, yeah.'

Declan said, 'Wow.'

'I teller bowt me actin' career, I givva some Charlie, yeah, she give me a number, says, "Call me." '

Shortly before Declan had joined the Posse household, Drake had been given a small role in a student film about London vampires. He played a vamp that had not seen daylight for several years. Although his only piece of dialogue had been '*Aaaarggghhh!*' as he tried to bite the lead female on the neck, he believed this was the beginning of his professional acting career.

He shook his head mystically and stared at Declan.

'Ralph Sweeney's makin' a new movie, isn't he?' he said, as if this were the most amazing thing since Hugh Grant got busted with a whore in Hollywood. 'An' she think she can get me a talkin' part. I'm gonna play some kinna East End thug, she says. Eh ha! Me! A cockney geezer, yeah. No method actin' there, eh? I just go in an' be meself! That's it!'

'You'll be awesome,' Declan lied.

Vivian came down the stairs holding her head and telling Drake to shut it. Drake ambushed her on the bottom step before she could make it into the living room.

'Viv! Guess what! I ben offered a role in the new Ralph Sweeney movie. Ralph Sweeney!'

'That's great, Drake,' Vivian said dryly, 'screw me in the ear why don't you.' She pushed passed him and searched over the bookshelf for some of Juliet's tranquillisers but found nothing.

'Bloody hell,' she said, throwing an empty packet on the floor. 'Where's Juliet?'

Tristan came down the stairs wearing pink slippers and a silk G-string. When Drake saw him he stiffened like an old dog and looked over at Declan anxiously. Drake and Tristan had been living together for almost two months now, and apart from their regular drug transactions they never spoke to each other. This morning, however, Drake was unable to ignore Tristan's choice of morning attire.

'What is this? A porno freak set,' Drake muttered. 'We don' wanna see yo skanky ass in the mornin'.'

'Fuck off out of my life for ten minutes,' Tristan said in his other voice, the growling thug.

Drake left the room without a word.

Vivian and Tristan glared at one another.

'Well?' Tristan said.

'Well what?'

'Who was he?'

Vivian continued searching the surfaces of the living room for prescription drugs but added a sneer of disappointment to her features. 'Are you still on about that?'

'Yes, I'm still on about that. You were virtually fucking him when I left.'

'It's called dancing.'

'You know what dancing is? It's the horizontal expression of a vertical desire!'

Vivian laughed. When Tristan realised his malapropism he grabbed Vivian roughly by the arm and yanked her around so that she was facing him.

'Listen you … If you think I'm going to put up with that shit you're wrong. I'm not some two-bit tart, slut, fuck that you walk over, all right? You're fucking my dick and you're gonna respect that!'

Vivian put her nose in the air and marched back up the stairs to Heaven. Tristan sniffed and turned to Declan.

'Women,' he said, 'you have to keep them on a short leash. You got a matinee tammazie for me?'

Declan shook his head and Tristan scratched his chin as if remembering something. He drew closer.

'Who was that girl on the sofa last night?' he whispered.

'Friend of a friend.'

'Wow,' he said, smiling slyly and shaking his head.

Juliet did not come downstairs all morning. Declan went up to her room around midday and she was lying in bed with her face in the pillow.

'What do you want?' she asked without turning around.

'You got anything?'

Juliet spun around and threw her pillow with considerable dexterity.

'You can all just piss off!' she shouted.

'That's a "no" then, is it?'

'Did you sleep with her? I know you brought someone home last night,' Juliet continued. She found some Ketonals by her bed and tossed the packet at Declan's head. 'Piss off then.'

'Hang on, Jules, you know, a little bit of perspective never hurt the Old Masters. How can you be upset because I had sex with a woman? What about Jake?'

'Don't start ... '

'No, I think I want to start,' Declan said calmly. 'You expect me to just wait for you?'

'Yes, why not?'

Declan and Juliet laughed, and he sat down on the bed beside her and gave her a hug.

'Look, I like you, Juliet. I just don't want to be treated like a man bag.'

'Are you sure?' Juliet kissed Declan on the neck affectionately. Then she kissed him on the ear and on the mouth, her tongue gently easing his lips apart. They fell back onto the bed and began groping at each other's clothes. Juliet took a condom from her bedside table and grabbed at Declan's dick with one hand, kissing her way down his body and letting her mouth replace her hand. The touch of her warm lips made Declan's body shudder.

Someone knocked and opened the bedroom door. It was a young teenage girl. At first Declan thought it must have been one of Tristan's groupies who had lost her way. Juliet screamed and pulled the duvet over her body. It occurred to Declan that she could have easily taken a bite out of his dick.

'Can't you people ever ... ' Juliet stopped. 'Susan? What are you doing?'

'Hi, mummy,' said the girl called Susan. 'Did you forget about today?'

'Today? Today?'

'It's my birthday.'

17

Juliet had not mentioned having a teenage daughter before. She explained things as she and Declan got dressed. A cigarette dangled from the side of her mouth as she spoke.

'I was eighteen. I had just finished my A levels. I couldn't go to university with a kid so I gave her to my aunt in Brighton. She was thirty five, no kids, said her husband was infertile but I know for a fact it was her who had the problem. She asked me if she could have it and I said OK. The plan was for her to raise Susan as her own, she chose the name. There's no way I would name my daughter after that Brady Bitch, but Susan found out when she was about nine.'

'How?'

Juliet looked cross, '*I* don't know! Maybe she's psychic. Anyway, I see her now a couple of times a year, for Christmas and birthdays and stuff.'

'What are you doing today?' Declan wanted to make a suggestion that involved him. 'Let's take her to the Tate Modern.'

The Tate Modern had been open for three months and Declan had already visited it five times. He got a rush of adrenaline entering the turbine hall of the former power station, now one of the world's great modern art collections. The sheer volume of the space was sublime in the oldest sense of the word. It inspired the kind of awe and dread that one might feel standing on the summit of a mountain, or the edge of a cliff. Everywhere people were walking and milling in small groups, literally tens of thousands of people from all over the world were walking around solemnly, as if in a labyrinthine church. The popularity of this collection of modern art had taken almost everyone in the media by surprise. Article after article trumpeted the *amazing* fact that, in the first six weeks of its opening, over a million people had visited the gallery.

Declan, Juliet and Susan made their way to the burgundy-soaked Rothko room. Declan said that the artist had slashed his own wrists. It was one of those stories he loved repeating just to hear the surprise in people's voices.

'I'm not surprised,' Susan said. 'These paintings look like suicides.'

Declan looked around at the immense burgundy and black canvasses and saw that she was right. He had only ever focused on Rothko's bright, cheerful colour fields, while all the time the artist had been producing these dark, heavy, sombre images. The room had a sepulchral gloom about it and Declan stepped back out into the well lit corridor, checking his gallery map to see what else was on show.

When they reached the Cornelia Parker installation, *Cold Dark Matter*, Declan felt his heart beating faster. It was visually thrilling, like a detonated Hitchcock image thrown up from a time before the age of Technicolor; a box-shaped explosion of wood with every splinter hung separately from the ceiling to collectively replicate an object frozen in space just moments after it had been blown to smithereens. A light was positioned in the centre of the frozen explosion and this threw sharp, eerie shadows across the walls, floor, and ceiling. It was as if time had stood still at the supernova moment. The energy and power of the work hit Declan's retina walls like a crash test dummy hitting a car windscreen. It made him want to do a million things. It made him want to live, now, live everything while he had time.

'Bang,' he whispered.

'Wow,' Susan replied.

Moving closer to the work they saw objects within the shards of cubic-formed timber: a wellington boot with a baby shark-bite taken from the Achilles' heel, an old hardback copy of a book called *The World of Children*, a plastic dinosaur, a bike tyre, a horseshoe, a watering can, the limbs of a plastic doll.

'What is it?' Susan asked, indicating the entire work.

'Well it's not a painting,' Declan said. 'I think it's a garden shed. Look, there's a garden rake.'

'She actually blew the shed up,' Juliet called from the entrance where a text plaque had been stuck to the wall.

'Don't read that!' Declan shouted. 'You haven't even looked at the work yet.'

'I want to know what I'm looking at.'

'No, no, that's totally wrong. You can't be told what you're looking at; you have to decide for yourself. Works of art are like people; you don't understand them through description, you understand them by looking at them.'

Juliet made a 'pfftt' sound to indicate what she thought of that idea. 'Jesus you're a pretentious wanker sometimes, Dec. I want to see what the artist says.'

'That's not important,' Declan insisted, loudly, and a well dressed couple frowned at him from through the shattered cube. 'What's important is what you see.'

Juliet sneered. 'What is this, Roland Barthes week?'

She finished reading and stood beside Susan in front of the installation.

'She filled a garden shed with lots of old rubbish from a family home: an old tricycle, sports trophies, plastic dolls, and books. Then she called in the army's demolition squad and asked them to blow the place sky high. Then she picked up all the bits and pieces and brought them to the gallery and hung them like this.'

Declan shook his head and said nothing.

'This is great,' Susan said.

Declan pointed out the burnt objects between the pieces of shattered wood.

'Look at the stuff she's put in the shed, they're all the things people don't want in their daily lives, shit they don't really need, but don't want to throw away forever because they might get sentimental one day. They dump it all in the shed instead and forget about it. Then, every year or so, when they're looking for a garden tool or something, they come across them, and then what?'

Juliet was chewing gum like a baseball pitcher. The shadow of a toy doll hanging from the ceiling obscured half of her face, masklike, and she smiled and left the room.

Declan shook his head in wonder. What on earth was he doing with a bunch of prehistoric paintings on his bedroom walls? This was the art of today. Titian and Caravaggio were dead and gone, nothing would bring them back. Declan did not want to bring them back. He wanted this vivid contemporary vision of a world that was both beautiful and frightening. He wanted it, but he was scared of it. It was the destruction of sentimentality. It was the harbinger of a dark future that he knew was drawing closer.

They had lunch in the café on the top floor of the gallery. Juliet ordered a bottle of wine and disappeared into the toilets.

'Are you a drug addict too,' Susan asked while Juliet was snorting coke in a cubicle.

'Your mother's not a drug addict,' Declan said.

Susan smiled ironically. 'My grandparents may be daft but I'm not. I'm fourteen you know. And I *don't* sell flowers for a living.'

'Look,' Declan offered, 'the traditional model for drug addiction is out of date. These days many people who do drugs are wealthy, well-adjusted and successful people.'

'You think my mother's well-adjusted? Her last boyfriend was seventeen.'

'Jake?'

'Philip.'

'Oh.' Declan tried to change the conversation. 'So you're in … what? Year nine?'

'I skipped a couple of grades. My teachers say I'm gifted. I just work hard.'

'Are you doing your GCSEs then?'

'I did my GCSEs last year.'

'You're doing your A levels at fourteen?'

'English Literature, psychology and German,' Susan said matter-of-factly.

'So you hang out with students four years older than you?'

Susan nodded, 'Girls mature much faster than boys. Most of the boys in my class are pathetic. It's the girls who do well.'

'Have you thought about what you want to do when you finish?'

'I want to work in Berlin. It's a romantic city. Do you love my mother?'

'We're … we just live together.'

'Do you always have sex with your flatmates?'

'Juliet and I don't have sex.'

Susan nodded her head. 'Right, so, you're just using her? What is it with men and commitment? What are you so afraid of?'

Juliet returned with a smile and a sniffle. She touched her nose self-consciously and Declan saw clearly, for the first time, how sad and lost she was. Susan remained solemn and put her hands together on the table as if she were about to lead the three of them in prayer.

'Mummy, there is something I need to speak with you about.'

'I'm not your mummy, Susan. I'm just the girl who gave birth to you.'

'Isn't that the definition of a mummy?' Susan asked.

'A mummy is the woman who takes you to the doctors when you're ill.'

'Remember I was having problems with my studies last year?'

'You were?'

'You said it was because I was too young to be doing GCSEs.'

'I did?'

'I saw the school counsellor and we have resolved the problem.'

'You have?'

'I'm ADHD.'

'You're *what*?'

'Attention deficit hyperactive disorder.'

'I know what it means, Susan, I sell the drugs. What did they put you on?'

'Concertol'

'Bloody hell.'

'What?'

'I don't want you on that drug.'

'I'm just telling you as a courtesy.'

Juliet reached out suddenly and knocked her wine glass over.

'Fine!' she yelled, as pieces of glass fell to the floor and a narrow river of red wine snaked its way across the white tablecloth. Susan looked at Declan with wide, frightened eyes. Juliet continued,

'Take the drug! See if I care. But don't come to me for help after you've hung yourself with chicken wire.'

Juliet and Declan took Susan to Victoria Station and watched her board the train back to Brighton. As the train pulled out, Juliet took a bag of coke from her jacket pocket. She licked her pinkie finger and dipped it into the bag of coke, then sucked it. She then offered the bag to Declan and he did the same. His lips were instantly numbed.

'That is so screwed up,' Juliet muttered, shaking her head.

'She seems really nice.'

'What would you know? You watch movies all day. You wouldn't know reality if it bit you in the cock.'

18

A month before Bridget's exhibition debut, Declan asked David to show him the shoe photographs. David was sitting in the lounge examining his camera, a cigarette hanging from the side of his mouth. He took the cigarette out of his mouth, pressed it into an ashtray overflowing with butts, and looked up at Declan.

'Why do you want to look at them?'

'I like shoes,' Declan said. 'I spend a lot of time inside them.'

In three years, David had taken over three thousand photographs of old shoes. He collected his pairs of shoes from the streets, from garbage bins and, if he was really desperate, from charity shops.

'You'd be amazed how many pairs of old shoes you can find on the streets when you start looking.'

He stored the photographs in shoe boxes, which seemed appropriate, and kept them under Bridget's bed. To photograph each pair, he placed them on a white pedestal like busts of Caesar, and threw tungsten light over them, drawing crisp, sharp shadows across the cut of the material, the laces and the surface of the pedestal. The power of the images was startling. David knew how to work a camera and his shots were far more advanced than the commercial flair of Bridget's shampoo catalogues and hardware store brochures.

'Cool,' Declan said, flipping through the photographs, 'it's like some luminous *Vogue* catalogue … for old shoes.'

David laughed. 'I'm going to call the series "FAMILY", in capitals.'

'They're amazing,' Declan said lightly.

After looking at the first dozen photographs Declan was amazed, by the time he had gone through them all he was enthralled.

'You have to exhibit these,' he said when the last shoe portrait was back in its box.

'I don't want to,' David replied.

'But why? They're fantastic. I mean, apart from anything else, they're a slick contrast to society's obsession with young, shiny, new things.'

David rolled a smoke and lit it. 'Exhibitions suck man,' he waved his cigarette in the air like a wand casting a spell over the syllables as he pronounced them.

'What are you Marcel Duchamp?' Declan asked.

'The whole art system sucks. Its soul destroying. There's the euphoria of the first exhibition but then it becomes like any job, an annual grind. The artist doesn't have to fight for exhibition space any more, he just produces enough work to sell on the gallery market once a year, but his hunger has gone, his soul has gone, he's a wage-slave disguised as an artist. Bridget thinks there's a distinction between her commercial photography and her artistic photography, but there's no difference, except her commercial work is actually pretty good. A gallery wall is just a glorified magazine advertisement these days.'

It was easy to forget that David did not work himself and chose instead to live off Bridget's income, an income that he often used to attack her with accusations of selling out.

'It's all shit, man,' David moaned. 'Artists open restaurants now. Yeah? Can you imagine Michelangelo opening a pizzeria?'

'But you wouldn't want things to be the same as they were in the Renaissance? Imagine people painting like Michelangelo today. It would be boring, we've been there man, it's not even old-school, it's dead-school.'

'You can talk,' David laughed. 'You've got dead-school stuck all over your walls.' He pointed derisively to Bridget's Polaroids attached to the wall. 'She'll fit in perfectly, you know, she produces more shit per cubic inch than a public toilet. She wants to open a solarium as some kind of art installation and charge people fifty quid for ten minutes under the lights. They go to the exhibition and walk home with a work-of-art tan.'

'What do you think about Juliet and Jake?'

If David was surprised by the sudden change in topic he did not show it.

'Juliet? I'd be her man-bag any day. She's hot and rich and stupid – what a mix.'

'I didn't know she had a daughter.'

'Why would you? She's about as maternal as a porn film isn't she?'

'Who's the father?'

'The father?' David's expression was the facial equivalent of a five-eighth dodging a tackle. 'I shouldn't say, really.' Declan kept a straight face and David continued. 'It was her uncle, I think, that's what I was told. The one married to the aunt who took the baby.'

'Oh? So … what, it was like an IVF thing?'

David shook his head slowly. 'He raped her. That's what Bridge told me. Makes sense doesn't it? I mean, that's why she's so fucked up, yeah?'

Declan sat in bed that night thinking about Juliet. He wanted to speak with her but she had gone clubbing with the rest of the Posse. It all made sense to him now. Juliet was just performing a role to protect herself from getting hurt. If Declan could make her trust him then he could rescue her. He often fantasised about rescuing women. It gave him a specious power and created the illusion that he was not more helpless and disturbed than the particular woman he dreamed of rescuing.

Declan woke to the sound of Tristan and Vivian watching a porn film in the living room. It must have been three or four in the morning

'Do you love me?' Vivian asked.

'Love you? No. I don't love you. I adore you. I worship you. I kiss your footsteps with each lip as you pass across my dreams.'

'I'm pregnant.'

Vivian spoke again after a lengthy silence. 'Say something.'

'Is it mine?'

'Of course it's yours.'

'What are you going to do?'

Silence.

'We can't have a baby, Tristan.'

'You see that painting on the wall?' Tristan said. 'What do you think it represents?'

'I don't know. It's just a few colours.'

'It's more than that.'

'I don't know.'

'It's about horizons, Viv. It's about what you set as your horizon. Is it there, or there, or there? And what are horizons? They don't really exist,' Tristan cleared his throat and Declan knew he was about to start singing.

'Take one step forward,' Tristan warbled, 'or one step back, and your old horizon has gone.'

'Did you just make that up,' Vivian said, her voice soaked with wonder.

'It's a work in progress. I've always got a few songs gestating.'

'You have a way of seeing the world. I wish I was half as smart as you.'

'You probably are.'

'No. You're like, one of those geniuses who come every hundred years or so. You become the voice for a whole generation. If only we were smart enough to speak like you.'

'Your hair smells of promises,' Tristan whispered, 'your throat tastes like the dreams I've never had, and each breast feels like the arriving moment of a deep desire.'

19

As the newest member of the Posse, Declan acquired the reputation of a good listener, but in truth this reputation was unmerited. He had no ambition; he was a cheerful loser, so it was impossible to lose face by talking to him.

Drake visited Declan three weeks before Bridget's exhibition opening. Drake was a minnow in the sea of illegal drug trading that floated largely unseen through London's streets. It was, after modelling, the most obvious career open to him. It was a business that required no start-up capital and consisted of no operational costs apart from a weekly trip to the supplier. The barriers to entry for anyone with good contacts in the industry were negligible: no special skills were needed to become a drug dealer except a willingness to break the law and the ability to retain a small but regular clientele. It was a market that experienced little volatility thanks to the constant high demand for hard drugs. In the market structure Drake was what you would call a sole trader. He dealt only with his supplier and his buyers. Like most people who got started dealing drugs Drake gained entry through a friend, Kieran, a fellow model. At first Drake only dealt casually, as a means of supplying his own habit, until one of his disaffected teenage customers carved the scar down his cheek with a broken bottle. Having put an end to his modelling career, Drake asked Kieran to introduce him to his 'manager'.

Kieran's manager, Mo, supplied about sixteen sole traders,

mostly in North London. His drugs were delivered to him in small shipments four times a week so that if he were ever raided by police, the amount he was caught with would mean no more than a two-year custodial sentence. Drake collected the drugs from Mo once a week. He would call him to organise a date, the scenario in which they met signified the type of drugs he wanted: a movie was cocaine; dinner and a movie was cocaine and heroin; dinner, a drink and a movie was cocaine, heroin and crack. Drake bought his ecstasy from another sole trader because Mo would not touch the drug.

Drake entered Declan's room and sat on the desk chair, looking at all the paintings on the walls.

'What's up?' Declan asked, expecting incomplete sentences and hoping that a line of coke might be his reward for appearing interested.

Drake stood up and sat down on the bed and held his hands together as if praying feverishly.

''Ave you ever loved someone?'

Declan shook his head, 'Yes,' and explained that he had loved Betty Boo when he was a teenager. He hadn't cared that Betty Boo never sang a note on any of her records, she was gorgeous and that was all that mattered to his fifteen-year-old soul.

'I love 'er man,' Drake whispered. 'I love 'er. I lie in bed and all I can think of is 'er … I stare at 'er photos an' me 'art breaks.'

It was the first coherent speech Declan had ever heard Drake complete. 'What?' Drake asked, noting Declan's look of surprise.

'Vivian?'

Drake nodded his head. 'I know what I am … I'm … I'm not … stupid. Look at me. I'm a loser. Dead-shit, dumb-arse model, fucked-up, drug-face,' he ran a finger along his facial scar. 'Nobody'd talk to me if I didn't 'ave drugs. An it's not just 'cos

I'm a black man. Me parents stopped talkin' to me ten year ago.' He paused for a moment, reflecting on some other memory of his parents that he did not want to convey in language immediately. 'I ring 'em up they hang up. I send 'em letters they never reply. I go round their place an' they don' open the door. Me mum tells me *piss off*! Shouts through the door. I just need some luck 'ere. I'm not a loser I just … just need some luck. Then they'll see. Viv too. I'm changed. It's the nu me.'

He took a photograph from his jacket and handed it to Declan. It had been taken when Drake was fourteen or fifteen; he looked like a teenage Tiger Woods and was kicking a football in Highbury Stadium.

'See that there; I was picked up by Arsenal Academy at fourteen. Coulda played for the Gunners … but the modellin' work, yeah … it was money for nuffin, yeah. No trainin', nuffin'. I must a made a few 'undred thousan',' he indicated the scar on his face, 'then this 'appened an' it was all ovah. Twenty-six I was,' he emoted. 'But this … the 'orror movie, yeah, it's my first step ta … 'ollywood, I'm on ta somethin'. If the Ralph Sweeney girl calls me, I'm … there, I'm right there, yeah?' he tapped the side of his head and glared at Declan in earnest. 'Think abou' it. There's no difference between me an' Tristan. Only difference is 'ee's famous and I'm noh. If I was famous, all the things she 'ates about me would make 'er love me. Think abou' it, yeah – 'ee robs old ladies on the street, 'ee rapes young girls, I never done nuffin' like that but she still wants 'im not me. Why? It's the fame bruvva. I just gotta get some, yeah.'

'Vivian's very young. I don't think she knows what … '

'No she's not! Maybe 'er body is but 'er mind … man, 'er mind … she blows me away. She's so smart, so together, an' so smart … so beautiful. She's got a beautiful 'art and, you know this … this is nothin' … ' Drake pointed to his face, paused, and then thumped his chest. 'It's what's in 'ere that's important.'

He started to cry, softly, almost imperceptibly, and then he began sobbing loudly.

'You'll be all right,' Declan offered. 'Come on.' When he looked into Drake's eyes he saw, for the first time, the depths of the man's suffering. It was easy to dismiss Drake as an insensate zombie because that's how he acted most of the time. Maybe it was all just an act like Juliet's. Drake lit a cigarette, wiped the tears from his face and took another photo from his pocket. It was of a young, dark-skinned boy, perhaps five years old, sitting on Drake's shoulders.

'It's me boy,' Drake said. 'He's the reason I get up every day. He's me foocha.'

'I didn't know you were a dad.'

'I don't like to boast abou' it, but truly, man, till you're a dad … you dunno what it means.' This was not an argument Declan could win and he remained silent and nodded his head. 'I'm noh the centre of the world any more,' Drake continued. 'I got somethin' to live for, someone else to think abou'. I jus' wanna do me best for 'im.'

'You'll be fine,' Declan lied.

'I know. I know. I tell ya … I look at me boy and … I feel connected. Before I was just floatin' aroun' like a ghost or somethin'. But this … this is what it's all abou'.' Drake smiled down at the photo for a moment then looked up. 'Can ya do somethin' for me?'

'Sure.'

Drake pulled out a bag of coke and cut up two lines with a razor blade that he had slotted into the leather band of his watch. 'Can ya talk about me wiv Vivian? Can ya tell 'er what's happenin' … abou' me foocha, me actin' career, the movies, 'ollywood? She won't listen ta me. Bridget, she fills Viv's 'ead wiv bad shit abou' me all the time. I know it. An' every time I try to speak wiv Viv, she don't wanna know abou' it. She'll listen to ya. Can ya tell 'er? Tell 'er I'm gonna make it, I'm gonna be somebody, noh just a nobody.'

Drake stood up and placed the half-full bag of cocaine on the table. Ordinarily Declan would have said nothing, but having just heard Drake's confessions he did not want to take the drugs.

'I'm good mate, keep the coke.'

'Come on?' Drake said.

'Nah, really, cheers anyway.'

Drake smiled and put the coke and the picture of his young son back in his wallet. His eyes were glistening, and the two men shook hands with a sequence of fancy movements that culminated in them both toking on imaginary spliffs between their fingers.

'I luv ya like a bruvva man,' Drake said, choking on the words slightly. 'You're me best mate.'

20

Bridget came to see Declan two weeks before her exhibition opening. Declan was lying in bed looking at his postcards. Bridget was worried about her imminent show.

'I mean, sometimes I look at those Polaroids and I think ... ' Bridget shook her head first. 'Do you know what I think?'

Declan shook his head second and said he didn't know.

'I think "Who am I kidding?" That's what I think. Sometimes I think "David's right, I am just a hack commercial photographer. I am never going to pull this off." '

'You will.'

Declan was not convinced by Bridget's performance. If she really doubted herself, if she really questioned her work, then she would never have been so bloody minded and hard working. More than anything else he resented her confident manner. She was as driven by ambition as he had once been, but she was not only ambitious, she was productive. As well as cooking Michelin star meals most evenings Bridget worked all day as a commercial photographer and then came home and worked all night preparing for her exhibition. As a young man Declan had worked consistently, despite all his doubts, because he was driven by something deeper than desire for success; but since the brain injury his ambition had capitulated before some frightening image of failure. His doubts and fears were translated into a wild cynicism that was directed at the commercial art world, and he quickly became far better at attacking other artists than producing any art himself. He attacked everything and produced nothing. He had tried to paint after being discharged from hospital but it was no good; his arm muscles quickly tired and after twenty minutes his hand would start to shake uncontrollably.

Now he worked as an art critic, the final act of cynicism, the final revenge of a failed artist. He criticised other people's creative efforts because he had lost the desire to produce his own art. Even as a critic he had lost his voice. Now he said whatever people wanted him to say.

'You don't know what it's like,' Bridget continued. 'I know I put on a confident façade! I act the tough bitch, and people think I'm the girl who got it all. The first eight years of my life were just mum and dad screaming at each other night after night. She threw wine glasses. That was her thing. When he got really angry he smacked her across the face. It never shut her up. Coming home from school was like coming home to a boxing ring. I know I'm harsh. I know what people think of me, "Bridget the bitch", but that was the only way I was ever going to survive. I had to toughen the fuck up. You can't stay sensitive and listen to that shit or it destroys you. And confidence? Confidence is easy once you've learnt to be tough. And you need to project an image of confidence to make people believe in you. It's like that real estate guy in *American Beauty* said, "If you don't act like you believe in yourself one hundred and fifty per cent then nobody will follow you." Nobody.

'But I get scared,' she continued, 'I have the same insecurities as you. I worry that I have no talent; that I'm never going to succeed. Then sometimes I worry I'm trying to soar too high like Icarus.' She fingered a painting of Breugel's then smiled and sat down on the bed. Declan pulled the duvet over his exposed leg and she rubbed it under the duvet. 'You're so positive, you know? It's so lovely having someone who is so … so artistically affirming. The stuff that you wrote for my catalogue, the way you give my conceptual work a literary value, it's just really phenomenal Declan. I'm going to use your words for my LCD screen speech.'

'You are?'

'David doesn't understand me like you do. All his negativity seeps into me and takes over my own sense of self. I find myself thinking about what David *says* rather than what I *believe* in here,' Bridget tapped her left breast where her heart was beating beneath the skin and behind the bone. 'You know what I love about you, you have an artist's soul and you appreciate people who have the courage to have a go, people who want to make a statement and live their dreams to the full!'

Bridget left. Declan wondered how much longer he could keep up his own façade. Should he tear it down one day, which façade would he choose? If he started questioning who he was he'd never stop, he'd tear down one façade after another, and end up with nothing. Maybe he thought badly of Bridget sometimes, maybe he judged her harshly and gave her the false impression that he respected her work a great deal. There wasn't any harm in that. There was nothing wrong in making her feel good and avoiding the sort of conflict that would arise if he voiced all the negative thoughts out aloud.

More than anything, Declan liked to avoid conflict, even with himself.

21

Drake auditioned for the Ralph Sweeney film and got a small role. Needless to say the Posse was gobsmacked, but everyone praised him for his astonishing success and then immediately contradicted their astonishment by saying they always knew he could do it. As soon as he had left the room Bridget wondered how big a coke habit the casting agent must have had.

'He does have that scar,' David noted. 'That's quite visually impressive.'

Eight days before Bridget's exhibition Drake entered Declan's room and asked him to phone his parents to pass on the good news. He gave Declan the number and stood beside him while he dialled the number.

An old woman answered the phone, ' 'Ello?'

'Hello, it's Declan Twist speaking, I'm just … '

'Ooo!?' the woman screeched down the phone line.

'Declan Twist, I'm just calling … '

'I don' know no Declan Twist. Whaddaya want?'

'I'm a friend of your son Drake.'

'I don' 'ave no son.' The woman hung up and the line went dead.

Drake must have heard what she had said, or he had heard it a hundred times before. He gave Declan a 'she's right' smile, swept the air with one hand and nodded his head.

'She does that. Just ring 'er back an' say abou' the film. Don't even introduce yersel', just say it.'

Declan rang back and the same woman answered.

'Drake's got a role in Ralph Sweeney's new film!' Declan said quickly and loudly. A moment's silence. Declan and Drake looked at each other, puzzled.

'Listen,' the woman said. 'I told you.'

'Wait here,' Drake said when Declan gave him the phone. He went and got his copy of the screenplay and returned to the room. He asked Declan if he could help him rehearse.

'I'm not an actor.'

'You're on the tele every week,' Drake said. 'Ya live in this nut-'ouse. It's all performance innit?'

Declan couldn't argue with that, and Drake smiled and handed him the screenplay. He had highlighted his lines with a pink fluorescent pen.

'Right,' he said, rubbing his hands. 'In this scene, me boss 'as just killed a guy and the body's in the boot of the car. Me boss 'as gone back inside and the dead man's partner comes up to me lookin' for 'is mate. I'm not 'elping 'im out. In fact I shoot 'im dead.'

'That is unhelpful.' Declan took a look at the scene

EXT: A CAR PARK – NIGHT

Roger approaches a man standing beside a Mercedes with the lights turned on.

ROGER

Where is he?

EARL

He ain't here.

ROGER

I'm not asking where he ain't.

EARL

Check inside with the boss then.

ROGER

Not likely.

EARL

You ain't holding my hand out here sunshine.

Earl pulls out his gun and shoots Roger in the head.

'Where is he?' Declan asked, being Roger.

Drake began lolling his tongue and strutting up and down like a black Mick Jagger with a thrush infection.

'You talkin' to me man?' he asked. 'Are you talkin' to me man?' Drake glared with considerable fury. Declan had never seen his nostrils flare like that before.

'What are you doing, Drake?'

Drake stopped. He looked suddenly deflated.

'I'm impravisin'.'

'I think you should just say your lines.'

'Ya think?'

'Definitely.' Declan took a breath. 'Where is he?' The moment he looked up into Drake's eyes he knew the rehearsal was going somewhere dangerous.

'Don't you fuckin' talk ta me like that!' Drake screamed.

They rehearsed for five minutes and every time Declan read the cues Drake began improvising like some hybrid Dennis Hopper / Robert De Niro-psycho.

'Drake, for fuck's sake!'

'I can't 'elp it!' Drake declared after the three hundredth improvisation. 'It's in me blood.'

'What? It's a virus? Just slow down your breathing. Speak slowly. Focus on me.'

'Focus on you?'

'Yeah, *I'm* the one you're trying to convince here. Doesn't matter what's inside you, you don't have to convince yourself that you're feeling any emotion, it's *my* character you want believing in your words. Just imagine I'm some dick at a club wanting a few lines of free coke.'

'That'd be 'ard.' The mere mention of coke made Drake reach into his pocket, take out a bag and rack up two lines on the desk.

'Exactly. You've got just enough coke for yourself ... and me ... so you're telling this guy you don't have any drugs, but you do. That's the tone you want.'

They went through the scene together once more and, to Declan's great surprise, Drake was entirely convincing. He did not sound like he was trying. It was pure and natural and simple. They each had a line of coke and looked into each other eyes. Drake appeared equally surprised. It was a *Kodak* moment.

'That was amazing,' Declan said, and they both laughed hard and loud. 'Really, Drake.'

'Yeah.' Drake nodded his head.

'Shall we go again?'

Drake's face lit up. 'Oh I almost forgot!' He took a gun out of his jacket and handed it to Declan. 'You can use this fer when you 'ave ta shoot me, fer realism.'

'Is it real?'

'Yea-uh.'

'What are you doing with a real gun?'

Drake flashed a wicked grin, 'Tristan Russell innit.' He took the gun and lined up imaginary targets. 'Just wait. I'll blow 'is 'ead off one day.'

'You're not serious.'

'Like shit I'm noh.' Drake looked at Declan deadpan; he then laughed and punched him in the arm. He gave him the gun and said he should have seen the look on his face, but Declan didn't have to, he knew exactly what he must have looked like. Drake said that he'd had the gun a couple of years for protection. Declan felt the weight of it in one hand.

'Is it loaded?'

'Course it's noh loaded ya think I'm a idgit?'

Declan was about to put the gun to Drake's forehead and pull the trigger to pay him back for the last joke, but he could not point a real gun at anyone's face, unloaded or otherwise. Instead he pointed it at the window and pulled the trigger. The sound of the pistol discharging was so loud and so unexpected that Declan dropped the gun and screamed as if it had burned his hand. Drake made some noise himself. The bullet pierced the window pane silently and sailed out over East London. Not for the first time, Declan appreciated being thirty feet higher than the surrounding buildings. Drake went to the window and wiggled his finger through the bullet hole. 'Shit,' he said quietly. 'Lucky we're high up, eh?'

'That was a surprise,' Declan shuddered.

Declan didn't tell the Posse about Drake's gun. He figured they probably already knew about it. Perhaps he could have mentioned that Drake had joked about blowing Tristan's head off one day, but he thought Drake was only joking. He was ninety per cent sure it was a joke, and there was no point creating imagined dramas when life is always sure to give you more than enough real ones.

22

Five days before Bridget's exhibition opening Juliet walked into Declan's bedroom and closed the door behind her.

'What's up?' she asked.

Declan knew it was a rhetorical question and said nothing. Juliet sat in the same chair that Drake had used the previous week, and lit a cigarette and asked how the gay film reviews were going.

'They're very gay.'

'Don't you worry what people will think?'

'I ridicule myself quite enough without having to worry about other people.'

Juliet laughed. 'I know what you mean.' She looked at the painting postcards and shook her head. 'We're all pretending to be something we're not.' she said.

'Yeah, you pretend to be an idiot.'

'You pretend you have no feelings. Deep down we're all just terrified, I think, all of us. Did you ever see Tony Blair *not* looking shit scared in an interview? He's simply nurtured a talent for controlling his fears in public. That's all success is: not letting fear overwhelm you. That's why you're so good on live television, you don't show your fear.' Juliet looked at Declan with an expression of faux-fear and rattled her eyes for a moment then smiled to show it was all for show. 'My parents are frightened little people,' she continued. 'They own a florist's in Bath, which is pretty ironic because my dad's about as romantic as cow. They think I'm the great success of the family because I'm the first

Cody to get a degree. And Jake … ,' she shook her head and smiled, 'he asked me to marry him yesterday.'

'Did you say yes?'

'I love Jake. He's great in the sack and emotionally he's far more mature than men your age.' She fingered a Picasso print of a young child holding a dove. The child's face was enigmatic, its gender was unclear. It was holding the dove like a prayer: covetous, frightened, perhaps melancholic.

'It's all gone to shit,' Juliet said. 'It always does.'

'What did you tell him when he proposed?'

'I told him to take a Mogadon and shut the fuck up.'

'Was he hurt?'

'He was surprised. God knows why. I've never given him any indication that my love extended to the idea of marriage.'

Juliet reached into her pocket, took out two blue tablets and popped them in her mouth.

'Bloody men,' she whispered. 'They're getting like women used to be, they're all soft and weak and … *sooo* sensitive.'

She sat down on the bed. The scent of her body was rich with an oriental perfume. Her dark hair fell from her shoulders like a cartoon fantasy. She put her hand between Declan's legs and pressed gently against his cock, bringing her parted lips forward so he could kiss them.

'Can I sleep here tonight?' she asked.

Juliet pulled her top off, slipped under the duvet and rested her chest on Declan's shoulder. He did not want to talk any more and when their lips met time was quickly forgotten. Juliet climbed on top and started riding Declan's body, her palms pressing into his chest. He opened his eyes and watched her as she moaned gently and thrust herself down using the full weight of her upper body. Her head was tilted back, her eyes were closed tight in painful concentration, shutting out the external images that might draw her out of herself. Her lips were tense and uncertain, her simpering voice was urgent. She was waiting, impatiently, perhaps in frustration, as her sensory world brought her closer and closer to a physical ecstasy that was as solitary as masturbation. It was as if Declan were not in the room at all. He felt like a very large, animated dildo.

An hour later they shared a joint and Juliet directed the smoke toward the postcards on the wall with a jerk of her head.

'They're almost all dead white men,' she said. 'Why do you like them so much?'

'I don't know. Why do you like peanut butter?'

'I don't like peanut butter.'

'Why don't you like it?'

Juliet handed Declan the joint, 'Because it tastes like shit.'

'There you go. I think those paintings taste beautiful.'

'And what's so special about beauty?'

Declan was sitting with his back against the wall as he took a long drag of the joint. 'Beauty demands nothing from us, really, it takes nothing from us. All you have to do is open your eyes and receive its gifts.'

'It's a total lie. It was an ugly world back when all this beauty was being made.'

'The media has always been a lie, hasn't it?'

'Especially if you were a woman. Do you know the story of Artemisia?' Juliet pointed to Gentileschi's *Judith and Holofernes*. 'As a teenager she was raped by one of the artists who worked in her father's studio. When it was taken to court one of the possible "punishments" was that the rapist would have to marry her.'

Declan nodded. 'But he gave her father money for her dowry instead because no man would marry a woman who had been raped unless she came with a lot of money.'

Juliet eyed him suspiciously. He felt something like happiness. He could feel warm blood flush through his body. There he was, lying in bed with a beautiful woman, both of them glowing with orgasmic satisfaction and discussing art as their hands moved gently over each other's body. Was he becoming human again? Had he finally found perfection? A beautiful woman with a degree in art history, they could make love and talk about art all their lives. What more could he ever want? He looked into Juliet's eyes hoping to find the warm light of love, but her eyes flickered restlessly from one postcard to the next. 'I have to go to Brighton tomorrow,' she said. 'Susan is in hospital.'

'Your daughter?'

'She's my aunt's daughter.'

'She seems to think you're her mother.'

'Yeah? Tristan thinks he can sing, Bridget thinks she's an artist; don't you see how deluded people are these days?'

'She's an amazing kid, Jules. I think most women would kill to have a daughter like Susan.'

'She tried to kill herself.' Juliet spoke as if she were discussing a drug deal gone wrong. She took the joint out of Declan's hands and smiled. 'It's that Concertal,' she said. 'I told her she shouldn't take it.'

'Do you want me to come?'

Juliet looked at Declan as if he had bull horns coming out his nose.

'Why? Do you want to?'

He did. He had decided that Juliet was ashamed of her motherhood and he wanted her to know that he was comfortable with it. He also realised it would enable him to be alone with her for most of the day.

23

They caught the morning train from Victoria to Brighton. If Declan had expected some intimate conversation during the train trip he was soon disappointed. Juliet bought a copy of *Marie Claire* at the station, and spent the whole trip reading about the lifestyles of the rich and famous. Declan looked out at the countryside; the cows, the sheep, the rolling hills, like a tourist on an African safari. He realised he had not been out of London in over a year. The closest thing to countryside he had seen with any regularity was Soho Square. He didn't even do parks in London because there never seemed to be enough time to just sit and look at trees. But now, sitting on the train and looking out over the countryside, he felt how soothing the space was, the greenness of it, and the relative emptiness. Then again, just about anything would be soothing compared to central London.

When they entered the hospital ward Susan was watching *American Beauty* on a laptop computer. She looked up and smiled:

'Mum!' she shouted.

'Susan, how are you?' Juliet asked, as if she were pulling splinters from her gums. She held out her hand and patted Susan's leg under the blanket. Susan continued to smile brightly. She nodded her head and said she was great.

'How are your parents?' Juliet asked firmly.

'They're OK,' Susan said, quieter now. 'Philip says hello.'

Not a muscle on Juliet's face moved. 'Does he?' she asked.

'He was wondering if you wanted to have Christmas with us this year.'

'I'm flying to Peru for two weeks,' Juliet said. 'You know I can't stand English winters. I feel like I'm being squashed by the clouds all day.'

Susan smiled shyly at Declan, who returned a shy smile of his own.

'Are you two together now?' she asked, and Juliet looked like she had just been asked what the square root of a cucumber was.

'Declan lives beneath me,' she answered quickly. 'We're flat-mates.'

They began to discuss the college situation. Susan's first year A level classes were under way and she was very concerned about missing them. Juliet was unsympathetic.

'If you insist on doing everything three or four years before you're physically or emotionally mature enough to do them, you're bound to suffer in some way.'

Susan put her chin out a little before replying, 'People do different things at all sorts of different ages these days, or not. There is no right age for anything any more.'

The girl has a point, Declan thought, but he knew better than to get involved.

'Susan, for Christ's sake, you were the one who decided to go on drugs in some kind of blind pursuit of better grades than Einstein!'

'Actually, I think Einstein flunked school,' Declan said before thinking.

'Shut up Declan! Look, Susan, you can't spend your whole life worrying about … '

'I want to go to boarding school,' Susan said before Juliet could finish. 'I don't want to stay with Aunt Brenda any more.'

'Why not?'

'I just don't. I thought if I went to boarding school then I could come home to your place during the holidays.'

Juliet waited, her mouth hung open.

'Come . . . ' she said gently, 'you've been to my place. It's a twenty-four-hour circus and no place for a young girl trying to study.'

'I can just stay at the boarding school all holidays. I don't care. I don't want to stay with Aunt Brenda any more. I can't.'

Juliet had stopped listening, she was glaring at a wind-up music box on the bedside table as if it were a micro-bomb packed with Semtex, counting down to zero. It was made of gilt-wood, about the size of a regular lunch box, with a glass front revealing a group of figurines dancing in circles inside.

'Who gave you that?' Juliet asked in a whisper.

'Philip.' Susan reached out and began winding the little arm so Juliet and Declan could hear the music.

Juliet looked like she might cry. Declan had never seen her so upset. In fact, he had never seen her upset. She turned and walked out of the room without even saying goodbye, leaving Declan standing at the bed wondering what he might say. He hated Juliet then with a righteousness that felt pure. *How could she walk out like that? How could she be so selfish? This girl needs her mother now.* He expected Susan to cry out to Juliet, implore her to come back but she remained silent. She did not say a word. She stopped winding the music box and looked to her laptop. *American Beauty* was still playing and Buddy Kane the real-estate king was hammering into Carolyn Burnham as she lay on her back in a hotel bed with her legs pointing to the heavens:

Buddy Kane: Do you like getting nailed by the king?
Carolyn Burnham: Yes, your majesty!

Declan cleared his throat. 'You, um, did you notice his hair is all black in that scene. In the previous scene, when they were having lunch, his hair was mostly grey.'

'He's no king,' Susan said. 'He's a loser.'

'I think it's an ironic title, isn't it? A parody of the male ego.'

Susan looked at Declan evenly and asked if he was in love with her mother.

'I think I am,' Declan said. 'She's a tough nut to crack, isn't she?'

'You don't know the half of it,' Susan muttered. 'She embalmed her heart years ago.'

'She could have had an abortion,' Declan offered in Juliet's defence, but from the look on Susan's face he could tell that she did not consider this a compliment.

Juliet returned on a train to London without waiting for Declan. He arrived home and went straight to her room but it was empty. She was probably out getting hammered somewhere. He fell asleep determined to prove to Juliet the next day that he understood her situation and was ready to help.

24

The painted blue sky and clouds covering Juliet's four walls made Declan giddy. He tried to sit down but he had too much energy and excitement to remain still. Instead, he paced the floor, going over all the things he wanted to say in his head, the things he had wanted to say for so long but was too scared.

Juliet entered her room. When she saw Declan she scowled.

'What are you doing?'

'I wanted to surprise you.'

'This is my room. No one comes in here!' Juliet looked genuinely afraid.

'What do you think I'm going to do?' Declan laughed 'Steal your drugs?' The manner in which Juliet's face tightened revealed he wasn't far from the truth.

'Have you touched anything?'

Declan was not going to let her sour mood distract him from his mission. He knew that as soon as she heard what he had to say everything would change.

'Juliet, I love you.'

'Fantastic, write me a poem.'

'There's so much I want to say to you, Juliet. I feel like I'm ready now.'

'Ready for what,' Juliet rolled her eyes.

'Ready to be honest.'

'Honest about what?'

'About how I *feel*.'

Juliet grunted fearfully. Declan moved closer to her.

'There's so much I've wanted to say so … I've … I've written you this letter.' He handed Juliet the envelope containing a typed confession of his love, among other things. Before Juliet could respond he left the room. He sat on his bed and tried to remember all the profound expressions of feeling that he had found a language for in the letter. He tried to imagine how Juliet was feeling as she read it. He agonised over the effect that some expressions might have, but ultimately he felt sure that his passion and his honesty would surprise and please her.

'Are you having a laugh?' Juliet was standing in the doorway. The letter was scrunched up in her left hand. She did not look pleased.

'I … I … I'm trying to be honest,' Declan said, 'about my feelings. It's not the brain damage, I've just been too scared to feel anything since … '

Juliet's face was wiped clean of emotion. She stopped blinking and Declan was not even sure she was breathing, but he was confident that at any minute she would fall into his arms, crying. This would be the beginning of the rest of their lives.

After a long silence Juliet started laughing.

'What's so funny?'

'You are.' Juliet looked at Declan squarely. 'You don't even *know* me, Declan. You've created some kind of fantasy of me in your head. I am not the woman who has made you feel human again.'

'I know you, deep down.'

'Yeah? I'll tell you what I know, deep down. I know I never want to be like the other women my age, looking in the mirror every morning, horrified, despairing, praying every night that it's not too late, dating men they wouldn't have looked at ten years earlier, leaving dinner parties early and feeling humiliated because they don't have a partner. And if they do find a man who'll stick with them it doesn't matter how pathetic and fucked up he is, they cling to him as if he were the King of Sheba. Look at Bridget, she has stayed with David for *six years*, and he never worked a single day in all that time. Why didn't she dump him years ago? Because she's scared of being alone. I don't want to be scared like that.'

'You don't have to be scared. I love you.'

Julia laughed. 'I love you too, Declan, I suppose, but we're just passing ships in the night. One day you'll go home, wherever *that* is, and I'll find another toy boy.'

'I won't go home,' Declan said. 'I can't, all my best friends are dead.'

He hadn't meant to say this. It had just come out. Juliet paused for a moment to consider her next move. Declan had given her a perfect exit and she took it.

'You can't run forever, Declan.'

'Me? *Me* run?'

'I don't know what happened to you, but you're kidding yourself if you think ... '

'What about you?' Declan blurted. 'What about your uncle?' Juliet whipped around, but she managed to restrain whatever her first instinct had been and remained silent. Her eyes clouded over like two polluted swamps.

'David told me,' Declan said.

'What? David knows *nothing* about nothing! What don't you know?'

'Juliet, look, all I'm saying is that you deserve to be happy. We both do. You deserve everything that ... '

'Oh so you're offering me *everything* now?' She smiled, took her

T-shirt off and crept into bed and under the covers. 'Just give me your cock and shut up.'

Juliet's body was warm and urgent. She kept her eyes shut tight until she reached orgasm and they lay together afterwards, staring up at the ceiling like two astronauts strapped into a shuttle.

'You know what I don't get?' Juliet said without looking away from the ceiling. 'You have all these paintings on your walls ... and not a single photo from your real life. You don't even own a camera, do you?'

'I don't own a camera.'

'Why don't you like photos?'

Declan could have said that he disliked photographs because he thought they trapped people; people couldn't move in a photograph, they were rooted to the spot, striking that one single pose for the rest of their lives, like a bush in a garden. Photographs gave people a false sense of understanding their pasts, of knowing how things were, how they themselves were. People arranged photos around their houses, those special chosen photographs, taken in an instant, started to define some greater period in a person's life – a weekend, a year, a relationship, a childhood.

But Declan didn't say all this. Instead, he said, 'I don't mind photos.'

Juliet tweaked one of his nipples, a light challenge that made him wonder if they were going to have sex again before going to sleep.

He laughed and said, 'Haven't you ever been shown a photo of yourself from an old friend, a photo that you've never seen before in your life? It's kind of disturbing and amazing at the same time. You know? There you are, it's you, and you recognise yourself, but it's a version of you that you're completely unfamiliar with. It's like, when you first see it there's this shock for a second, a recognition that you don't quite know yourself as well as you thought you did.'

'Bloody hell, Declan.'

'It's true, isn't it? As much as people love to look at themselves, they only like to look at the same versions of themselves over and over again until those versions become who they are, and all the bad version get deleted. For every nice photograph people should have an utter shocker, you know, the ones with half-closed eyes and lolling twisted, corpse mouths and bird's nest hair.'

'I don't keep photographs of people I don't like,' Juliet said. 'I think that's funny. School friends would take photos at a party and some girl who stole their boyfriend would be in one, and still they'd keep that girl in their album.'

Later she explained what had happened with her uncle. She had been staying in Brighton over the summer and she returned to her auntie and uncle's house drunk one night after a beach party. Her uncle came into her room while she was lying in bed trying not to vomit. He pushed her down and took her panties off and eased himself into her.

'Does your aunt know?'

Juliet shrugged. 'It might have been her idea.'

'What about Susan?'

'Maybe she knows,' Juliet nodded. 'If she does she's not letting on.'

'Why didn't you go to the police?'

'It didn't bother me, really,' Juliet said, clenching her jaws as if trying to shatter her teeth. 'I'd always quite fancied my uncle.'

Declan was sure she was lying and the lie surprised him.

'How can you be so casual about this? He *abused* you?'

'What business is it of yours? Who are you to tell me how to deal with my past?'

'I was with you today, remember? I was there when you walked out on your daughter.'

'Excuse me. I don't even ask you about your past, let alone advise you. I respect your right to deal with your life in your own way!'

'That girl needs her mother,' Declan whispered. He did not speak with any conviction, he spoke like a man commenting on the colour of a sofa, and perhaps this was why Juliet looked so hurt. She ordered Declan from the room before she realised it was not her room, then she leaped out of the bed and slammed the door on her way out.

25

The day before Bridget's exhibition opening at EX Gallery the curator phoned with a new plan to generate publicity. He was going to fill a rubbish bin in the gallery space with fifteen of Bridget's Polaroids. The next day cleaners would take the rubbish away and the curator would contact the media to say that it was one of the key works in the exhibition, worth fifteen thousand pounds. He would make sure the rubbish was not in the skip when the cleaners were called back to search for it and when they failed to find it he would threaten to sue the cleaning company for the value of the work.

'Do you see how brilliant this is?' Bridget asked Declan when she got off the phone. 'So many people think contemporary art is rubbish, so we give journalists the perfect headline. The story will make the front page of all the tabloids *and* feature on TV news bulletins. It will be one of those quirky "What in the World?" kind of stories, such a brilliant artistic statement, and *so* ironic.'

The opening night of Bridget's exhibition was a refined mix of glamour and grunge thanks to a carefully balanced guest list that Bridget had spent six weeks developing like a work of art. She had allowed her mother Abigail, a born socialite sheepdog, to round up the majority of the guests because, she explained, her mother's friends were the ones who were going to plant a red spot beside her Polaroid photographs. Bridget had then carefully selected friends from her own London coterie to contrast nicely with her mother's moneyed set from Chelsea and Kensington.

She invited a lot of loud and flamboyantly dressed media people, mostly from film production and advertising, a handful of struggling artists from her university days, and one or two very good looking drug addicts whose sharp, angular features and dusty eyes gave heroin chic considerable artistic appeal.

When Declan stepped out of the taxi with David, a row of photographers jostled on the pavement, raising lenses in their direction. They stopped and peered out from behind the cameras when they realised they didn't know who the hell the two men were. Not one flash went off as Declan and David made their way up the red carpet that had been paid for by Bridget's mother.

Abigail, dressed in a black and white hounds-tooth jacket and black skirt, was a picture of pure class as she passed from group to group, mingling for no more than ten minutes wherever she went. She had invited several sitting members of parliament, two judges, a handful of media personalities, a fashion designer and some extremely wealthy art collectors. Critics from *The Times* and the *Guardian* sipped champagne and studied the Polaroids while several gossip columnists munched on hors d'oeuvres and chatted with the guests.

Bridget's father, Pierre Defond, flew in from France with a dozen crates of Veuve Clicquot, a bottle of Viagra and several tablets of ecstasy which he soon put to good use. He said a polite hello to his ex-wife, kissed Bridget on the forehead and preened his new toupee, the colour of a foxy-nugget bangle with flecks of natural silver. He then wandered over to the side of the gallery where Bridget's younger friends were quaffing his champagne.

Bridget approached David and Declan, took a couple of photographs, nodded a cursory *hello* to David, and then whisked Declan across the room, photographing people as she went. She held him close and whispered.

'You know the only brilliant thing about my mother's friends? They always want to out-spend each other. It's like a competition between who can care less about money. Other than that they're complete wankers.'

Bridget's massive face was bigger than the bull-bar on the front of a Mac truck. It stared out at everyone from the four LCD screens on the gallery walls. Her recorded voice was firm and confident, but with a gentleness that Declan did not recognise although the words were his. He blushed at the thought that anyone might see through the artifice: '*Photographs offer a two-dimensional impression of the two-dimensional world as we perceive it.*'

The room was neatly divided into two groups, each standing on opposite sides of the LCD screen in the middle of the back wall. To the left side, Bridget's mother and her society friends gathered, talked quietly, with the occasional grave inflection, and looked up at Bridget's massive face with an admiration bordering on uncertainty. To the right were Bridget's friends and her father, who tried unsuccessfully to chat up several young women whom he seemed to single out for their kiddie-porn fashion sense.

'Are you a friend of Bridge's?' he asked Vivian, who was wearing a mini-skirt, a cropped top and no bra. Vivian's body was a soft golden colour, with finger marks smudged over the gold on her shoulders and forearms in the places where she had scratched herself. She and Tristan had shot a music video that day to promote the duet they had recorded. The director had wanted Vivian to look like a golden statue. Now she was standing by the bar looking out for Tristan, who was late again and had ruined another photo opportunity for her. Vivian nodded 'yes' to Pierre and he took a bottle of pills from his jacket and shook them in the air. 'Look what the Candy Man can do,' he smiled, taking two ecstasy pills from the brown glass bottle and offering one to Vivian.

'*Measuring finite space is an exercise in mathematical deception in so far as we can never, finally, ascertain the smallest space between two points, in mathematical terms space is infinitely expansive and regressive.*'

After their third glass of champagne some of Mrs Defond's friends felt game enough to approach the Polaroid photographs Bridget had stuck to the wall. They pretended not be looking at the crude female nudes. Declan overheard Bridget behind him, talking to a woman in a fur-lined jacket.

'Diane bought five of them.'

'Did she?' the woman said. 'Five? I'll buy ten.'

'Are you sure? Do you want to choose?'

'Any ten, they're all fabulous Bridge, just put a red dot next to ten of them.'

Bridget turned to Declan and winked. He looked up at her enormous face on the LCD.

'*The notion of a three-dimensional reality is an illusion. Nobody sees in three dimensions, we all see the world on a flat retinal screen, similar to the image of me on the screen that you see before you now.*'

Bridget had a champagne glass in one hand and was leading another two society ladies towards a small patch of Polaroids on one wall.

'I'll buy fifteen,' said one of the ladies.

'Me too,' said the other. Bridget looked disappointed.

'*Time was once measured in seconds, now it is measured in nano-seconds, and these images present all the nano-moments that flash by us every day. Sometimes we catch a face, a cup of coffee, a parking metre in the haze of experience, but most of the reality that stands in our immediate and peripheral vision is lost forever. Tonight, I give you the opportunity to reclaim and ponder the experiences, the "you" that you have lost.*'

Declan shuddered and finished his glass of champagne.

Tristan strutted in like Byron without the limp. He was dressed up in a princely, red velvet suit and a billowing cravat that Vivian said he had stolen from a shop in Regent Street the previous day. He had flecks of whipped cream smudged around his ears and on his neck. Abigail's guests gaped in shades of horror as Tristan sidled up to the bar and dropped two pills into a glass of champagne before downing the entire contents with a practised flash of the wrist. He turned to the crowd, adjusted his cufflinks like James Bond, and gazed out across the sea of guests like a sailor on the bow of a ship. Wherever his eyes wandered people turned and began to talk amongst themselves quickly.

Any guest with political associations dropped their drinks and ran for the cloak room as soon as they saw Tristan. It was as if a suicide bomber had entered the building. Abigail rushed over to speak to them as they collected their summer coats.

'I had no idea he was coming,' she said. 'I'm so sorry.'

Bridget approached Declan with open arms and said that the monologues had turned people on with a force that was palpable.

'I could never have explained my artistic intention with the same style and ... conviction,' she confessed. 'You reached down into my soul and captured the essence and beauty of this work in a conceptual language that was beyond my ability. I can create the images but you ... you give them the language they deserve.'

'It was my pleasure,' Declan lied.

Red dots were spotted across the room like measles. Each dot represented a Polaroid sold.

'You're selling them individually?' Declan asked, 'Isn't that like selling pieces of a mosaic.'

'I can't sell it as a single work, I wouldn't make any money.' She drew closer and whispered conspiratorially. 'I've been selling them for one thousand pounds each, and I've already sold fifty!'

Declan did some quick mathematical calculations, his jaw hung loose, while Bridget swept herself away and spoke confidently with some older men dressed in expensive suits. They were eying the fuzzy female nudes and their lips were wet.

Declan revisited the bar with David and each dropped a pill before ordering a glass of champagne.

'You could do this with your shoes,' Declan said, 'three thousand shoes at a thousand a pair, think about it.'

'I have,' David said. 'Many times, and every time I think about it I imagine myself stuck in a room full of people like this, drinking expensive champagne like this, talking shit … the idea makes my skin crawl.'

'Don't you want recognition?'

'I don't want to get it by shouting nonsense. Did she even pay you for the catalogue?'

Juliet and Jake came to the bar and Juliet kissed Declan's cheeks defiantly, grabbing a glass of champagne like a praying mantis grabbing its boyfriend. Declan could see she was on her third or fourth pill, but the ecstasy in her blood could not still the fury in her heart. Jake looked sullen and cold. He slouched against the wall and kept his eyes on Juliet's feet.

'I'm so sick of trying to sell drugs all day,' Juliet snapped. 'There's got to be a better way to make a living. Don't look at me like that Declan, what if the wind changes? You'll be a monkey-face the rest of your life'

'How's school,' Declan asked Jake. 'What book are you studying?'

'*Macbeth*,' Jake said, and pulled a face to show what he thought of Shakespeare, or *Macbeth*, or both. Declan tried to think of something interesting and impersonal to say.

'You know, some people say that Banquo was a son of a bitch.' This raised Jake's eyes momentarily.

'I thought he was the good guy,' he said uncertainly, 'the one who wasn't corrupted by the witches.'

'That's one way of looking at it. But maybe he could see the writing on the wall; maybe he could have stopped Macbeth while Macbeth was still indecisive.'

Declan saw Jake was stewing over this possibility and continued quickly. 'What I'm saying is, maybe Banquo sat back and *let* Macbeth do the dirty work, maybe he secretly *wanted* Macbeth to kill Duncan because that meant his sons were one step closer to the throne that was prophesied by the witches. I think the popular term these days is passive-aggressive.'

Jake shook his head and finished his glass of champagne.

'That's not what the papers say.'

'No,' Declan nodded. 'But you can't believe what you read in the papers.'

Drake approached the group in a manner that suggested a remarkable eagerness to talk, which was somewhat unusual for him. He punched Declan in the arm and grunted hello.

'Guess the fuck wha!' he said excitedly. His hands fidgeted in the air as if he were playing an invisible Rubik's Cube.

'What the fuck?' Declan asked.

'I got a promotion at work today. I meet Ralph Sweeney, yeah, 'ee sees me do me bit, 'ee says I'm tha bizness. That baldy geezer pulled out and 'ee offered me lead on the spot.'

David shook his head. Juliet frowned and touched her bottom with a ring finger. Drake continued, explaining that the character he was now playing had eighty-six lines and a sex scene with

Minnie Driver and some other honey. By this point everyone was reacting to each piece of news with surprise and joy. They must have made a lot of noise because people from Abigail Defond's side of the room looked over like disapproving teachers at a school assembly. When the Posse faction had finished its mini-celebration they all looked at Drake and waited until he remembered what for.

'An' I got the party players!' he added, flashing a lopsided grin. He offered everyone a pill each and they washed them down with the dregs of their champagne.

'This is posh,' Drake said, looking to his left and right with theatrical intention. He was standing upright and he was smiling. Declan could hardly believe it was the same man he had met just a couple months earlier for the first time.

'What?' Drake asked.

'Nothing. Thanks for the pill.'

'Buncha toff faces 'ere ... Your kind, eh David?'

'I'm not kind,' David said, and smiled to show that he was still there.

Drake took Declan aside for a private conversation.

'I got to thank you mate,' he said with tears in his eyes. 'Ya were the only guy oo believed in me. You were the one got me through. And I know it's not jus' the drugs. I offer 'em to ya and ya don't take 'em.'

'I take them ninety per cent of the time.'

'See wha' I mean?'

Declan didn't.

'You really 'elped me wiv me lines,' Drake explained.

'You're lucky I didn't blow your head off in the process.'

'Ow many times we go over them lines? Ten? Twenty? Sweeney watches teday an' 'ee loves me. Absolutely *loves* me ... a natural

’ee says. And it’s yoo-hoo made me like that.’ Drake reached into his pocket and gave Declan his mobile phone. ‘You wanna do me a fava and phone up me muvva for me. It’s ringin’. Just straight out wiv it, no introducin’ yerself.’

The same old woman answered as before and Declan spoke rapidly.

‘Drake’s been promoted and now has a major role in the next Ralph Sweeney film.’

The phone went dead. Drake’s look of hope folded over into something more realistic. He took his phone back and mumbled gratitude.

A loud scream pierced the gentle hum of voices and everyone turned to see a well-dressed woman clutching at her throat as if she’d just been poisoned.

‘My pearls!’ she screamed. ‘My pearls have gone!’

Tristan snuck up beside Declan and dug his knuckles into his side.

‘Let’s go to Heaven people,’ he said.

26

They came in through Purgatory like a 4th-of-July parade. Bridget tried to silence everyone so she could say thank you, but even she was powerless to command attention on this occasion. Instead she took photo after photo of the posing pilled-up Posse. It was the first time Declan had ever seen Nathan socialising with the group. He was looking relaxed and smiling, enjoying a hit from somebody's crack pipe and blowing the smoke out in spirals. He had just got Tristan out of a media-saturated public event without any arrests, injuries or deaths and he must have wondered what could go wrong now.

Bridget toasted each person for helping her realise her dream. The biggest cheers were reserved for Drake, the star of Ralph Sweeney's new film. Everyone banged the table like drunk Germans at a beer festival when Declan made the announcement. Only Tristan seemed displeased. He pretended that it was because nobody had told him.

'We're telling you now,' Vivian said.

'Yes but you didn't tell me at the exhibition, did you!' Tristan screamed. 'Nobody told me.'

Bridget misread the dynamics of the moment and tried to crack a joke.

'You better watch out now, Triz, he might end up twice as famous as you.' Everyone laughed while Tristan shook his head bitterly and said that pigs would fly first. Bridget and Juliet pretended to stir an imaginary pot in front of him.

David was the only person in the group who remained sedate. He went up to Heaven and sat out on the balcony by himself, looking across the city lights. Declan followed him upstairs, offered him half a pill and washed his half down with a swig of whiskey.

It was Declan's third month in Purgatory and he had enjoyed about three good nights sleep. He had not been for a swim or a run and his body felt like sewage in a bag of skin.

'How are you feeling?' David asked.

'Great,' Declan said, and heaved several mouthfuls of wet cement-like vomit over the balcony into the night sky to prove it. 'You?'

'Great.'

They looked out over the city horizon and Declan cursed.

'I just threw up my half of that pill.'

'Jump over and find it.'

Declan leaned over the edge of the balcony and vomited again instead.

'Do you ever imagine jumping?' he asked, once he had emptied most of the champagne from his stomach. 'When you look over the side of a tall building, don't you wonder, what if?'

By the time David answered 'no' Declan was already sailing through the air in his imagination, the wind whistling past his ears, his heart surging up toward his throat. In seconds he would hit the concrete below. He closed his eyes and tried to imagine that moment of impact. Would he feel any pain or would death come so instantly that the pain would never get the chance to be processed by his brain. He had been told that most people who fell from tall buildings died of heart attacks before they hit the ground, but how could that be when the body seemed programmed to try and survive almost any physical catastrophe.

Even Icarus would have been imagining a way of cheating death right up to the final moment.

Declan heard a glass smash downstairs and people screaming. As he stumbled back into the flat he could make out Tristan and Drake's angry voices. Vivian and Bridget were both screeching like frightened bats in the background. Declan laboured down the stairs just as another wave of euphoria zapped his senses, his head started to vibrate like a tuning fork leaving him with blurred vision and chronic feedback humming down his auditory canals.

'I'll tell ya how it is!' Drake threatened.

'What are you saying?'

'What?'

'I'll … '

'Drake shut up!' Bridget screamed.

When Declan got downstairs he could not distinguish anything more than the outlines of figures moving toward the balcony. He heard Tristan's voice and hardly recognised it. The sweet, ethereal tone had been replaced by the incubus once again. Drake was attempting to compose a sentence of some description, but he was so angry he could not get past the first few words.

'You two are … you're … you fuckin' … '

The voices bounced around inside Declan's head and he collapsed onto the table just as everything went eerily silent. He found a seat with one hand and dropped into it, trying to regain enough focus to see what was right before his eyes. Heavy breathing was punctuated by the sound of uncertain footsteps moving away from the balcony and back into the house. He tried to speak but the words would not come out.

'Wozappen'd?' he whispered.

Vivian started crying. 'What have you done?' she asked.

Declan put his head on the table and the night was swallowed up in one vicious gulp.

'Oh my God, please, you have to come quickly!'

Declan opened his eyes and saw Bridget rehearsing in front of the mirror. Her voice painted with emotion.

'Please, you have to, you have to ... There's been a terrible accident ... He's fallen off ... He's fallen off the balcony!'

After testing several other lines she dialled a three-digit number and Declan felt himself slipping away once more.

When Declan regained consciousness he saw six cops in the room. The only other Posse member he could see was Bridget, who was sitting on the sofa, dabbing her eyes with a handkerchief and talking in a high-pitched voice. Several police officers sat and listened and one scribbled notes. Bridget saw that Declan had regained his senses and glared in his direction for a millisecond, with eyes that threatened castration, before continuing her story.

A police officer approached Declan, and Declan asked what had happened.

'A man went off the balcony,' the officer explained. Declan stared at the Rothko print hanging on the wall. 'Drake Preston,' the officer continued. 'Did you see anything?'

Declan looked to Bridget again and, once more, her eyes flashed a warning. He shook his head and lit a cigarette, saying he didn't remember anything.

27

Declan awoke eighteen hours after Drake had fallen to his death, staggered straight up to Juliet's room in Heaven and dropped five Mogadons. Juliet was not home, neither was anyone else. Bridget's digital camera lay on the table in Purgatory. Declan picked it up and turned it on, hoping to look through the photographs from the previous night, but the memory card was empty: all the photographs had been deleted.

The next day Drake's death was reported in three of the daily papers as a tragic accident. Bridget entered Declan's bedroom with the newspapers around midday. She put the papers in a pile on his bed, and then started marching up and down in a sequence of attitudes like a mechanical soldier with a faulty wire.

'When are you going to get out of bed?' she asked.

'I'm tired.'

'Yeah, I'm tired too, Declan. I'm exhausted but you don't see me hiding under a pillow all day. Drake's in the papers. I can't believe he's dead. I can't believe it.' She was unable to remain brisk and angry, she put her hands to her face and sobbed in genuine despair. Her body began to convulse and Declan was suddenly moved to put a hand on her shoulder, but he could not reach her. She wept loudly. 'It's just horrid-horrid-horrid!' Declan looked at her face all twisted up, and it occurred to him that this was one of those moments she would never like to be reminded of in photographic form. Her internal pain had taken away whatever external beauty she possessed, she looked like a beast from a fairy-tale that had leapt out from under some bridge into the real world. Her whole face had turned to dirty water and even her sobs sounded like they were drowning. Declan wondered what impression she had of him. He was sitting passively in bed with his knees up and his hands around his ankles. She probably thought he did not feel anything; that he did not care. His bowels suddenly needed to express themselves beyond his will, and he did a massive fart that almost blew the duvet from his bed. Bridget stopped marching and gave him a withering look.

'Jesus, Declan.'

'Sorry,' he said, as the air around him surrendered to the fumes of stale champagne.

Bridget stepped away from the bed and fingered a print of a Bernini sculpture, *Daphne and Apollo*. Apollo was chasing Daphne, intent on having sex with her. The myth says that Daphne had cried out to her father, the river god Peneus, to help save her from Apollo's lust and in response Peneus turned his daughter into a tree.

A tree. On what level, exactly, is that helpful? Why couldn't the father, if he has the power to turn flesh into wood, have moved Daphne somewhere safe and out of harm's way? Did he know there was nowhere safe, no matter how far away; nowhere Daphne could walk without looking over her shoulder?

Bernini's sculpture captures that moment just after the metamorphosis begins. Daphne's mouth forms a circle of surprise, or maybe it's horror. It's unclear whether her horrified look is in response to Apollo's intentions, or her father's method of assistance. It was probably a bit of both. What was she going to do as a tree all day? Maybe the myth was saying that trauma can turn people into trees sometimes. They just stop moving.

'What happened?' Declan asked. 'Where has everyone gone?'

Bridget wiped the tears from her cheeks and exhaled as if her lungs had filled with liquid.

'They've all run home to mummy and daddy, the spoilt babies. They *hate* their parents and bitch about them, but as soon as there's trouble it's back to the old-school bedroom. Will you hold me?'

Declan held his arms out and Bridget hugged him fiercely. 'He was such a beautiful boy,' she wept. 'How will we cope without him?' Then, with a self-deprecating laugh, she added, 'Where are we going to score our drugs?'

The newspapers reported the story of Drake's death in three-hundred-word summaries. *Man Falls to Death from Russell's Turin Street Den* was one headline. *Russell Flatmate Dies in Mystery Fall* was another. Declan flicked through the newspapers and found a story about Bridget's exhibition, a work of art reportedly valued at fifteen thousand pounds had been thrown out with the rubbish. *IT'S NOT RUBBISH, IT'S MODERN ART!* screamed the headline. Declan pulled a face to show that he was impressed, and Bridget waved one hand, 'It would have been front page if it weren't for poor Drake.'

'How did they find out about him?' Declan asked, slurring his words.

'Are you high?' Bridget asked, 'You are, aren't you, you're off your head.'

Declan shook his head. 'It's just when I'm tired.'

'You know what the media's like,' Bridget exclaimed. 'Ruthless blood-suckers – they hang out at the morgue just to see whose body comes in.'

Bridget was named in the *Daily Mail*. Her exhibition was mentioned as the venue where Drake had been drinking before he went home and fell, or jumped, twenty metres to his death.

The structure of the stories was uniform in each paper, with quotes from Bridget holding everything together like cement.

'They rang yesterday,' she explained.

Drake had been to Bridget's exhibition at EX Gallery, he had returned to the flat with Bridget and another male tenant, Bridget had taken a shower and at some point Drake had fallen to his death from the balcony. The story ended with a statement that read like a quote from a satirical television programme, 'For once in his life, Tristan Russell is not in the wrong place at the wrong time'.

'Wasn't Tristan with us?' Declan asked.

'I had to cover for them.'

'Why?'

'Everyone was fucked up, Declan. You can be fined five thousand pounds and spend six months in jail just for being under the influence of a class A drug.'

Declan did not know if this were true or not but it sounded believable, or Bridget sounded believable, so he said nothing.

'Besides,' Bridget continued, 'imagine the scandal if Tristan were here. All he has to do is be present in a room and he's accused of crimes against humanity.'

Bridget's mobile phone rang and she left the bedroom to answer it.

'Yes ... Yes I am ... Yes, that's right, at EX Gallery. Well, I'm devastated, of course I'm devastated. I just hope it wasn't the power of my images that drove him to this end. It was such an intense exhibition, so visceral, I heard several critics saying that their stomachs were literally turning.'

The aspect of the story that finally moved Declan was the memory that Drake had been offered a lead role in Ralph Sweeney's film. *Just when he'd got what he'd been dreaming of,* and suddenly the tears came. As soon as Declan started crying he began convulsing, and it was not long before he was barking like a bull-whale on steroids. He had not cried for many years and it confused him: was he crying for Drake or was he crying for himself, crying because he was feeling something without the help of a drug? He had never really liked Drake as a person. At least, now Drake was dead, he did not believe that he had liked him. He had felt pity for him, a sly kind of pity that placed Declan firmly in a position of superiority. He had thought he was better than Drake. Christ, that wasn't hard to do, Drake was not the kind of guy that anyone looked up to, and yet, at the same time, there was something about him, a kind of innocence that floated serenely over all the degradation and corruption. It gave him character, and the more you saw that character the more substance you saw in the man. Or maybe it was just the fact that he gave Declan bucket-loads of free drugs.

Vivian returned home that afternoon and went straight into her room without speaking to Bridget. When she came out fifteen minutes later she had metamorphosed into a stunning Italianate widow, shrouded in a black scarf and wearing a black Ted Baker dress with black Jimmy Choo shoes.

'Wow,' Declan said. 'The funeral's not till the weekend.'

'I have a photo shoot with the *Sun*.' Vivian started to cry, then realised she was ruining her mascara and cried even harder. Her sorrow was not as ugly to look at as Bridget's, but she certainly lacked the natural beauty that characterised her usual appearance. 'I can't believe he's gone,' she sobbed. 'I can't … '

She went to her room to do her face again and when she returned Bridget was in the kitchen roasting some peppers. Vivian stopped when she saw Bridget, it appeared she might reverse back out of the room. Bridget closed the oven door, looked up, and her face iced over. Declan sat on the sofa looking from one to the other, and waiting for someone to say something but Vivian turned and walked out the front door. Bridget sucked her teeth and finished basting the peppers. Declan was no Freud, but there was definitely something going on between those two women.

When David came downstairs for a coffee he was equally frosty toward Bridget. She asked him if he wanted some roasted vegetables and he shrugged and turned the kettle on.

'There's not enough water in it,' Bridget said, and she took the kettle and filled it and replaced it on the element. David did not thank her but turned and sent a weak, 'hello' grunt Declan's way.

A Posse meeting was held that night – just the four members: David, Vivian, Bridget and Declan. Bridget found some pain-killers in Juliet's room and they divvied them up and drowned them with glasses of water. Vivian sat with her hands in her lap and her eyes downcast. She did not speak or look at anyone. Bridget had the newspapers spread over the table and checked the *Guardian* before tossing it contemptuously to the floor.

'They hardly even mention my exhibition,' she grumbled, shaking her head. Her expression grew sombre. 'Not that that's important.'

Silence.

'I still don't know what happened,' Declan ventured. Bridget answered before anyone else could.

'Drake was totally wasted; he was leaving the room, but he clipped his heel on the balcony threshold and fell back and over the side. I waited ten minutes until everyone had left and then phoned the police.'

'Ten minutes?' Declan repeated. 'He could have been alive.'

'From the seventeenth-floor balcony?' Bridget snapped. 'He might have been a dildo, but he wasn't made of rubber.'

'Bridget?' David warned.

'*Don't you Bridget me!* I'm as upset as anyone but I won't let sentimentality turn me into a liar, David. Come on, we all thought Drake was a dildo ... I mean, he gave us a lot of pleasure for free.'

'He could have hit a tree,' Declan said. 'A guy in Australia fell more than two kilometres when his parachute failed, and he lived.'

Vivian started crying. Bridget looked unsure for a moment then glared at Declan like a wildcat. She stopped playing defensive and tossed the conversational ball to her offence team.

'Great, well done, Declan. Are you determined to be a total cunt? What are you suggesting anyway?'

'Nothing.'

'Well your tone is not appreciated.'

Vivian continued to cry.

'What tone?'

'That fucking *suspicious* tone. You think any one of us is responsible for this? Is that it? I'm trying to keep everyone out of trouble, you included.'

28

Declan bought the *Sun* newspaper the next day and read the interview with Vivian. 'I can't believe he's gone,' she was quoted as saying. 'I've never lost someone close to me before. It makes you realise how precious life is and how easily we can lose it. It's such a reality check when this happens.' The photo showed her looking with deep yearning toward a photo of a youthful, pre-scar-era Drake.

Nathan also gave a statement to the media. He wanted to be clear about Tristan's whereabouts at the time of Drake's death. 'We was at the exhibition,' Nathan was quoted as saying in the *Mirror*, 'but after that Triz come with me and some mates to a place in South London.'

It was amazing that this version of events was accepted by the press, but then, with no story to contradict it, why wouldn't it be? None of the papers suggested that Tristan or anyone else had fled the scene but it was assumed that drugs had played some part in Drake's death.

Nathan visited Declan in his room the day after the Posse meeting.

'Y'all right?' he asked, closing the bedroom door behind his massive frame. He perched himself on the side of Declan's desk and glared toward the bed, then at the paintings on the walls, then at Declan once more.

'What's up Nathan? Where's Tristan?'

Nathan stared for a long time before speaking. He shook his head.

'Yer a good kid and ya got a good foocha. Triz likes ya.'

Declan nodded his head, realising this was not a conversation that required his involvement. Nathan continued, 'I know. Ya feel bad about what happen', we all do. Jus', keep ya 'ead on, right? Don't get silly on us.' Then he stood up and left, closing the door behind him quietly.

Declan lit a cigarette and his hands were shaking. Was Nathan threatening him? Was it a threat? It certainly sounded like a threat. What could Declan do?

Biographies of Drake were quickly composed in the press thanks to interviews with people who had not known him for years. None of the stories represented the man Declan had shared drugs and living space with over the summer. He was the son of a retired naval seaman who had served in the Falklands. His proud mother told the press her son was one of the top male models working in London, a loveable rogue and devoted young father, who lived for his own son. The photos accompanying these biographies were all professional headshots taken from his early modelling career when he was a white-toothed, fresh-faced beauty, well before drugs had ravaged the topography of his face like a hurricane ravaging a suburban town. His acting career was given a celebrity injection when Ralph Sweeney expressed his great sadness, having met Drake for the first time just hours before he died.

Mr Sweeney gave the following statement to the press:

'Initially Drake Preston had a minor role in my film but as soon as I saw him act I knew we had to give him something more substantial. I met him just the once, but he had enormous talent and he was a wonderful human being.'

Mr and Mrs Preston praised their son's 'devil-may-care' attitude, they called him a people's person and reminisced about his sporting prowess as a young boy. They did not believe Drake would have killed himself. 'Our son loved life,' Mr Preston was quoted as saying in the *Sun.* Asked if he thought his son was experimenting with drugs he was adamant, "Drake wasn't like that. He's just wasn't that kind of person".

The mother of Drake's son, a large African woman, praised Drake as an affectionate and attentive father to his young boy.

The *Mirror* carried a photograph of Mr and Mrs Preston sitting on their sofa and holding each other while looking down at a framed photograph, artfully positioned between their laps, of a youthful Drake laughing.

The former head of the Arsenal Academy said that Drake had showed great promise as a cadet but he had chosen to focus his energies on becoming the best male model he could be. Once it became known that Drake had trained at the Arsenal Academy when he was a teenager, his story become the biggest tragedy since Diana's death in Paris. *Sporting Star Turned Actor Had the World at His Feet* was the most understated headline. His one-year training stint at the Academy was soon turned into more charming epithets like *Former Arsenal player, Drake Preston.* The Prime Minister Tony Blair spoke outside parliament, looking suitably shaken as he wished Drake's parents well.

Even though no newspaper could place Tristan in the flat at the time of Drake's death, some newspapers intimated that Tristan Russell's influence had led Drake to experiment with drugs, and that this had predicated Drake's leap from the balcony.

Vivian held a press conference outside the Chocolate Block to announce the up-and-coming single she and Tristan had recorded.

'We're releasing the single and the video this Friday,' Vivian told the journalists. 'It's called "Lick Me All Over".' She gave an impromptu performance of the first verse and chorus, and a cameraman for the BBC clapped enthusiastically.

'Where is Tristan?' a journalist from the *Independent* asked. 'Is he upstairs?'

'Tristan is devastated by this tragedy,' Vivian told the journalists. 'Drake was a dear friend and Tristan has left the city for a few days in order to grieve in private.'

Vivian told Declan later that Tristan had bought a UN-medical-supply load of heroin and holed himself up in a hotel somewhere in Surrey. No one knew where he was, in fact, because he wasn't answering his phone. Vivian rang him fifty times a day without getting through. She also phoned her agent and Nathan several times a day. Nathan kept telling her he had no idea where Tristan was but she would not listen to him.

'Nathan I need him!' Vivian screamed. 'I need him by my side!'

Vivian needed Tristan because their debut single was being released on the Friday and they had to promote it as widely as possible: radio interviews, television performances, shopping-centre appearances. Without Tristan, Vivian was going to have to do everything by herself, and people would no doubt question how stable their relationship was if he was not by her side.

It was as if Vivian and Bridget had each placed Drake's death into a small compartment in the back of their memory warehouses. Meanwhile, in the immediate world, they busied themselves unpacking all the boxes of publicity that Drake's death was generating, and setting up their display windows in the 'minor-celebrity' shop front. Declan knew they were both hurting. The more Bridget dismissed Drake as a dildo, the more upset she appeared. Everyone deals with tragedy differently, don't they? Some people run away and hide, some people busy themselves with work, while others get drunk or take drugs; some simply cease to function properly, they cease to move, they lie in bed and mope and feel sorry for themselves or for the people they have lost, or both.

Vivian and Tristan's duet, 'Lick Me All Over' was released the day before Drake's funeral. The record label had little trouble securing time slots on the major weekend music programmes and when they received a copy of the video, most of the programmes requested an interview with both Tristan and Vivian. Vivian's voice was tuned with a voice synthesiser but it did not matter how badly she sang, because Tristan had the voice of a barking goat with haemorrhoids in his throat.

In the music video, Vivian appeared naked. Her entire body was coated in gold paint. She had a feline tail attached to her rump and she moved like a lynx around Tristan, who sat on a stool and smoked a cigarette, staring dolefully into the camera. Tristan was also naked apart from the bird-nest hairdo, which he wore like a hat, and a pair of Speedos, which were completely hidden by the few inches of whipped cream that had been spread over his entire body. As Vivian moved around him she licked the cream from his nipples and his belly-button, as well as other suggestive areas of his body, so he began to look more and more like a white leopard with skin-coloured spots.

The video created a minor scandal when it was screened on BBC1's 'Saturday Music Show'. The station's switchboard received over a thousand complaints from parents disgusted that their eight-year-old children were watching such filth while eating their cornflakes. The government regulator, Offcom, quickly banned the video clip from television broadcasts before nine o'clock. This was a stunning achievement, and it offered the single the kind of publicity that money could not buy. Every website, newspaper and magazine ran a story on Tristan Russell's latest scandal: a 'salacious' and 'offensive' music video. The articles were invariably accompanied by stills from the video, showing Vivian in all her voluptuous gold-leafed glory, her full breasts swinging freely as she leaned forward to lick Tristan.

The song was a top ten hit, which meant Tristan finally had some money. Vivian attacked the media like a cluster bomb, exploding in a hundred places at once. She appeared on several radio and television programmes daily, she was in the newspapers, magazines and even granted interviews to some fledgling online media websites. Questions about the controversial video clip were easily deflected.

'Why do people have such problems with nudity? We're all born naked, we all have showers naked, don't we?'

Over the years Tristan's absences had cost the Rods thousands of pounds in cancelled dates and recording studio sessions. Now, suddenly, he had made a lot of money and none of it was for them. For the other band members it was the final insult. They announced that he was no longer a Rod, and called up a young man from Bristol, who had a much better voice and a slightly more manageable drug habit, to replace him as lead singer.

While Vivian's public profile was that of a young, sex-bomb, Bridget, whose physical appearance was curious if not attractive, presented herself as a visual intellectual and a sassy-lipped business-woman. The media threw superlatives at the amount of money she had made from her debut exhibition. She had sold two hundred Polaroids on the first night of her exhibition, earning her a cool two hundred thousand pounds in a little over four hours. The *Guardian* noted that this equated to profits of about eight hundred pounds a minute. Art critics and commentators praised her boldness, her self-belief, her ambition, her calculating *genius.* Her show at EX Gallery became the most talked about exhibition in London since 'Sensation' three years earlier, and within a week every single Polaroid had been sold, netting Bridget a fortune. Financial success and artistic credibility may not have always been consubstantial in British art circles, but it was very difficult to sell four hundred thousand pounds' worth of blurred kiddie-pornesque Polaroids and not be hailed as a genius. Bridget was instantly welcomed by the established Brit Art pack. Soon the thousand-pound price tags were viewed as bargains and collectors who had missed out began offering twice as much for groups of ten. Polaroids that actually contained recognisable images, particularly the nudes of Vivian, were selling for up to six thousand pounds.

Bridget was interviewed on ITP's *Culture Show* and *The Arts Show* on ALB radio. *Time Out* put her on the front page with the blurb, *The Most Exciting New Artist in London? Probably.* She was pictured drinking at Soho House and the Groucho Club with some of the elder statesmen and women of Brit Art. A journalist from the *Mirror* christened her Bridget DeFabulous and overnight she had a new name. Curator James Judd rang her and said Pink Disc Gallery wanted to put on her next show. In the 1990s Pink Disc was arguably the most successful contemporary art gallery in London, and possibly the world.

'You're big now,' Judd told her. 'But I'm going to make you a superstar.'

Femme magazine offered Bridget a job reviewing different hotels around the world every month.

'They're going to fly me around the world,' Bridget explained. 'They give me a free room for a weekend and all I have to do is write about the hotel!'

Declan and Vivian were watching a porn movie when Bridget entered the living room to inform them of her latest success. Vivian did not even look up when she replied.

'Great, Bridge, maybe I should die too, then you'll be really famous.'

'Fuck you, Vivian,' said Bridget, 'the only reason you've been wearing black all week is to take five pounds off that arse.'

Vivian lunged at Bridget and the two of them went to ground clawing and screaming at each other like trailer-trash guests on the *Jerry Springer Show.* Declan wanted to get up and do something, but he had stolen four Temazzies from Juliet's room in the afternoon and was unable to move from his seat.

'Hey,' he said weakly. 'Don't ... don't do that, guys.'

David came down from Heaven to see what the noise was all about. He leapt down the last few stairs and ran to where Bridget and Vivian were thrashing on the floor, pulling Bridget away from Vivian with a gentle tug. The girls looked like they'd each been tumble dried. David led Bridget upstairs and Vivian grabbed her mobile phone and rang Tristan's number. She was choking and sobbing when his answering machine clicked on.

'Tristan, come home, please, take me away from here, please.'

The Posse was falling apart: Drake was dead, Tristan had disappeared, Bridget was making rude remarks about Vivian's arse, and Juliet was hiding out in Bath. At least David seemed to be coping pretty well. Declan went back to bed and wondered how it could get any worse. He could not sleep. His body was awake with fear. He felt confused.

29

Juliet rang from Bath the next day and asked if Declan could deliver a bag of prescription samples to Caspar Darling the chemist that evening. Caspar had finally summoned up the courage to collude in Juliet's scam, but Juliet wouldn't be home in time to meet him in Kentish Town that evening. Declan wondered why she couldn't wait until the following evening to make the drop but said nothing about this.

'Where are they?' asked Declan.

'They're under my bed. Don't worry, he's not expecting you, he's expecting me, so if anything looks suspicious you can just keep walking.'

Declan looked under Juliet's bed and saw two black sports bags. He drew one out and opened it but there were no drugs inside. There were wads of fifty pounds notes, all bundled up like you'd expect in a heist movie. There must have been at least ten thousand pounds. Perhaps Juliet had left the bag there as a test, to see if she could trust Declan. He put it back under the bed and took the other bag, half-expecting to find more money. This one was filled with the drug samples, and he put the packets in his own sports bag and threw Juliet's empty bag on her bed.

There must have been at least three hundred packets. How many years jail was that worth? Luckily Declan hadn't shaved since Drake's death and with a baseball cap on his head, he was sure Caspar would never recognise him. He took a couple of packets of Mogadon for himself, dropped three pills and stashed the rest in his bedroom before leaving to meet Caspar. Even the drugs couldn't calm his nerves and all along the bus route to Kentish Town he felt a pale dread chilling his body. All of his instincts were telling him not to meet Caspar but there he was, on the bus, with God knows how many drugs in his lap, and all because Juliet had asked him to.

If someone told you to jump off a cliff would you do it? he asked himself.

He entered the Kentish Town KFC at eight o'clock and saw Caspar sitting in one corner of the family restaurant. Caspar was looking far healthier than the last time they had met, and a lot more nervous. Declan ordered a chicken burger, fries and a Coke, and sat down where Caspar could not see him. Several tables away, two men dressed in blue jeans and Arsenal jackets were drinking coffee. Declan loosened his neck, stretched and swivelled his eyes around the room. On one semi-rotation he noticed one of the men wave a finger at Caspar. Caspar had been staring at the door for ten seconds and the finger directed Caspar back to the food on the tray in front of him.

Declan did not want to get up and leave immediately. He finished his burger and fries before taking what was left of his Coke. He did not turn around, nor did he run, but as soon as he had walked several hundred metres from KFC he dropped to the ground and felt his body shake with fear.

Juliet was lying naked in Declan's bed when he arrived home.

'I thought you weren't coming home today,' Declan whined.

'I thought I'd surprise you. Are you ready for a surprise?' she asked.

'Are you ready for one?' His tone was not flirtatious and Juliet pulled the sheets over her breasts.

'What happened?'

'I've just been released from the cop shop. They questioned me for two hours.'

'Not funny, Declan.'

'I'm not joking.'

'Did you tell them about me?'

'They already knew about you! You were the one supposed to meet Caspar, remember.'

'He didn't know my real name!'

'Hang on, you throw me to the lions and now you're worried if I grassed you up?' Declan changed his tone so Juliet could see he was telling the truth. 'Don't worry, they didn't catch me. I saw it was a set-up and got out before he recognised me.'

Juliet screamed relief. 'God! I hate it when you do that, it's like some obsession with you, you love scaring people with bad news that isn't true. Come on; don't look at me that way. I couldn't have gone, could I? He'd have recognised me straight away.'

'He had as much chance of recognising me.'

'You've almost got a beard now.'

'You didn't know that. Why couldn't you ask someone else? Someone whose face he hadn't seen? What about David?'

'David! Are you kidding me, he's an idiot. He'd be at the station right now ratting me out. I knew I could trust you.'

Juliet tried to reach up and kiss Declan on the mouth but he averted his head and sat down on the bed. *Come on,* he commanded. *Get angry! Be angry!*

'You could have warned me, Juliet.'

'I did warn you. I said if anything looks suspicious.'

'You didn't say you thought there was a good chance things would be suspicious.'

'I didn't think there was a good chance things would be suspicious!'

'Bullshit. You're lying.'

But Declan could not win this argument. It was true, Juliet had warned him and he still went. He could have said no but he didn't, and now he was angry.

Juliet sat up in the bed so her breasts were fully exposed.

'I can't believe we're arguing like this and Drake is dead.'

Declan could not ignore the subject of Drake's death and return to arguing about the Caspar situation. Maybe Juliet knew this.

'What happened that night?' he asked. 'Nathan came over and threatened me the other day.'

Juliet did not seem surprised. 'I suppose Tristan's still MIA?'

'Why is Nathan giving me the heavy word?'

'That's his job, isn't it? Keeping Tristan's back to the wall. Maybe he thought you'd go to the cops … not that Tristan did anything, but if the cops found out that he was in the flat when Drake died – think about it. They'd find out that Drake was Vivian's ex-boyfriend too. There wouldn't be any court case, but Tristan would be crucified in the media.'

Declan relaxed a little as Juliet's words sunk in. When he had spoken to Bridget nothing made sense. Now it did and it bothered him that Juliet's naked beauty might have helped him understand the truth better. He shook the thought away. It had nothing to do with the way Juliet looked, it was the words she had arranged into an explanation. He understood now why Tristan had to leave the flat before the police arrived. It was not an admission of guilt, it was as much as an effort to avoid the inevitable assumption of guilt that the press would have made if they had learned the truth.

'Every time I visit my parents I remember why I never want to get married,' Juliet said. 'Dad is such a grumpy bitch. "Fuck this" and "fucking that" and "where's me fucking smokes?" and "where's me fucking dinner?" – I don't know how my mum has put up with him for thirty years.'

Juliet started to cry. Declan wanted to hold her, to take her in his arms and tell her everything would be all right, that he was there, that he would protect her, that he loved her.

'What's wrong?' he asked.

It was a ridiculous question and Juliet did not bother to answer. She hid her face in her hands and continued crying. Declan really should have been holding her at that point, but he eased back on the bed and waited until she stopped. She wiped the tears from her eyes and gave him a crooked smile. In the movie version of his life he would have told her to leave him alone, he would have said that he did not want anything more to do with her.

'I don't know what you want from me,' he said, hoping Juliet would reach out and comfort him, that she would cover his face with kisses and tell him that she wanted him to love her; that she wanted him to take care of her.

'I don't want anything from you,' Juliet said defiantly. 'Why would I want anything from you? Why would I want anything from any man?'

'You don't like men much, really, do you?'

Juliet gave a sneering laugh. 'Why? Because I don't kneel before them and do as I'm told?'

'Love is not about kneeling.'

'What do you know about love?'

'Well, not much, I admit that, but I do know a bit about kneeling. I used to kneel in church every Sunday. If that's love then I admire your decision to avoid it.'

Juliet laughed and they were close again.

'Do you ever think about, you know, starting a new life?' Declan asked.

'Why? I'm never going to make this much money in another life?'

'Money isn't everything.'

'What would you know?' Juliet sneered. 'You've never had any.'

It was intended to hurt. Declan was suddenly relieved that he had not taken Juliet in his arms while she was crying. He was glad he had not uttered any ridiculous platitudes about love and support. He saw clearly now how different they were. Juliet was wealthy, beautiful, successful, and addicted to prescription drugs. Declan was a film critic for a gay magazine; his most prized possession was the collection of art postcards he had stuck to his walls. He was just a bit of fun in the night for Juliet. Even if she did want a genuine and committed relationship with a man one day, she had no intention of falling in love with a man like Declan. He couldn't support a goldfish. He was financially unreliable.

'Seen any good films?' Juliet asked.

'I saw a preview yesterday of a film called *Memento*. It's about a guy who suffers a brain injury and loses his long-term memory.'

'Is it one of those 'insider films' where you have to have brain damage to appreciate the subtleties?'

'You don't need brain damage to enjoy the film. It's a great film. You know what? One advantage of losing your memory is that you lose your conscience. You don't ever have to feel guilty again because you forget everything you do after five minutes, as long as you don't take photographs.'

'So what's the down side?'

'You don't have any idea who you really are any more.'

Juliet smiled sadly. 'Do people ever have any idea who they really are?'

'They don't have to, they just have to believe.'

'Believe what?'

'That they have an idea. That they are making choices based on the understanding that they know themselves.' Declan sat up straight in bed, warming to his theme. 'I was thinking about Drake yesterday, and I realised that this life is all we've got and it doesn't last long. You can look the wrong way at the wrong time and it will all be over in a second.'

'Sometimes it seems to drag on for an eternity.'

'It doesn't have to be that way.'

'I know; that's why God invented drugs.' Juliet rubbed Declan's arm affectionately to draw him out of his thoughts. 'Can I sleep here tonight?'

He wanted to say no. He wanted to tell Juliet that he didn't give a damn, like a hero in a movie, but he had a painful erection so he lifted up the duvet and slipped into bed beside Juliet. She rode him hard and loud, they gripped each other's hands and formed double-edge fists.

'What am I going to do with Susan?' Juliet asked when they had finished. A wash of guilt drifted over Declan because he had forgotten all about their visit to Brighton.

'What's happened?'

'You heard her. She wants to get away to boarding school.'

This conversation closed the distance between them even more than sex could. As they discussed what to do with Susan, Juliet put one hand on Declan's thigh and smiled sweetly into his eyes as he imagined a wife would do if she loved her husband. They agreed that Susan had to be removed from her aunt's house when she was discharged from hospital. She should be placed in a boarding school as soon as they found one that was willing to accept a fourteen-year-old girl studying A levels.

'Actually, I found one,' Juliet said, reaching down to the floor and taking a brochure from her trouser pocket. 'Royal High School in Bath. I checked it out while I was at Mum and Dad's. They do this new curriculum called the IBO and they're offering Susan a scholarship. I told her last night and she's excited because she gets to study six subjects and something called 'Theory of Knowledge' instead of just the three A levels.'

'So why are we discussing what to do if you've already decided?'

'I haven't already decided. I wanted to know what you thought.' Juliet rubbed his cheek with the back of her hand and he smiled, but something did not feel right.

30

Just five people stood outside the church when Juliet, Vivian, David and Declan arrived. The media was absent because Vivian had told her agent that the funeral was going to be at another cemetery. She did not want any photographs of her crying to appear in the papers. Apart from the Posse, Drake's parents, Drake's young son, the mother of his son, and an Asian man wearing a smart black suit waited solemnly for the church service.

Everyone introduced themselves to Drake's parents outside the church and apologised. They did not apologise for anything specifically, they just said 'I'm so sorry' and left it at that. Declan found it impossible to connect them with Drake. They were in their late fifties, bitter-looking London people; they were the sort of middle-aged black people you imagined spent most of their early lives subject to racial abuse, being a minority in East London in the Seventies. Standing in front of Mrs Preston it suddenly occurred to Declan that she had actually given birth to Drake. He got horrific flashes of Drake's tiny head popping out of her vagina for the first time. He could hear her screaming. He could hear the doctor saying, 'push, push!' He could see Drake's black hair bursting out all smooth and bloody.

'Are you all right?' Mrs Preston asked. Declan blinked and nodded weakly. He didn't know why but he was expecting the Prestons to abuse him, to accuse him of complicity in Drake's death, but they each held onto his hand as if the earth was about to suck them down forever. Their eyes were filled with tears but they were smiling.

'We know about you,' Mrs Preston said gently. She nudged her husband. 'This is the fella what rung me up ta speak about Drake's film career. Thank you.'

Mr Preston smiled nervously. 'Oh you're that guy are ya? Right. Drake told us lots a stuff about ya.'

Declan must have looked incredulous because Mr Preston began to stammer and search for something to add that might suggest he had spoken to Drake recently. 'You … you … you're the guy, ain't ya?'

Declan nodded and Mrs Preston nodded, and her eyes begged or defied him, he wasn't sure which. He felt sick in his stomach. No wonder Drake wanted him to give the eulogy.

'We spoke to the police,' Mrs Preston said. Her lips drew in. 'We don't believe Drake killed 'imself.'

Mr Preston shook his head in agreement. ' 'Ee never would 'ave done that.'

'But 'ee can't defend 'is name. There's nuffin we can do.'

'We wan ta at least find those responsible. Drake oughta be compensated for the career ee's lost now. 'Ee was gonna make good money.'

'I was there,' Declan said, 'but I'd … I'd had too much to drink.'

Mrs Preston put one hand on his forearm reassuringly. 'We know,' she nodded. 'If there was anyfing you could a done for Drake, you'd a done it.'

Declan informed them that in the will he had found in Drake's room, there was a request that he say a few words at the funeral, and they looked at each other uncertainly.

The Bee Gees' 'Staying Alive' was playing softly when Declan entered the church. He looked across to the Asian man in the black suit and saw that he was smiling and lip-syncing the first verse. David nudged an elbow into Declan's ribs.

'That's Mo,' he said.

When the song finished, the priest, who had never met Drake, spoke about death, Jesus, precious gifts, lambs, flocks, children, glory and a lot of other things that Declan was not really listening to. He was looking at the copy of Raphael's *Deposition* on the church wall. The hill of Calvary was in the distance and, like the disciples of Socrates in David's painting; most of the figures in Raphael's *Deposition* were swooning.

My God, Declan thought. *How many images of this dead man have I seen in my life?*

When it was his turn to talk, he walked to the front of the church and turned to face everyone.

'The one thing I can say about Drake,' he said, 'if I were honest, is that he was a good drug dealer. Otherwise he was a pretty hopeless human being. He was fucked five ways to sunset every day of the week. He knew it, too. He knew I knew it, and I think he asked me to speak here today to make sure it was said. We often used the word "wasted" to describe Drake. He wasted most of his life, he *was* wasted most of his life, and yet we still feel his death is a waste. There is nothing romantic or nice to say about it. The great tragedy is he died just when it looked like he might use his life for some good.'

Drake's father and mother looked like they had just swallowed raw elephant dung. The Asian man grinned from ear to ear. David slowly closed his mouth and blinked, Juliet and Vivian smiled vaguely.

At the burial, two elderly grave diggers covered Drake's coffin with soil. Declan listened to heavy clods of earth thudding against the coffin and found it difficult not to think about death. How could he have ever seriously contemplated suicide? Fast-forwarding his life to some personally determined fatal conclusion? Did he really think that being dry bones in a box would solve his problems? He shivered. Life lacked anything that could be considered a logical explanation, it didn't make much sense, but death, death was a chilling nothingness. Life was the only thing he had worth living, and it was so short, a person could blink and it would all be over.

When the grave diggers finished, the small group of mourners dispersed in different directions except for Mo, who came up to Declan and David.

'You two, I want to talk with you,' he said.

They went with Mo to a nearby café. Mo spoke in short crisp sentences, cutting up his thoughts like rolls of sushi for them to digest. Apart from a dragon tattoo on one forearm, Mo looked more like the middle-aged owner of a laundrette than a drug wholesaler.

'Did Drake talk about me?' he said, spooning the cream from his cappuccino into his mouth. David and Declan shook their heads. 'He was my yubi-yubi,' Mo continued. 'My little yubi-musubi, but could not live with himself in truth, and he could not live with me.'

David looked at Declan uncertainly.

'Hang on … what?' David asked.

Mo took his wallet from his pocket and gave David a roll of passport photographs that showed Drake hugging Mo in a photo-booth. In the last frame they were kissing. David held the photo closer to his eyes as if this might tell him something more, but there was nothing else to see.

'Drake never say he was gay?' Mo said. 'He tell parents when he seventeen. They kicked him from house. They tell him "*you not our son.*" '

'Drake's got a son,' David said.

'Lots of gay men make sons.' Mo rested his forearms on the table. David looked at Declan, wanting him to challenge a story that neither of them could believe.

'He never tried to hit on any of us?' Declan said, like a question to David, who nodded and shook his head at the same time to indicate this was correct.

'Maybe you no his type,' Mo said proudly. 'Now he is dead, I want to know what happens. How happens.'

The two men told Mo what they knew. Mo nodded his head and thought for a long time before speaking: 'You think he jump from balcony?'

Of course that was not what they thought.

'We were all wasted,' David said. 'None of us could see straight.'

'And you speak with Tristan?' Mo asked. Declan shook his head. 'That man hides his face. You know he owes Drake fifteen K? He rack up a fifteen-K debt on his habit?'

David and Declan stared like two cops in a B-grade comedy.

'He owed Drake *money*?' they said together.

'Five-hundred-a-day habit and no cash? He make the papers but who buy his records? You know what I think?' Mo lowered his voice a decibel as if the three of them were now entering into a dark cave of conspiracy. 'I think he try to clear debts the old fashion way.'

Mo left and David and Declan waited for someone to say something.

'You don't think ... ?'

'Are you kidding?' David replied. 'If Tristan wanted money there are plenty of ways of getting it. He doesn't have to kill people.' David smiled as his mind changed tracks. 'God, "My little *yubi-yubi*"?' he said dryly. 'What was that all about?'

'Maybe it means honey-bunny or something ... honey-honey.'

'Come on, Dec, you don't think Drake was gay?'

Declan shook his head. 'It would explain his parents' bullshit.'

'What about Vivian?'

'Maybe he was bi? I dunno. My guess is he just took Mo for a ride to get some free blow. I can imagine Drake fucking anyone for a discount. It would be like part of the job, nothing sexual about it.'

'I have to get to Paddington Station. If I were you, Declan, I'd get out of that house and hide away somewhere for a while.'

They walked to the Underground and said goodbye, and then Declan walked all the way back to Aldgate. It took him two hours but he needed some time to contemplate. Part of him felt like he was now involved in a very exciting murder mystery. He imagined his character in a movie. He would be the one trying to uncover the truth about the mysterious death of his friend while all around him people were trying to cover things up. Declan Twist would be a crusader for truth, justice, and the cinematic way. But to be involved in a murder mystery there needed first to be a murder, and a murderer and, try as he might, Declan couldn't see anyone in the Posse playing that part. Even if Tristan owed Drake fifty thousand pounds he was no killer. Or was he? What about those times he had turned on Vivian; those explosions of violence and intimidation? He had once grabbed Vivian by the hair and dragging her off the dance-floor at the Shoreditch. If the past few months had taught him anything about the Posse it was this: nothing was entirely as it appeared to be, and everyone was hiding something. This was often the case with murder. How many times had he read news stories about the neighbours of some murderer, saying how surprised they were to hear the news?

'He was such a quiet, shy man.'

'He didn't seem the type.'

'He helped my grandmother build a trellis in her front garden.'

Drug dealers and criminals who murdered might look the part in the newspapers, but crimes of passion admitted to no profile. The mousiest looking housewife could turn into a killer if her heart was enflamed at the wrong moment, in the wrong place. But if Mo was right then this was not a crime of the heart, Tristan had pushed Drake over the balcony because of a fifteen thousand pound drug debt. As David had explained, that did not seem plausible.

What could Declan do? After all, he had other priorities now. His relationship with Juliet was no longer a complete debacle. After months of circling each other suspiciously they had come together and now shared some nascent love and trust. Did he want to jeopardise that development by trying to pry into Drake's death? Did he want to question the version of events that Juliet had already said was the truth? Did he really believe Juliet was still hiding something?

31

The Monday after the funeral was also the Monday after the video for 'Lick Me All Over' first appeared on television, and Vivian finally got the call she had been waiting for. She had done a screen-test for a presenter's role on a children's television programme called *Pimp my Room.* The producers rang and offered her the position. *Pimp my Room* was a programme in which kids phoned up and asked young gangsta rappers to redecorate their bedrooms to make them look funky and cool. Vivian had worn a loose-fitting strapless dress to the screen-test and leaned forward at regular intervals while talking with the production team. The team voted five to one in Vivian's favour; one woman was on the team.

The Posse did not get together and celebrate Vivian's success because nobody was around. Juliet had been working late every night, probably dismantling her illegal drug empire from the ground up so she wouldn't get busted. Bridget was in Moscow reviewing a hotel, leaving Vivian and Declan alone in the house. They smoked a joint and watched one of the porn films that Vivian had bought for Tristan as a 'welcome to Heaven' present.

Vivian was wearing a pair of cotton panties and a loose T-shirt and her long legs folded over themselves on the sofa. Her breasts rose and fell beneath her T-shirt in subtle rhythms that seemed to correlate with the humping on the television screen. Declan tried to position his erection comfortably in his trousers without making it look too obvious. He tried to imagine himself cleaning a dirty bathtub in an effort to bring down his heart rate. He wanted to speak with Vivian about Drake's death but the sight of a beautiful woman swallowing a nine-inch cock was quite a distraction. Vivian touched his leg casually. Her fingertips sent a surge of lust that drilled through his nervous system and cramped his sphincter. He had to cool the mood quickly.

'Drake's film starts shooting next week,' Declan said. 'It's hard to believe he would have been up there in front of the cameras. He would have been more famous than Tristan. Now he's dead.'

'It's funny this fame business, isn't it, Dec?'

'I don't know. I'm not famous.'

'You're on TV every weekend.'

'Nobody watches that show. I've only been recognised once in public, by a short Mexican man who sounded like Cheech and Chong.'

'Who?' Vivian asked, making Declan feel every year of his age.

'Just a Mexican guy. I was waiting to cross the street and this guy pulled on my sleeve and I looked down and he said,' Declan put on his best Mexican voice, ' "*Hey man, I tink I see you on the TEEEVEEE.*" That was my fifteen minutes and it only lasted three seconds before the lights turned green.'

Vivian did not seem to know how to respond to this so she asked why Declan didn't try to get an agent.

'You've got a great face for television,' she said. 'Really, and you're smart, and you're so good with words, those reviews you do are fantastic.'

'If someone offered me representation I'd probably take it,' Declan said. 'I take everything else people offer me. But going out of my way to pursue an agent? It's like admitting that you want it.'

'What do you want?'

'I don't know. I always wanted to be a painter but after the brain damage … Now when people ask me what I do, I feel like a liar. If I had to choose, I don't know what I'd do. I don't know who I'd be any more. Maybe that's the difference between you and me.'

Vivian sounded hurt by this remark, 'I'm not kidding myself that I've got where I am because I've got talent. I've had to fight all the way, but a guy like you? I could imagine you being, like, really famous.'

'You reckon I'd be happy with that?'

'I don't know,' Vivian nibbled on her bottom lip. 'I always wanted my face in the paper. I always wanted to be somebody. And these days, if people aren't talking about you, well, what are you? And now it looks like I'm going to succeed … *at last*.'

'You're only nineteen, Viv.'

'My agent made me quit my job at the Shoreditch because it wasn't good for my image. I can't even go there socially any more because all these people just stare. It's creepy. And the only men who approach you are complete tools. They're all City boys who think they're gods because they have a penthouse flat with views over the Thames.'

'Why don't you go to a place where other celebrities hang out?'

'Like where Bridget goes? I can't do that. I get too self-conscious.' Vivian sighed. 'So here I am, the biggest day in my life, my first presenter's role, and what am I doing? I'm smoking a joint at home with some random guy.'

'Gee thanks, Viv.'

'You know what I mean.'

The porn film cut to a close-up shot of a woman preparing for a man to ejaculate all over her face. The man beat his dick with one hand and the woman's face glowed as if she were basking in the sun for the first time after ten years underground. Suddenly a rope of pearl-coloured jism leapt from the man's dick and went up the woman's nose. She jerked back, repelled instinctively for a moment, before relaxing once more and forcing a smile back onto her face.

'She didn't enjoy that … thing,' Declan noted.

'It's called a facial,' Vivian explained, making Declan feel his age for the second time in less than a minute. He pointed to the television.

'If you ever wanted proof that God was not a pornographer you just have to look at the female orgasm. They're about as visually stimulating as the idea of an idea of an idea.'

Vivian laughed and he felt young.

'Really,' Declan continued, 'they're the bane of pornographic films aren't they? Why couldn't they do something visual like … like pop a few smoke rings out their vaginas?'

'That would be good.'

'And the man could shoot his load through the smoke rings.'

'Yes!' Vivian laughed.

'Maybe that's too active. Maybe God wanted women to look like passive receivers in pornographic films; dirty old patriarchal bastard that he was.'

Vivian touched Declan on the thigh once more and took the joint from his outstretched hand. He knew he had to change the subject very quickly.

'I met Mo at the funeral,' he blurted. Vivian did not bring the joint to her lips; she held it in the air as if her shoulder had just locked up.

'What did he say?'

'He said Tristan owed Drake fifteen thousand pounds.'

Vivian shook her head convincingly. 'That's not true, that's not true at all. Triz owed Drake a couple of thousand at the most.' Vivian seemed to realise where this conversation was going. 'Jesus, Declan, you don't think Tristan … ?'

'No, of course not.' Declan lied. It wasn't a lie so much as a half-truth, part of him did not think Tristan had anything to do with Drake's death, but part of him was unsure.

With that, Juliet came down the stairs and stopped when she saw Declan watching a porn film with a near-naked Vivian.

'Bridget's back,' Juliet said, and took the stairs back up to Heaven two at a time.

Bridget entered Purgatory with two bags of luggage and a look of gladiatorial victory in her eyes.

'Fuck-aye!' she said as she entered the room. 'What a place!'

Vivian bristled and pouted and kept her eyes fixed on the television screen.

'How was it?' Declan asked.

'Amazing! I was treated like a goddess. The full Monty baby. I mean they *really* look after you when you're in the media. They put a seventeen year-old boy on full room service duties. Juliet has *so* got the right idea about young boys.' Bridget pulled out a Sony DVD camera and held it up like a trophy. 'And I've got the tape to prove it. You want to see how big this boy's cock was?' Vivian and Declan shook their heads. Bridget swallowed the disappointment and looked around the room as if expecting to find someone hiding. 'Did Tristan show his face yet?' she asked uncertainly.

Drake had been dead for over a week now and nobody had seen or heard from Tristan. Vivian shot Bridget a look of pure cancer.

'He doesn't want to see you!' she snapped.

'He doesn't seem to want to see you either,' Bridget replied coolly. 'How was the funeral, Dec?'

'It was quiet,' Declan said.

'I wanted to go but what am I going to do? Everybody wants a piece of me now and there's only so much *DeFabulous* to go round.'

Ever since Bridget's exhibition opening and Drake's death, Bridget's agent and her publicist were receiving multiple invitations daily to A-list parties: exhibition openings, film premieres, magazine launches, music awards, supermodel birthdays, charity dinners, restaurant openings, fashion shows – the list went on and on. After unpacking her bags from the Moscow journey Bridget put on a black dress, had two lines of coke and went off to a private party in Soho House that was organised by a French publisher hoping to launch a new magazine in the UK.

Bridget DeFabulous was not divertingly attractive like Vivian, but she was reasonably good looking, except for her nose, which seemed to have been made out of a large slab of wet plaster rolled in poppy seeds and squashed onto her face in a snoutish manner. Despite this unfortunate and prominent feature, the media loved Bridget because she was loud and brash – if there is one thing that makes a big nose forgivable to the media it is an even bigger mouth. Bridget had a quote for every occasion and was heralded and celebrated as the new 'party-babe with attitude'. She got drunk before going on a chat show; she offered to give Ali G a blow job under his desk while the cameras were rolling; she called Tony Blair a 'silly cunt' on the Jonathan Ross radio show. The media called her 'refreshing', 'daring' and 'a new challenge to the stuffiness of the British art establishment'. The daughter of serious money, she was praised for moving East to the artistic heart of London and turning her back on her upper-class roots for the sake of personal liberty. Much was made of her hand-to-mouth existence as a poor photographic student, her struggles to pay bills and produce good work. She was hailed as an artist with a conscience because she sponsored an African child.

Her publicist wanted her to get into more trouble.

'A bit more controversy and your career is going to sky-rocket,' the publicist explained. 'Look at Tristan. He can do no wrong. He could murder someone and the press would love him.'

'What can I do?' Bridget asked Declan the day after she got back from Moscow. She was preparing some red snapper fillets with tequila mayonnaise. 'I don't think I've got the stomach for murder.'

Declan looked at the poster of Pamela Anderson on the living room wall.

'Why don't you release that sex video,' he joked.

Bridget's eyes lit up. 'Perfect,' she said, kissing him on the forehead. 'You should be my publicist.'

32

The summer was drawing to a close and the evenings were getting shorter. After shooting *Massive* that weekend Declan had three drinks with the crew and arrived home in near darkness. He saw someone pacing the pavement outside the Chocolate Block and, when he realised it was Nathan, he feared for a moment the big man might have come to take care of him once and for all. He wanted to turn and run but the fear was not strong enough to move his legs. Nathan saw him and nodded without smiling.

'Come on,' he said, walking away and expecting Declan to follow. 'You're coming with me.'

This was one of those moments when Declan felt he really should have said no. But how could he? If he said no Nathan would construe it as an admission of guilt and, in truth, he had nothing to feel guilty about. So he did as he was told and followed Nathan to the van. Before starting the engine Nathan put some high-spirited dance music on which seemed as suitable to the atmosphere as gangsta rap in a cathedral. Declan started tapping his feet instinctively to the music, and could almost feel a pill coming on as the thumping bass-beat drilled his senses. Nathan offered him a smoke and as he lit it he was thinking about all those movies he had seen when a man was given a final cigarette before he was executed. They were almost out of London before he summoned up the courage to ask Nathan where they were going.

'You'll see,' was all Nathan said.

Perhaps this was a test; perhaps he was trying to scare Declan into making some kind of confession, assuming he had a confession to make. Declan started to reflect on his life, on all the regrets and the tragedies great and small that had brought him irrevocably to this moment. In the past he had always believed, no matter how terrible things had become, that everything that happened in his life was leading him somewhere good, that at some point he'd reach a good place and he would lose all his regrets, he would realise that all his mistakes had lead him to goodness.

Serendipity is the name people give to mistakes that turn out better than expected. Many of the processes by which certain foods are made, for example, were supposedly discovered by accident. It has been suggested that tofu was first created when a Chinese cook accidentally spilt a pot of soy beans over a kitchen floor and mixed them with a bag of impure sea salt. Another theory suggests tofu was discovered by a process of deduction, but if Declan had to guess which theory were true, he'd go with the human error. His life was supposed to work out like that: something great was meant to be created from all the mistakes. He was not supposed to die like this but he was strangely incapable of taking any evasive action.

They stopped at a petrol station and Declan waited sedately in the van while Nathan went and paid for the tank. He had plenty of time to leap out of the van and run. Nathan would never have risked shooting out in the open. As Declan sat there, rooted to the seat, he understood in some small way how all those people could have marched so calmly to their deaths in the Nazi gas chambers. Even when the body is pumped with fear and every instinct warns that your life is in danger there can be something greater, some stubborn logic of the heart that convinces people that no one is ever going to just kill them without reason.

After driving for over an hour Nathan turned down a dirt road that led to a farmhouse four hundred metres back from the surfaced road. Declan had no idea where they were. It was pitch black and only one light was on in the stone building. Nathan parked beside a chicken coup and told Declan to get out of the van. They walked together to the farmhouse and Nathan opened the door and guided Declan in with one hand. This sign of respect, standing back and allowing another man to enter a room first, was traditionally a means of making sure the other guy could not stab you in the back, just as shaking hands was a way of showing another man you were not carrying a dagger. *How much of our good manner is derived from a basic mistrust of other people?* An image came into Declan's mind: television footage of an Israeli Prime Minister fighting with Yasser Arafat over who would go through the door to Camp David first. *Why the hell am I thinking about that now?* Declan wondered.

'*ARRGGHHH!*' he screamed when he saw a group of teenage girls sitting on the sofa. They screamed like three queens of the night, Declan screamed again and Nathan smacked him on the head.

'What's wrong with you, man?'

It was a cosy room with an open fire burning and several rocking chairs covered with crocheted woollen rugs. A large print of a Paolo Uccello painting hung on the wall opposite the fire-place, and several cow hides covered the wooden floor boards. In the centre of the room a massive wooden log served as a coffee table, with Rizlas, a hash-mix, and other drug gear scattered across it.

Tristan came out of the kitchen to see what all the noise was. His face looked like the flesh of a dead rabbit that had been flattened by a truck: raw scabs festered on his cheeks and neck, his eyes were yellow and his lips were dry and cracked, but when he saw Declan his face beamed and he held Declan's face in his hands and said his name warmly.

'Don't worry 'bout the face,' Tristan said. 'Fell over didn't I? Smacked myself face-first into the gravel.' He turned to Nathan. 'Take the girls home Nathan they got school tomorrow.'

The girls all groaned but Tristan spoke with the paternal authority of a head teacher, 'No argument girls, you've got homework no doubt so get off and get to it.'

After they had gone the two men sat down and smoked a joint that was seventy-five per cent pure hash.

'Whose house is this?' Declan asked.

'Me parents.'

Declan looked around nervously but Tristan told him not to worry, they wouldn't be home for another hour.

'What about the smell of the hash?'

'Ah they don't care about that,' Tristan said.

'I thought your dad was fire and brimstone.'

'*I* don't care what he is. I don't care about anything at the moment. I can't even fuck. I'm lying in bed all day staring up at the ceiling.'

Declan looked into Tristan's eyes; his suffering seemed acute, but how was Declan to tell if this suffering was an admission of culpability or a reflection of his sensitive nature.

'We all killed him, you know,' Tristan continued. It was not a question. 'We all killed Drake. He was digging a hole and burying himself for months, right before our eyes, and none of us tried to stop him.' Tristan held his face in his hands. 'I hated him that night, hated his guts. I mean, he was a loser, but that night he was, he was so proud, so high an' mighty and it pissed me off, and I hated him … but I didn't want him to die. If

I could bring him back now I would, but I can't and I feel like shit.'

'Did someone push him?' Declan asked. He was beginning to think Tristan wanted to make a confession. Tristan seemed genuinely surprised by the question.

'What? No. Dec, he tripped over the entrance thing and went backwards. Everyone was falling everywhere that night; he just fell the wrong way.'

Tears formed in Tristan eyes and the heavy drops fell silently down his cheeks. He covered his face with his hands to hide his ugliness from sight. *Is it vanity that makes people cover their faces when they cry,* Declan wondered, *or is it shame?* His mind bent one way, then the other, like heated metal. The thoughts were hurting him and nothing looked real. Nothing seemed true. It did not seem possible that Tristan could fake this kind of tragic emotional response.

The front door opened and Declan turned, surprised that Nathan had taxied the girls home so quickly, and even more surprised to see that it wasn't Nathan but an old man standing on the threshold with a grocery bag in either hand. He looked a bit like Christopher Plummer: a kind face and a full, thick head of silver hair. If he were angry or surprised by the smoke and drug gear on the table he did not show it.

'Hello there,' he said cheerfully.

'Dad this is Declan, he's a friend a mine.'

Mr Russell shook Declan's hand heartily and asked if he would like a cup of tea.

'He doesn't drink tea, dad, give him a beer.'

Declan said that a tea would be fine.

'Have you been smoking inside, Tristan?'

'No.'

'I'm just worried you'll burn the house down.'

'You worry too much,' Tristan grunted.

Mr Russell turned back to Declan and asked if he wanted any tea, as in, dinner.

'I can cook something for you, no problem.'

'That all right,' Declan said.

'Are you sure? I've got some pasta in the fridge. I could warm it up for you.'

'He said no dad, *Jesus*!'

Mr Russell looked at Declan, who saw he was blushing. The old man's bottom lip wobbled uncertainly and Declan felt ashamed to be in the room at that moment.

'Actually I wouldn't mind some pasta,' he said. 'If it's no problem.' Mr Russell's grateful smile was not enough to assuage Declan's guilt and as he searched for something else to say his eyes passed over the Uccello painting on the wall. 'I've seen that painting in the National Gallery,' he added, 'Uccello, isn't it?'

'Yes!' Mr Russell exclaimed, delighted or surprised or both. 'That's right.'

'Declan writes stuff on art,' Tristan muttered. He had got off the sofa and was rummaging through one of the shopping bags that his father had left by the front door.

'Is that right?' asked Mr Russell.

'Sometimes. I've got a smaller version of that painting stuck on my wall.'

'His wall's like an art gallery,' Tristan said. He found some chocolate chip biscuits and returned to the couch.

'Mind you don't eat all of those Tristan or you won't have room for your tea.'

'Jesus, I'm not a baby!' Tristan roared. 'I can't breathe in here!'

He got up and stormed out the front door. Mr Russell and

Declan stood facing each other and wondered what to do, then Mr Russell went to make a cup of tea and by the time he came back, Declan had formulated something interesting to say about Uccello's painting.

'I love that painting,' he said.

'Yes,' smiled Mr Russell. He sipped his tea. 'The perspective may not be perfect, but as least he was trying, eh?'

'Very trying his wife used to say. I read once that he used to sit up late at night, and his wife would call him to bed and he'd whisper to himself, *What a sweet thing perspective is.*' They repeated this quote together and laughed with surprise at the sound of their unscripted duet.

Tristan came back in, slamming the door. Mr Russell took the grocery bags into the kitchen.

'You don't have to eat anything, you know. Don't feel like you have to do anything,' Tristan said, once his father had gone.

'I thought your dad was all fire and brimstone,' Declan repeated.

'He's always nice to strangers,' Tristan spat. 'Don't let that cheerful façade fool you, underneath it all he's a total hypocrite and a monster.'

Nathan returned an hour later with lipstick on his cheek. He said hello gruffly to Mr Russell, and asked Declan what time he wanted to get home in a tone that Declan understood to mean he wanted to leave immediately.

Tristan gripped Declan in a bear hug that was surprisingly powerful for a man who seemed close to death. He handed his friend a piece of paper with a phone number on it.

'That's the number here,' he said. 'Don't give it out, please; you're the only guy I trust with it.'

On the way back to London Declan felt like he was enjoying the first night of the rest of his life. When he had entered the farmhouse two hours earlier, the terrifying journey down had been instantly forgotten, but now, back in the same space with the same brooding man, he remembered just how frightened he had been travelling out of London. It seemed stupid now, the irrational fear of an excited imagination, and yet something still gnawed inside, a sense that, even if Nathan had never intended to hurt him, he had certainly wanted to give him a fright, and perhaps Tristan had wanted to frighten him as well.

33

Juliet and Declan hired a car and drove to Brighton. Declan's breathing relaxed once they were out of London and he told her about the previous night with Nathan. Juliet thought it was a fantastic joke.

'No, seriously,' Declan said. 'I honestly thought he was going to kill me.'

'Why would Nathan kill you? Are you mad?'

Declan did not want to talk to Juliet about his suspicions. After all, she had been in the room when Drake had fallen from Purgatory, if Tristan was trying to cover up the truth then so was Juliet.

The brochure for the Royal High School was in the glove compartment. Declan took it out and flicked through the pages.

'You don't have a licence, do you?' Juliet asked.

'No. Cars scare the bejesus out of me.'

The brochure was filled with photographs of grand, old Victorian mansions, lavish grounds, and pretty girls in uniform. Declan whistled loudly in a descending pitch.

'Jesus, Jules, it looks bloody expensive.'

'Eighteen thousand pounds per year.'

'*Eighteen thousand pounds.* How will you afford that?'

'It's only two years,' Juliet shrugged. 'I've got about one hundred K sitting in the bank under my bed.'

Declan had known that Juliet made a lot of money as a project manager for Phebron, and he had always suspected she made a lot with her side business selling drug samples, but he hadn't known it was that much. They had never discussed money before and for someone so rich, she lived a relatively frugal life, which had kept her financial situation well and truly hidden.

'I saw a bag under your bed; it didn't look like one hundred thousand pounds.'

'The rest is under the carpet,' Juliet explained. 'There's a little compartment in the floorboards.'

'That's such a drug dealer thing to say,' Declan said. 'Why don't you buy a house with the money instead of waiting for someone to steal it?'

'I have bought a house,' Juliet said, with that special smile reserved for people who know they are revealing a spectacular personal secret, a smile of excitement tinged with guilt or fear. 'Actually, I've bought two. But I've got to keep some cash under the bed or people will start asking questions. Don't you dare tell anyone. I don't want Jeremy Taxman coming down on me like a gang-banger in a porn film. And if you tell the Posse they'll all start lifting a few hundred pounds a week, the scumbags.'

Declan stared at the white lines on the highway. 'You sure know how to keep a secret, don't you?'

Juliet laughed and honked the car horn three times for fun, but Declan couldn't laugh yet. 'Why are you living in that shit-hole if you own two houses?'

His whole estimation of Juliet was changing because of this revelation, and as a consequence he was suddenly aware why she might have kept her wealth hidden: two houses and a hundred thousand pounds is not something that can be easily dismissed when the wealth belongs to a newly beloved. Declan wondered whether she was telling him this as a kind of penance for using him as a drug mule. He wondered, too, how long it would be before she suspected his feelings for her might be flattered, and then compromised by her wealth. Declan's spectacular lack of success as a thirty-something male crystallised into something hard and tangible, and he realised that to maintain any relationship with Juliet he would have to make something of his life quickly. He was no David, to be sure, and Juliet was no Bridget. He could feel resentment poisoning his blood. He resented Juliet not for her wealth so much as for her telling him about it now. It might not have been an expression of confidence at all, it might not have been a sign that she was moving closer to him; in fact, the opposite might have been true. Perhaps she was telling him this now to show him how different they really were, how impossible it would be for them to ever remain together. But when he looked at Juliet's smiling face he thought he could see a new desire reflected in her eyes, a desire to be truly known by someone, a desire to be truly loved.

And she had chosen him.

'What other secrets do you have?' Declan asked. 'I wouldn't be surprised to discover you've had a sex change. I'll come home one day and you'll show me this photo of little *Julian* when he was sixteen. "Who's that boy?" I'll ask, "That's me," you'll say, "I used to have a *cock*." '

They both laughed. Juliet kissed him quickly on the cheek and smiled as if she were being wicked for taking her eyes off the road. It was a smile of such beautiful, cheeky confidence. Her eyes shone with gratitude and Declan knew again what he had just doubted: this was a sign of something big – she had taken a risk and revealed something to him and he knew it was because she trusted him now. He had shown her that he could be trusted to do anything.

'You can talk about secrecy,' she said. 'Nobody knows anything about you. You act like an insensate zombie most of the time.'

'It's the brain injury.'

'That's just an excuse. And we don't know where you're from, we don't know what you've done, who your parents are, what you studied, where you studied, if you studied. You seem educated but you may have grown up in a squat. We know there are dark secrets in your past, Declan, we just don't know how dark they are.'

'So you've discussed this have you?' Declan asked. Juliet nodded her head and licked her lips. Declan shook his head. 'And? What? You're the designated Posse driver sent to pry all my secrets away.'

'You once told me you couldn't go home, wherever that is, because all your friends are dead?'

'Yes.'

'What happened?'

'They died in a car accident when I was nineteen. Four of them.'

'Fuck. Is that how you got your brain damage?'

'No. That was another time. A few years later.'

'Really? Have you got a black cloud floating permanently over your head? So what happened?' Juliet looked down her nose at Declan and gave him a look that was a simple request to continue.

Why not, Declan thought. *It doesn't matter now.* He took a deep breath and related the story, in full, as a passionless monologue, like comedian Steven Wright performing stand up.

'I was waiting for a train. I was sitting down beside a group of teenage girls who were standing and smoking, sharing a bottle of rum and talking about sex. They were all sloppy, solid, big-breasted girls with greasy hair and Duran Duran hairdos, with lots of colourful bangles around their wrists. They were talking about oral sex as if it were a new television programme for kids. You know: "He's probably got herpes!", "He's got a huge cock!", "He's a helmet?", "Great for blow jobs!", "Hardly get it all in me mouth."

I must have been staring with an open mouth because one of the girls glared at me and shouted angrily, "Who you looking at fucksmith?" She actually said that: "fucksmith". Her friends all turned to look at me. I realised they were all quite drunk and their red eyes and snarling voices indicated a level of hostility that I generally associate with football hooligans and prison rioters. I tried to defend myself but they all shouted over me.

'I don't remember much after that. I do remember one girl giving me a roundhouse kick to the side of the head. I have a clear image of a pink shoe attached to a thick leg coming into my field of vision from the left at rapid speed and connecting to my head. I don't remember any pain.

'I think the popular modern term for this sort of thing is "happy slapping" but this was before mobile-phone cameras and these girls did more than slap me. Two of them were black-belts in karate. They kicked me in the head for ten minutes. I was in a coma for twenty-four hours and suffered a severe brain injury. My head looked like a mutant blue pineapple. After two weeks in hospital the doctors said that I might only regain ten per cent of my mental functions. They said I might regain more, or I might regain less, it was impossible to say because every brain is different and every brain injury is different. I understood what they were saying but I couldn't communicate. There was nothing I wanted to say. I just didn't care. It took me two years to learn how to walk and talk properly again.

'The police came to interview me in hospital three weeks after the assault and I told them in a slow-mumbling slur that two large men had attacked me. I described the two men as very tall and well-built but I forgot about the CCTV footage from the train platform's cameras. The media got hold of the story and I made page four of the newspaper, *Teenage Girl Gang Assault Man at City Station.* A number of columnists received good money to comment on the story; they said that it was part of a growing trend among young girls who were emulating the violent behaviour of certain post-modern female role models. The girls were caught and told police that it was self-defence. They said that I had called them "whore bitches" and threatened to rape them. The media did not sympathise because the CCTV footage showed clearly that I was the one being threatened. I've suffered post-traumatic stress ever since. I'm terrified of teenage girls.'

'Hah!' Juliet laughed. 'And you move in with *Tristan*!'

Declan laughed too. Juliet was laughing so hard she almost swiped a Volkswagen in the overtaking. She had to swerve back the other way and almost went off the motorway.

When it was over Declan rested his head on the window. He wiped tears from his eyes and wound his window down to release some of the fun into the wind.

'You see?' Juliet said. 'You're not incapable of feelings, you've just forgotten how to use them.'

'I think you should go to the police,' Declan said. 'I mean, you don't know how many other young girls he's interfered with, do you?'

Juliet did not answer. She turned and gave Declan another quick kiss and he could taste her lipstick. He did not want to spoil the togetherness they shared at that moment. He did not want to fight or argue ever again, it was easier to say nothing, to smile and look at Juliet and feel an emotion which may or may not have been love, but was certainly pleasant in a sensual sense. Whatever else she may have been, Juliet was always beautiful and when she kissed him he felt alive. She had decided to take responsibility for her daughter and this made him hopeful that more changes were on the way. Maybe Drake's death had created some change within her. He liked to imagine their love had helped her to change as well, such was his vanity. *Maybe now she is going to clean herself up*, he thought, *and maybe, just maybe, I can be by her side and continue to enjoy the beauty of a new, clean Juliet.*

34

With love came a new responsibility: Declan knew that he needed to create something with his life. He could not go on living without direction or ambition. He needed to make money. He needed a career and, consequently, he asked Vivian if she could set up a meeting with her agent.

'Of course!' Vivian answered. All Declan had to do was give her some tapes of his movie maestro segments and she would pass them on with a glowing reference. 'And you'll have to learn two monologues.'

'Monologues? From plays you mean? But I can't act. I … I … I thought I could do presenting work.'

'It's all the same thing, Declan; it's all acting. You need to show them you have range.'

'I don't have range.'

'Well you'll have to find some range. And choose two monologues that have some meaning for you.'

Declan chose a monologue from a new play called *Blue/Orange*, which he'd seen in April, and another from Ibsen's *A Doll's House.* For research purposes he read through a book called *True and False* by David Mamet. It was a book on acting that Declan had bought thinking it was a book about Mamet's life.

When Declan went into the agency for his interview he was surprised by how nervous he was. The interview had meant nothing to him the previous day, when he was learning the monologues, but now suddenly he could feel the sharks in his veins.

The agent was a beautiful woman about thirty-five years old. She moved like a model and was probably an actor who had started temping at an agency between acting jobs. She smiled brightly and said her name was Emma, and Declan knew, as sure as his name was Declan, that this woman loved sex. Everything about her oozed sexuality, even her red stiletto shoes seemed to declare *I-love-sex*. She was a woman who exhibited her sensuality proudly, like something precious, something sacred in a church or a gallery, and Declan relaxed immediately. He knew that this interview would go well because in his imagination they had already enjoyed the most amazing sex on her office table.

The first thing she did when they sat down was fill out a generic form with all Declan's vital statistics.

'Age?'

'32'

'Height?'

'Uh, I think, 182.'

'Hair colour, black, eyes are blue. Weight?'

'74 kilograms.'

'OK. That's OK, but you'll need to add a few extra kilos. A bit of gym work to buff up the upper torso. The over-seventy-fives get at least fifty per cent more work than the under-seventy-fives. It's just one of those things. You've got naturally broad shoulders, so it shouldn't be too difficult to add some definition to that body. You're a little above average height but these younger boys are shooting up. I don't know what it is but males seem to be evolving rapidly into taller and taller specimens, so my advice is whenever you have a casting call, wear a good set of heels. Cowboy boots are good but keep them tucked under your jeans, nobody likes the Garth Brooks. What else? Hair, I see you've got one or two greys in there, which is only natural, I guess, but again, it's not going to help you in castings so you'll have to dye it. You can keep it black, that black hair and blue eye thing is a killer combination, just look at Mel Gibson! Your age won't be a problem so long as we come up with some kind of suitable excuse for you starting so late.'

'I suffered brain damage when I was twenty-five.'

'Urgh, no, not that. I'll say you were in the army, served your country in Desert Storm and blah-blah. We get quite a few calls from American casting agents and they love that kind of stuff. OK, so why do you want to be an actor?'

Declan didn't know how to answer. The truth was he wanted to get some sort of a career to impress Juliet, but he knew he couldn't say that.

'I have wanted to be an actor my whole life,' he lied. 'I've always felt that acting gives a person this great power of … transformation; you can be someone else; you live another life; you escape your own existence and create something beautiful. Acting is the highest form of liberation.'

Emma pulled a face. 'That's a bit Harvey Keitel, isn't it?'

'I don't know?'

Emma rolled her eyes like an Indian Bhagwan and explained that Harvey was totally 'guru' about the transcendental power of acting.

'The only reason he doesn't do interviews is because he sounds like a total tool whenever he speaks as a real person.'

Declan answered a couple of other questions and then they reached the final stage of the interview: the monologues. Emma asked him to do the *Blue/Orange* piece first because she didn't know it. Declan gave her a copy of the monologue and explained that it wasn't quite a monologue and showed her the line that she would have to speak, then he stood back, took a deep breath and turned himself into a psychiatrist with a dead, monosyllabic voice.

'For example,' he said, 'people used to say "schizophrenic" all the time. "Such and such is schizophrenic", being two things at once. OK. It was used to denote divided agenda, a dual identity, the analogy of split personality. Except we know now that schizophrenia doesn't mean that at all. Split personality? Meaningless. OK? So it's an unhelpful term. It's inaccurate. What we call a "misnomer" and this is a sensitive subject. We must think carefully, be specific, because you know ... it's serious.'

Declan looked into Emma eyes and tried not to think about sex.

'You were diagnosed with "Borderline Personality Disorder". What does that mean? Borderline Personality Disorder. OK? Key word – *Borderline.* Because, clinically speaking, you're on the *Border* between Neurotic and Psychotic.'

'Just ... on the border?' Emma read.

'Yes. And that's a very useful term, isn't it? Because if we get the word wrong – if people just get the meaning of the word wrong, how can they get the person right? How can there be any awareness. People don't know anything about it. They have stupid ideas. You lose out. So we try to "demystify". We try to explain. Which is why I want to talk to you today. Your diagnosis. This term, this label, and what it means, because the thing is, I'm beginning to think, now ... it's ... well, it's a little inaccurate.'

Declan took a step back and waited for Emma to say something. She was staring in silence. She looked down at the text, then back up again. Declan waited, a colourless sense of nausea rising from the pit of his stomach.

'That was *brilliant,* Declan!' Emma lied. It occurred to Declan that she was probably a very good actress in her day. 'Honestly, that was utterly, utterly convincing. You're a natural. You were born to act. You didn't even seem to be acting.' She clapped her hands together. 'OK, next please, this is delicious!'

Declan read the monologue from *A Dolls' House.* It was a scene near the end where Torvald tells Nora that he has forgiven her, just before she sits him down and enlightens him on some home truths before leaving their home to find herself.

35

Declan caught the train home contemplating life's infinite possibilities. A whole new world of fantasy had opened up before him, he was going to be an *actor*. Just like that. When people asked him, 'What do you do?' he could now answer them confidently. He was going to be paid money to pretend to be other people, people who were not even real. He might even go to Hollywood, meet beautiful actresses, he might … But then he remembered Juliet, and smiled to himself. She was the only woman he ever needed.

That night in bed he talked furiously about his meeting with Emma. Juliet played happy, but there was something bothering her. Her eyes were restless, her responses short, and she smoked a cigarette as if it were the last thing she might ever put between her lips.

'Listen,' she said, after Declan had repeated the same story five times with only minor variations. 'I was thinking we could move out of here. Get a place together.'

Declan remained passive. 'You and me?' he asked. Juliet looked at him defiantly and he winked and said, 'I don't know about that, Juliet. I'm not sure I want to shack up with a single mother.'

For some reason Juliet did not understand and she was halfway out of bed before he calmed her down and convinced her it was a joke.

'It wasn't funny.'

Declan kissed her eyes, lips and neck, and murmured sweetly

into her ear until she was soft and happy again. When they fucked it was like actually making love, she looked deep into his eyes and smiled.

The next morning they took a taxi to a Camden, where Juliet had arranged for an estate agent to show them around several properties. Susan phoned Juliet while they were in the taxi. She called Juliet 'mum', Juliet called her 'darling' and Declan felt a flush of pride because he knew he had played some small part in the reformation of this relationship.

The first two properties they looked at were horrible but they fell in love with the third apartment instantly. It was a beautiful two-bedroom place above a chemist shop in Camden High Street. Juliet assured Declan that her feelings had nothing to do with the fact that they would be sleeping above a parlour of drugs, but as soon as the agent went into the bathroom she pulled a bag of coke from her jacket and did two quick lines on the table.

'What?' she asked. 'Do you want some?'

'I thought we were going to finish with the drugs.'

'Who said that?'

'I just thought ... I thought things ... that we were moving out by ourselves because ... '

'Because what?' Juliet laughed. 'Because I want to stop taking drugs? Noooo. I like drugs. They're my job. I don't want some *tofu* existence.'

'Tofu?'

'You know, really, really good for you, really healthy, but light and fluffy and tasty as solidified air.'

Declan nodded his head. 'I thought it was shorthand for "totally fucked up", or something.'

The sound of the toilet flushing was a full stop to the

conversation and the agent came out of the bathroom and asked if everything was OK.

'Fine,' Juliet answered. 'Everything's great.'

They took a taxi home in silence and when Declan went to pay, Juliet pushed his hand away and gave the driver a tenner. 'Keep the change,' she said.

'I was going to pay for that,' Declan said, 'you didn't have to pay.'

'Relax, Declan? It's just a taxi fare.'

'So why didn't you let me pay.'

'Because you don't have any money.'

Declan feared he might cry. He got angry instead and this overwhelmed the tears, but it also made his voice so shaky and squeaky that he couldn't string a sentence together. 'That's … you know that's … that's so … '

He turned and as he walked away he was hoping that Juliet would call out his name, that he would hear her footsteps coming after him, but neither of these things happened and it was too late to turn around.

He went to the local pub and drank three beers. When he got home Bridget and Juliet were in the living room in Purgatory watching a grainy home video of Bridget blowing a young boy in a Moscow hotel room. A picture of Hitler hung on the hotel wall above the bed.

'He's got a nice cock,' Juliet said. 'I didn't know the communists cut cock.'

'They must cut some. Maybe he's Jewish.'

'What's this?' Declan looked at the television screen and noticed the portrait above the hotel bed. 'Is that *Hitler*?'

The girls looked up nonchalantly when they saw him and smiled hello.

'It's my bellboy from the hotel in Moscow. They had themed rooms. I was given the Hilter Room,' Bridget explained.

Juliet took an ecstasy tablet and offered one to Declan.

'Try these, Dec, they're to die for.'

Declan hesitated for a moment and tried to appeal to Juliet with a look so earnest she probably thought he was going to say no. But he took the pill and washed it down with some whisky from the coffee table.

'Come sit down with us,' Bridget directed.

'Ask him,' Juliet said.

'What do you think, Dec?' Bridget asked. Declan sat down in the space she had made between herself and Juliet. She pressed the menu button on the remote and showed excerpts from several short films she had made with the bellboy in the Hitler Room. 'Juliet thinks I should release the shower scene, but the shower scene doesn't give us a shot of Hitler on the wall, which is what it needs to spice things up.'

'Is that a banana?' Declan asked, and Bridget fast-forwarded to the next clip. 'Are you seriously going to make this public, Bridge?'

Juliet and Bridget looked down their noses at each other and grunted like cave-women.

Twenty minutes later the effects of the pill registered in the base of Declan's neck and he began to smile unconsciously. Juliet noticed and looked over to Bridget.

'I think he's ready,' she said. She took a small hand-held Sony digital camera from her jacket, opened the viewing screen and pressed record. Bridget moved toward Declan and licked her lips. Her nostrils were quivering and her hand reached out to touch his thigh. Declan leapt from the sofa.

'What the hell?' he screamed, his voice high and squeaky.

Juliet lowered the camera and chewed her gum.

'Relax, Dec, everybody's doing it.'

'Do you want this,' Bridget cooed, exposing her right breast and holding it like a fruit salesman might hold up a cantaloupe. 'Do you want to come on the Bridge to Heaven?'

Declan looked up at Juliet, whose face was obscured behind the camera. When she saw the look in Declan's eyes she pulled the camera down and frowned.

'What's your problem?' she asked.

Declan pushed Bridget off and left the room without replying.

'Fine, run away,' Bridget screamed.

The next day, Bridget's porn film with the young Russian bellboy starting circulating on the internet. Pretty soon the mainstream media had copies of the tape and edited versions were posted on news websites and screened on the television news. Much was made in the conservative press about the age of the bellboy.

He can't have been more than seventeen, wrote one columnist. *Once upon a time it was our male soldiers who took sexual advantage of the poor in developing countries, now it seems our female artists do too.*

Sex with a young Russian Jew beneath a portrait of the leader of the Nazi party – Bridget had really hit the jackpot. Some media commentators condemned Bridget as anti-Semitic, others countered that the boy in the clip was circumcised. For the first two days Bridget vehemently denied that the grainy video footage was her. Later she claimed that she had been set up; the bellboy must have placed a hidden camera in the room before taking advantage of her. She did not speak to the press herself, of course, but spoke through her agent.

'At this point in her career Bridget is focused one hundred per cent on her art,' her agent announced the day after acknowledging that the woman in the video was Bridget. 'These kinds of tawdry, sensationalist, money-grabbing, muck-raking stories take the focus off what is important –what is important is Bridget Defond's incredible art.'

Bridget's agent issued another statement the following day. 'The release of this sex tape, recorded without Bridget's knowledge or consent on a concealed camera, is extremely distressing, it is exploitative and shows very poor taste. We are in communication with the authorities in Moscow and hope that anyone involved in this enterprise is swiftly brought to justice in a court of law.'

The Russian bellboy, who was seventeen, claimed he knew nothing about the video camera. He asked where he would have got a camera from; he earned the equivalent of forty pounds a week. Bridget finally broke her silence and made an impassioned plea to the boy to just tell the truth. Two days later, after the boy continued to deny any knowledge of the camera, Bridget tore into him like a panther tearing into a wildebeest. 'He's a lying, ruthless, manipulative, evil, scumbag,' she said, before covering her face with her hands and breaking down once again for the cameras. Fearing a backlash from Western media and foreign tourists the hotel management sacked the bellboy without notice, and condemned him publicly as a stain on the hotel's reputation.

The media were evenly divided in their coverage of the story; half the press condemned Bridget while the other half praised her as a woman of the twenty-first century. *This is what I was doing forty years ago,* sneered one old feminist. *Bridget is simply trying to follow in my footsteps and if she were a male artist nobody would bat an eye.* The one thing that united the media was their interest in the story (only Pamela Anderson had a sex tape at the time) and within a day it was the highest Google search term in the UK. Within a week an estimated one million people had downloaded the tape, and Bridget sealed her fame with the ultimate tribute: she became the inspiration for several awful school-yard jokes.

What's the difference between Bridget Defond and Pamela Anderson? About seven minutes.

How many Russian bellboys does it take to change a light bulb? Just one – they all know how to screw.

36

Declan did not see Juliet for a week after the incident on the sofa. They each stayed in their bedrooms and only went to the kitchen to get some food or make a coffee when they knew the living room was empty. It was a stupid game but it was one Declan was determined to win. Finally, after five days, Juliet knocked on his door and asked meekly if she could come in.

She opened the door and stood there, her whole body was slumped in a kind of physical apology but it was not nearly enough. Nothing would be enough. Juliet sat down at the desk and rattled her necklace a couple of times with one hand.

'All right, I'm sorry,' she said. Then, realising she sounded more angry than apologetic she changed her tone and said, 'I'm sorry,' once more. Declan did not respond. 'Look, I've never done this before, Declan. I'm scared. I'm scared of you. I'm scared of us. I'm scared of not having anything to prop me up.'

'I don't care,' Declan said, and he made sure that Juliet could see it was not entirely an act. 'I don't care, Juliet. I'm moving out. I've found a place.'

Juliet started crying. The more he could see that she was hurting, the colder he became. He was determined to end this now. Whatever hope he had, whatever love he felt, he knew now that it had all been a fantasy. He had idealised Juliet, turned her into some glamorous, grotesque goddess. And now it was all gone. Nothing was real any more except his anger.

'Going where?' Juliet sobbed. 'What do you mean?'

'I've found a place. It doesn't matter where. I'm moving out in two days.'

'But what about us?' Juliet waited until she realised he was not going to answer the question. 'Was that all just a game for you? Was I just some challenge? Let me see if I can make Juliet fall in love with me. And now that you've succeeded you're not interested?'

'No.'

'I said I was sorry. What more do you want me to do?'

'I don't care what you do, Juliet. You can take vows of chastity and pray to Jesus for all I care. I don't want to see you any more.' The novel thrill of hurting Juliet surprised him. He should have stopped there but he wanted to hurt her in some deeper place. There was a passion inside him now that was wild and free. 'You act *so* tough but you're as weak as a daisy chain. You'll be alone all your life because you're too frightened to let anyone get close to you. You hang out with seventeen-year-old boys because you haven't matured since your uncle fucked you, and you use that one single experience as some excuse for this … life you've got. Take a look around, Juliet, you think one uncle-fuck is such a massive deal on the scale of things? It's like a grain of sand on the Himalayan Mountains of human suffering. And even if you want something more sometimes, you don't have the consistency to keep wanting it. You're unreliable, Juliet. You can't cope with the down times when they come, and when things get bad you don't know how to make them good again, all you know how to do is destroy, either yourself or others, and you'll keep doing it until there's nothing left to destroy. You'll be an ugly rotting hag left to die alone in a filthy bed.'

Juliet usually had the ability to lift her chin at anyone, but this time she was beaten. Declan had won, and in his victory he was a loser, for as soon as Juliet turned and left his exultation was replaced by an overwhelming sense of regret. How could his emotions turn so quickly? How could they trick him so easily? Everything he had said to Juliet was a projection of his own guilt: he was weak, he was inconsistent, he was destructive. He threw himself onto the bed like Scarlett O'Hara and cried into his pillow, and when he had finished crying he began taking all the postcard paintings down from the wall.

An hour later he heard Juliet sobbing up in Heaven and decided to apologise. He knew she would lash out and abuse him, but that was OK, she could not hurt him now. He walked upstairs and as he passed Vivian's room he realised the sobs were coming from there. He knocked on the door before opening it, and turned on the light. Vivian was lying on her stomach in bed with her head under a pillow. She held each side of the pillow as if awaiting a loud explosion.

'Go away!' she screamed. Declan closed the door and went back downstairs.

It took him a couple of hours to peel the Blu-Tack from all the postcards and pack them into boxes. He put the boxes under his bed and went back upstairs to see if Vivian was all right. When he knocked on her door there was no answer. He opened the door and saw Vivian lying face down with one hand slumped over the side of the bed.

'Viv?' he asked, quietly. He repeated her name a little louder but she did not respond, so he went over to the bed and touched her on the shoulder. Her flesh was cold. A bottle of prescription pills was empty on the floor beneath her limp hand. It seemed she had been dead for some time.

'Oh no,' Declan said out aloud. 'Oh, Vivian.'

Vivian stirred and turned over. 'What do you want?' she asked.

'You're alive! I thought you were dead.'

Vivian curled onto her side like a foetus. 'Tristan dumped me. He's with his PA. She's seventeen years old!'

'I met her,' Declan said, sitting down on her bed. 'Liz, isn't it? She's got blonde hair and a crack habit?'

Vivian threw her arms around Declan and he could feel her breasts pressing against his chest. It seemed like the most extraordinarily inappropriate moment to start fantasising about sexual congress with a woman, but there it was. Vivian wasn't wearing a top and the skin on her back was soft and warm against his fingertips. *She'd probably have sex with me now,* Declan thought. *She's desperate for some physical consolation.*

'Maybe he just wants some space,' Declan said, taking a shirt from the floor for Vivian to put over herself.

'You don't know anything do you?' Vivian stopped crying and wiped the tears from either cheek. She put the shirt on, and when she looked up her eyes were two glistening pools of fear: depthless, fragile, crystal fear. 'It was Tristan pushed Drake off the balcony,' she said. 'He murdered Drake.'

'What?'

'I was there, wasn't I?' Vivian snapped. She sank her head back into the pillow and wailed loudly. 'I was theeerrreee!!!'

Declan picked up two of the pills that were scattered around the bed and fed them to Vivian. He told her to get some sleep, then he went downstairs to his room and rolled a joint and smoked it.

What the hell was he going to do now?

37

Two days later Declan moved into a small bedsit in Kings Cross. He didn't say goodbye to anyone and nobody came to say goodbye to him. The *Daily Mail* received an anonymous tip-off from a woman who claimed to have been in a neighbouring flat on the night of Drake's death. *Russell Flees Death Scene* was the heading to the story on page eight. An anonymous female neighbour was quoted as saying she had heard male voices arguing and had looked through the spy-hole to her flat. She had seen Tristan Russell, several girls and a second man come running out of the flat. They had not even waited for the elevator, but ran to the stairwell and disappeared in a hurry.

The police were unimpressed that someone had gone to the media rather than call them. They questioned the validity of the claims. 'It may just be someone wanting to get a headline,' the investigating officer claimed. 'If anyone does have any information regarding the death of Drake Preston I ask that they come down to the station and give us some of their time.'

Bridget phoned the *Daily Mail* and spoke to the journalist who had written the story. 'You're a parasitic fuck-worm!' she screamed. 'You have no idea who you are dealing with. I am going to fuck you to tears and then I'm going to sell the tape.'

The journalist responded by investigating Bridget's past. He interviewed many of her old school and university friends, and the people she worked with in the commercial photography industry. The week after Declan moved out, the *Daily Mail* journalist published a damning profile in which he claimed that Bridget had had two abortions at university, she had cheated in her final year exams, she had stolen wallets from her school friends at Saint Paul's, she was a sexual predator who bet other university students she could seduce a male lecturer, she caused the marriage of another lecturer to end in divorce, she did not always pay her assistants on commercial photo-shoots, and she sometimes overcharged clients when invoicing for jobs. At the end of the profile the journalist published a transcript of his phone conversation with Bridget: *You have no idea who you are dealing with. I am going to fuck you to tears and then I'm going to sell the tape.*

The fact that Bridget was a young woman abusing an older male journalist was unhelpful. If she were a man her outburst might have been put down to stress, or disappointment, but as a woman the judgements were potent and she was freshly cast as a modern-day Medea.

Over the next month things unravelled quickly. The editor of *Femme* rang to say the magazine had 'reconsidered' Bridget's position as hotel reviewer. Pink Disc rang to say they had 'reconsidered' her next show. Art critics who had claimed that she embodied BritArt's entry into the twenty-first century decided they had been fooled by a clever publicity machine. Bridget's profound insights were, in fact, pedestrian waffle, her photographic skills were ridiculed, the thousand-pound-a-pop Polaroids were the greatest swindle since Ronnie Biggs: in short, Bridget Defond betrayed an unscrupulous ambition posing as talent. The value of her Polaroids dropped to the price of a cup of coffee in a greasy spoon café. She was accused of being responsible for the release of her sex-tape. Journalists sneered at her cynical attempt to generate publicity. The bellboy in Moscow was given his job back, and the hotel apologised to him and his family by offering a one-week holiday in the Polish mountains as compensation.

Bridget was called to the police station and questioned for several hours about the first *Daily Mail* story. When she returned to the Chocolate Block she was surrounded by cameras and microphones and insolent voices demanding answers to any question they could think of:

'Bridget, why did you lie to the police?'

'Why did you release a sex tape of yourself?'

'Have you ever had an abortion?'

'Are you a drug addict?'

'Did you seduce your university tutor?'

'Did you know he was married with three children?'

'Were you on cocaine the night Drake Preston was killed?'

'Did you steal from your friends at school?'

Bridget responded by grabbing a camera lens and smashing the camera back into the cameraman's face, leaving a small gash above his eye that required three stitches. The wounded cameraman, who also happened to be a haemophiliac, almost died of blood loss before an ambulance arrived to take him to hospital.

38

Declan followed developments in the press, but had no direct contact with the Posse. He did not leave a forwarding address or a telephone number in the flat. He sent a polite letter to Emma at Cooper & Whitely, thanking her for her trouble and explaining that he no longer wished to pursue a career in acting.

Apart from the box of postcard paintings and three boxes of papers, Declan had almost nothing connecting him to the Posse. Sometimes one painting or another reminded him of a particular conversation he had shared with a Posse member, but he did not have one photograph to remind him of his time in the Chocolate Block, and after a month the memories began to fade. In November he started teaching English to foreign students at a small school in Marble Arch. It may not have been his first choice as a career but it was his choice. Nobody had made it for him. He continued to present the film segment on *Massive* each weekend and wrote the monthly reviews for *Fluid* magazine, and he sensed a change was about to mark his life forever.

Although Tristan tried to hide himself away he did not stay out of the news for long. In early December Tristan was found unconscious in a flat in Brixton with two young girls naked and dead at his feet. Both girls had died of a heroin overdose and one had cigarette burns on her arms. When Tristan regained consciousness in hospital he told police he had not even been in the flat when the girls had injected the drugs, but a camera had been found in the flat, and it contained photos of Tristan injecting both girls and performing various sexual acts.

Declan read the news in *Metro* on his way to the school in Marble Arch. He felt a dread chill wash through his veins as if someone had injected him with gallons of liquid nitrogen. It was difficult to believe the story and yet, almost immediately, he seemed to know that this was always how things would end.

It was the end of the media's love affair with Tristan Russell. In the past whenever he had been criticised, it was the breathless sensation of a scandal that would raise newspaper circulation. Two or three journalists usually wrote op-ed pieces supporting Tristan, contrary to popular sentiment, but now that two young girls were dead the criticisms were imperious and sanctimonious, and nobody championed Tristan Russell as a subversive hero in a cynical and commercial world. The tabloid newspapers claimed that they had been warning the public for over a year that this was a dangerous man and a menace to decent society. They had been accused in the past of being sensational but now they felt their critical stance had been vindicated. Tristan Russell was not a romantic hero, he was not a rebellious youth, he was a disgusting and amoral criminal. If only the public had listened to the newspapers earlier, perhaps this young girl (sic) would be home with her family tonight.

Declan's initial shock was checked-mated by reality, and the first emotion he felt was overwhelming guilt. He finished teaching and went straight home. He lay like a stone in bed, staring up at the ceiling, trying not to cry. He was disgusted with himself because even now, as two young girls lay dead, his only response seemed to be one of self-pity. Logically, in terms of direct cause and effect, Declan knew that he was not responsible for what had happened, but emotionally he felt that he was in some sense accountable. Tristan had come into his room one morning and called himself a monster, and Declan had merely shrugged and discussed things reasonably, as if the two of them were talking about a person's taste in music. When Tristan had tried to express the depths of his self-loathing, Declan had pushed him out of his bedroom. He had not wanted to know. He had not wanted to feel in any way responsible for Tristan's welfare, let alone the welfare of the young girls who flocked around him like moths around a flame. He had not wanted to *feel* anything.

What had Declan felt, honestly, in all the time he had lived in the Chocolate Block? Had he felt nothing, or had he betrayed his feelings by deferring to some philosophical idea of a world where nothing could ever be proved to be true absolutely; where everything was just appearance and nothing was reality? Now two young girls were dead, really dead, and Declan had done nothing to prevent their dying.

As he lay in bed, Declan wondered what would happen now. He had no idea. The idea of changing his life was a nice dream, an admirable commitment, but he knew he would not change. His cynicism was a habit, an addiction, which over the years had become invincible. He might make some dramatic gesture of change for two or three weeks but things would soon settle once again, and the old cynicism would always win. It always did.

Tristan was refused bail and gave a brief statement to the press through his lawyer: he said that he had been sexually abused as a young boy. He said he needed help. He said he had reached rock bottom.

Declan knew that if he had been any kind of friend to Tristan, if he had felt any great compassion then he would have supported him then, when he most needed it. He would have gone to visit him in prison and simply by going, he would be saying that he was not judging him, he would have been saying that he could forgive him for what he had done.

But Declan did not offer Tristan anything. He did not forgive him. When his guilt subsided it was replaced with a narrow and righteous disgust, and the disgust was directed solely at Tristan. He did not phone, or write a letter, or visit him in jail, and eight years passed before he saw him again.

39

Declan felt like he had sunk to the bottom of a great ocean, down into the black depths where the pressure of the past, like the weight of a million of tonnes of water, made every moment and every movement a labour. He shaved his head raw as a peeled potato, and over the next few months he trawled through possible modes of suicide like a shopper trawling through clothes in a basement sale. The shopper contemplates buying a T-shirt only because it is cheap, not because he particularly likes the shirt's design. Similarly, Declan contemplated suicide, not because he had any great affection for death's design, but because it represented a cheap escape from life.

By the spring of 2001, the idea of suicide had begun to thaw and Declan started swimming regularly. Within a month his lungs were clean and his strength had started to return. His body language slowly reformed, and he started walking with his shoulders back and his chin up.

One evening he was catching his breath at the shallow end of the pool when an older woman took off her swimming cap and tossed her blonde hair in a manner that was hard to ignore. She was probably in her late forties, but she had the youthful beauty and the bright eyes of a woman who had always extracted pleasure from life's simple gifts. She smiled like a young girl. She wore waterproof hot-red lipstick, and tiny balls of water beaded on her lips, trickling down to her chin as she spoke. Declan was unaccustomed to red lipstick in a pool but he did not flinch.

'Eurgh!' she exclaimed, as if Declan had leeches on his eyeballs. 'Your hair is so short! Are you a Buddhist?' She spoke like a caricature of a French diva, and offered the final question with a familiar smile that made Declan feel he should say yes.

'No,' he said.

'Have you ever tried shaunt-inge?'

'Shaunting?'

'Shaunt-inge.' The woman put her hands together and began to chant in an Asian language. Declan said that he had never tried chanting. They arranged to have a coffee after showering.

Half an hour later when Declan arrived at the pool café, the woman was waiting in an open jaffa-red jacket with ear-rings that complemented her lipstick. Her long, blonde hair was divided into two thick pigtails, like Pippi Longstocking. She wore an Iron Maiden T-shirt.

She introduced herself as Cherie.

Declan stared at the Iron Maiden picture on Cherie's T-shirt and became aware of her breasts pulsing slowly with each breath. He was suddenly transported back to the shallow end of the pool where they had first met. He could feel Cherie's blood-red lips on his neck and her fingernails in his shoulders as he thrust into her and came like a beast.

Cherie smiled. 'I used to be a roadie for them back in the Seventies, "Ion Miden". We had so much fun!'

The days of being a roadie for Iron Maiden lit a fire in Cherie's eyes, and then she returned to the present. She leaned forward and handed Declan a card with the name of a Buddhist group on one side.

'Shaunt-inge is simply fantastic!' she said. 'You focus on something you want, something you really want, and you shaunt for whatever it is, and you get it.'

As Declan walked back to his bedsit he considered Cherie's advice, laughing at himself; was he seriously thinking about doing something as ludicrous as *chanting* over and over again, while dreaming that something good might happen in his life? This was surely an indication of just how emotionally desperate he had become. What would he try next: a horseshoe on his bedroom door; Feng Shui; astrology; a lottery ticket every week; some other form of fatalistic hope that describes a man who no longer believes in his innate power to control his own destiny?

On the other hand, Declan knew he needed to change the stories that had been playing inside his mind for so long. He knew that he needed some new ones: positive and optimistic, regardless of how ludicrously artificial they sounded. What new story did he have?

I want to feel happiness.

For the first time since his brain injury, Declan said these words without any shame or cynicism, though with a sense of startled wonder. Basic happiness now seemed like a decent thing to want. For many years he had viewed happiness as a superficial goal for weak people unable to face the truth. He had told himself that he was too cynical and too bad a person to be happy. Now he wondered if he hadn't been confusing the pursuit of happiness with the pursuit of pleasure. There was something in Cherie's manner, a strength of happiness that he knew was rare and good. She may have suffered, but her face was warm with her life's stories. Perhaps sometimes the truth is simply whatever story you keep telling yourself again and again.

Declan went to Cherie's Notting Hill flat the weekend after meeting her.

'Don't be fooled by the location,' she smirked, as she led Declan down the hall and into the living area. 'It is the only thing my father left me.'

Creamy silk curtains covered the bay windows and a Picasso etching hung from one wall. Cherie lit some incense, opened up her small Buddhist shrine, and put two cushions on the floor. She showed Declan how to sit with his legs crossed and his back straight. She positioned herself beside him and banged a small gong several times.

'Nam myo-ho renge kyo, nam myo-ho renge kyo, nam myo-ho renge kyo.'

To repeat the chant consistently Declan had to control his breathing in a way that was not dissimilar to the breathing required when swimming freestyle at three-stroke intervals, but instead of sticking his head under water, he was shouting some Japanese slogan over and over again.

After fifteen minutes his back was aching. He was bored and he felt ridiculous, but he remembered what Cherie had said and tried to imagine a string on the top of his head, a hand pulling the string, pulling his spine toward the ceiling.

See how spineless you are? he thought, and he remembered something else Cherie had told him, the power of positive thought. He must not allow negativity to creep in while he was chanting.

Loser, loser, loser.

They stopped chanting after half an hour. As soon as Declan stood up he felt oddly exhilarated. His whole body buzzed with vigour. They sat down to drink a coffee and the atmosphere was unusually, almost poignantly pleasant.

'So what do you do, Declan?'

'Now? Not much. I … I wanted to be an artist as a young man, but I suffered brain damage and I stopped.'

'Why did you stop?'

'Laziness maybe. Maybe something else. Fear. I think I was

talented, I certainly had opportunity and ambition, but after my brain injury the doctors said I would never fully recover. They said my emotions were sluggish and my coordination was weak. I used the brain injury as an excuse to stop feeling. I lost my confidence.'

Declan was not just talking about confidence in himself either; he had lacked confidence in the world. As a young man his ideals had been floodlit with the arrogance of youth and while he was repulsed by the society in which he lived – the greed, the waste, the indulgence, the pollution – he saw nothing wrong with succeeding in such a world. Now he felt justified and righteous in his failure, but he realised that all the toxic waste, all the environmental pollution that had so angered him in the real world, was nothing more than an outward manifestation of the toxicity that had swamped inside his own being after he was beaten up.

'One day I stopped projecting all my self-loathing onto the world and started to direct it inward. I was disgusted with myself and in my disgust I admired my insight.'

'And now?'

'Now I think I want a change. I want a new insight. I want to feel again.'

Declan started chanting at home, twenty minutes every morning and every night. Forty minutes of chanting a day was, Cherie told him, a disciplined start.

'What you are doing is making your mind *strong*. This is like lifting weights with your mind every day.'

Declan continued to feel foolish even though he knew nobody was watching him. He did not believe in it, but could think of no alternative. He did not believe in reincarnation, or chakras, or energy "vibrations", or any such thing. He knew that his mind was addicted to cynicism, and that this had crippled his emotional life more than his physical brain injury ever had. He told himself that changing mental habits was like learning to dance a waltz: at first the new thoughts would feel unnatural and false, he would stumble many times, but if he continued despite the stumbles, if he refused to give up, then at some point this new way of thinking would start to feel less awkward, it would develop a natural rhythm of its own.

He was right. After just a month of chanting he began to feel a rhythm coming to his positive thoughts. He just repeated the idea; *I want to feel happy*, again and again, no matter how ridiculous it sounded, and then slowly it started to sound less ridiculous. He knew it was too late to start painting again, and his relationship with Juliet had disabused him of all notions of love and romance. He did not want to find love. He was too superficial, too easily seduced by beauty and romantic idiom. It left him incapable of evaluating his feelings for women rationally, so he chanted only for happiness.

He visited Cherie's flat every Saturday to join her Buddhist meetings. One particular Saturday, he was the only attendee. He arrived with a chest infection that made breathing difficult, and he was wheezing and spluttering so badly that they finished chanting early and Cherie cooked some tofu with spinach.

'Tofu is so good for you,' Cherie said, and she disappeared into her bathroom. 'Hang on,' she called excitedly. 'I have just the thing for your chest!'

Cherie came out of the bathroom with a tub of Vicks VapoRub. 'This is wonderful, take your shirt off.'

Declan did as he was told and Cherie knelt in front of him and rubbed the ointment into his hairy chest. Her long bony hands rubbed Declan's flesh with a slow, subtle sensuality that he did not notice immediately. She continued to rub her hands across his chest and up around his neck and shoulders, well beyond medical necessity. The moment became sexually charged. Declan imagined Cherie's hands moving down to his stomach, and disappearing into his trousers to massage the erection that was already responding to this idea. He looked at Cherie but she had been transported into another world. She was gazing at her own hands, her lips slightly parted, her eyes glazed over. Declan wondered whom she was thinking of. It was not him. He was simply the conduit through which she could revisit a vision she had lost.

Cherie massaged Declan's chest for fifteen minutes. He was embarrassed but did not want her to stop. Finally, she brought her hands together, and looked up and saw him again.

'Was that OK, hmm?' she asked innocently.

'That was great,' Declan said.

After three months of chanting things began to happen rather magically. Declan bought a mobile phone, which may not sound too magical, but for Declan it was a miracle, a connection with the real world. Optimism was flying through his veins like doves. It became a habit. Something great was about to happen in his life. He no longer had to try to convince himself. Even if he did not know what that great thing would be, he knew it was coming.

40

The first few times Declan visited the National Gallery, he had rushed through every room, in every wing, within two hours and left exhausted. He had been impatient to get the full gallery experience in a single day. After the fifth or sixth visit he began to develop a different approach; he chose a particular art period from a particular region, and spent his time looking over the works in those rooms. Since leaving the Chocolate Block he would visit the gallery and sit for an hour in front of just one painting. It was a habit his legs were grateful for. Walking the streets for two hours was nowhere near as tiring as walking through a gallery for twenty minutes. Perhaps it had something to do with the power of mental activity combined with the legwork. Thinking really does hurt your legs sometimes.

Gazing up at Velazquez's *Venus* one day, Declan did not notice that a woman had sat down beside him until a young man walked passed, stopped, and addressed the woman.

'What are you doing?'

The man was wearing a suit that was several sizes too small and the middle button of the jacket was done up. He looked like a youthful Benny Hill.

'I'm sorry?' the woman asked, in an accent that sounded Eastern European.

'Are you looking at that painting?' the man pointed to the *Venus* on the gallery wall.

'Yes.'

'How old are you?'

'I have twenty-five years.'

'Why don't you come with me, I can show you around the other rooms.'

'Thank you, I'm sitting here.'

'Where are you from?'

'Poland,' the woman said.

'The Pope is Polish.'

The woman did not seem to know how to respond to this statement. She faltered for a moment.

'Yes that is true,' she said.

The man looked across at Declan.

'Who's that? Is he your boyfriend?'

Declan looked at the woman. She had the widest, greenest, brightest eyes he had ever seen. Her face was delicately made-up. Her blonde hair had obviously been put in curlers that morning, giving it a glamorous *Charlie's Angels* kind of bounce. She sat with her knees together and kept her back perfectly straight. She was elegantly dressed in a dark summer-dress with purple flower-buds scattered across the material. Her shoes were black, well-polished, with inch-high heels and silver buckles on the straps.

Lines of Byronic poetry fluttered through Declan's mind and his heart expanded for a moment, but he marked her instantly as a person of superficial character. The kind of woman he imagined dating wealthy footballers, shopping for clothes every day, and watching *The Bold and the Beautiful* every afternoon while talking to girlfriends on the phone. Perhaps she had come to London to find a rich husband. Maybe she had intended to sit down in front of the Velazquez until a wealthy looking man showed up. Benny Hill was not him. Declan was not him either.

'Are you her boyfriend?' the man asked Declan.

'No,' Declan replied.

The man appeared emboldened by this answer. He sat down beside the woman.

'I would like to ask you out,' he said, boldly.

'Thank you, I cannot.'

'I want to take you out to lunch.'

'I must meet my friend,' the woman said.

The man continued to pressure the woman with solicitations. Declan expected her to stand up and walk away, but she declined again and again without moving. After five minutes Declan felt he should say something. Perhaps she did not feel comfortable being rude because she was a foreigner in London.

'Mate, give it a rest. She doesn't want to go out with you.'

The man turned to Declan, who imagined several different outcomes, few of them appealing. He tried not to show his fear. Apart from anything else, a room filled with seventeenth-century art did not seem like an appropriate theatre for violence. The man did not look violent or aggressive, just highly strung, and sure enough after muttering some last words he stood and left.

The Polish woman smiled and thanked Declan.

'There are many strange men in London,' she said, shaking her head in genuine disbelief.

'Maybe it's all the naked bottoms,' Declan explained, pointing to the Velazquez painting. The woman laughed and Declan stared at the naked butt of *Venus*. He went over his options: he could get up and leave now; he could make small talk, be polite and leave; or he could say nothing and wait until the woman went away. But saying nothing seemed deliberately rude. No harm in talking is there? Why was he so anxious? What was he going to do, follow Farrah Fawcett back to Poland next week?

'Do you want to grab something, a coffee maybe?' Declan asked. The woman's eyes shone with extremely convincing desire.

'Yes,' she said, as if her whole body was speaking.

'I don't have much money,' Declan said, not because he did not want to pay for her coffee, but because it was true. He did not want to waste this woman's time if she was attempting to pick up a wealthy man.

'I have money,' the woman said, and she told Declan her name was Beata.

Many people say that you should not judge people by their appearances but that's a bit like saying you shouldn't hold your breath when you are underwater. Perhaps when people say, *you shouldn't judge,* what they mean is *you shouldn't pre-judge* others based on appearance. Declan's senses had imported a lot of information about Beata in the first few seconds after he turned to face her in front of Venus's form. She was a sensual woman with a heart-shaped face and bright green eyes, and it was only natural that his passions should be inflamed.

They went together to Bar Italia in Soho. Declan lounged back in his chair and prepared for a casual, empty, yet pleasant conversation. He ordered a coffee and Beata ordered a glass of red wine.

'Red wine for lunch?'

'Why not,' Beata said, with a wicked smile. 'I have the holidays.'

She really was gorgeous, no doubt about it. But Declan saw something else; looking at her face, into her eyes, her capacity for love suddenly appeared overwhelming.

'What do you do in Poland?'

'I'm a doctor.'

'Wow,' Declan said, in a way that was, ironically, supposed to hide his genuine surprise. 'What kind of doctor are you?'

'I want to specialise in child's haematology, for the blood diseases like leukaemia and aplastic anaemia.'

'Leukaemia? That's like cancer, isn't it? D–d–do–don't they die, then, the kids?'

'It's not so bad with the child; they have eighty per cent who live.'

'But twenty per cent die?'

'Yes, but eighty per cent live.'

'That must be hard.'

'It is hard work,' Beata shrugged. 'But I love the work. You save many lifes, this is no better feeling than to save the life of the innocent child.'

'Do people mistake you for a nurse?' Declan asked.

'Much times,' Beata laughed. 'You would not believe it.'

'No, no, I think I would believe it.'

'I see you,' she said. 'I know you.' Beata smiled; a sense of mischief in her eyes.

'You know me? What? From the language school?'

'No, on the television. You make the film critics.'

Declan did not try to hide his surprise. 'You saw that? It holds the record for the most unwatched programme on television.'

'I see that!' Beata squealed. 'I love films!'

'I love films too. I love art, but, you know, compared to your work … films don't save lives.'

'How do you know?' Beata looked directly into Declan's eyes and smiled without pretence. 'How do you know what the world would be without stories, without art? I cannot imagine. I think without stories we will be like dead. Stories keep us alive.'

'Some of them do.'

Declan swapped mobile phone numbers with Beata, and when they parted he wondered if he would ever call her. She was lovely, and not just to look at, but she would be gone in a month.

41

'Uergh, but you must call her!' Cherie said when Declan told her about Beata the next Saturday. All the other divorced women agreed. They had finished chanting and were having coffee together. The sun bathed Cherie's apartment in a clear light and the creamy silk curtains rustled in the breeze.

'Come on, girls,' Declan answered, 'she's twenty-five, I'm thirty-two, she's Polish, I'm … I'm not Polish. She's a successful doctor, and I'm … I don't even know what the hell I am. If I call her, it will be a complete disaster. I can't even afford an incomplete disaster at the moment.'

'Uergh, listen to you. You sound like a scientist concerned about an experiment. You must listen to your heart, Declan. In this matter you cannot think with your mind, do what your heart desires.'

The women all clucked agreement and nodded their heads.

'My heart is a … a … a fucking retard!' Declan said. He apologised for swearing. 'I'm emotionally retarded.'

Cherie took hold of Declan's wrist. 'Listen to me,' she said. 'You're just scared to feel. Nothing else. I had a man many years ago. I never lost him, I dumped him, he gave me his heart and I dropped it. I thought I could live alone. Now I live alone.' Cherie's dark eyes shone and her lips contracted. 'It was a mistake.'

Declan phoned Beata that night and she sounded genuinely overjoyed to hear his voice. She actually said the word, "Hooray".

'Declan you call me! *Hooray!* Shall we meet?'

They went to a film preview in Soho the next day and had dinner at a Japanese restaurant. Beata had never tried sushi before, and Declan had to stop her from eating a large ball of green wasabi in one gulp.

'It's very hot,' he explained.

'It looks so sweet and harmless,' she said.

'So did Bill Clinton.'

Declan wanted to pay the bill but Beata insisted on paying for her meal.

'I don't like the men pay for me,' she said.

'That's good,' Declan said, 'because I tell you something now, I don't earn much money.'

'I think you have something more than money. Yes. Anyway, no one in Poland has much money. When I was young girl we didn't even have food. We wait for hours just to buy bread but the shelves were often empty. Even now I make less than you.'

'A doctor?' Declan guffawed. 'I doubt that. I work three jobs and I make about a hundred and eighty pounds a week.'

'I make ninety pounds a week.'

'But … you're a *doctor*.'

'I'm a doctor in Poland,' Beata smiled. She seemed to find this rather funny.

Declan offered her some free English classes. 'There are three hundred students at the school,' he explained. 'You can come into my classes and I'll check the register and pretend to tick you off. Nobody comes in to check on me.'

Beata came to English classes every morning at 8:30. Two weeks later she was sleeping at Declan's bedsit most nights. She phoned the head of the haematology department at her hospital and said that she wanted to take all the holidays that she was owed.

'Now I can stay six weeks until the end of next month!' she told Declan after making the call.

In the afternoons they went swimming together. They attended film previews and discussed the merits of each film. On weekends they did tourist things that Declan had never bothered to do. They went to Windsor Castle, the Tower of London, Hampton Court Palace and Kew Gardens. They went to the stately Wallace Collection, filled with Baroque furniture, Canaletto paintings, and spears, pistols and cannons. They walked up the grand staircase arm-in-arm, pretending they were aristocrats back home from the country, preparing for the London season. It was like being on holidays in a movie, and sometimes Declan had to remind himself that it was real. They often laughed at things that were not funny; and Declan realised he was laughing because he was happy.

Whenever Declan invited Beata somewhere she said yes. She often said, 'hooray' when she heard his voice. He had never known any woman to be so consistently determined and over-joyed to see him. She never seemed to want to do anything else, and he could not quite understand why. Maybe he had changed and did not even realise it.

Of course she keeps saying yes, a cynical voice inside Declan offered. *She's on holidays and she can practise her English for free.* But every morning and every night as he was chanting, this cynical voice was overwhelmed by a gentle, powerful truth; Beata genuinely liked him. Maybe she loved him. And maybe he loved her. It was not a rational thing. His thoughts challenged his dream:

You're an idiot!

'I'm happy!'

Retarded chanting Chinaman.

'It's Japanese, actually.'

You think you're a good person now? After all that's happened?

'I can be good if I choose to be.'

Why? Because you tell yourself that same shit over and over.

'That's right.'

You're not good, you're weak and selfish and deceitful.

'Why does Beata like me then?'

She just wants a passport!

'So she's easy to please.'

You don't deserve her!

'That's not my decision.'

You're just running away.

'Maybe I'm running the right way.'

Beata and Declan spent two months together. On her second to last day in London, they walked through Regent's Park and the mood was funereal. Beata was catching the bus home the next morning and Declan would be teaching so this was their final goodbye.

'Do you think I could move to Poland?' Declan asked.

'Really? You would do that?' Beata glowed with surprise.

'I don't know, it's possible, I suppose, isn't it?'

'Yes! For the native speaker it is always possible in Poland. I will find something if you want it,' and she slipped both arms around Declan, and held him tightly as they moved down the path.

Almost immediately the idea of leaving London filled Declan with dread. It was a ridiculous romantic fantasy. Declan and Beata had made love and laughter in London, but in Poland everything would change. London was not his city but English was his language, and Beata had often depended on him when they were together in public. In Poland he would be dependent on Beata. He would not be able to communicate with her friends or her family. He would feel ignorant, even foolish, and slowly he would start to resent Beata for these feelings. All the differences between them that seemed attractive now would become annoying and divisive. Declan would start to complain. Beata would be sympathetic at first but then they would begin to argue and fight, the fights would get more and more frequent until finally, when each of them had come to their senses, Declan would leave Poland, alone, and go God knows where.

How can you project yourself into a future that is not yet known?

Beata was crying silently when they passed through the main gates of Regent's Park. The tears ran like tiny roller-skates down her cheeks every time she blinked. They walked to Tottenham Court Road and waited for the bus, and Beata kept looking down at her feet.

This is a woman who works with dying kids, Declan thought, *and she is crying because she's leaving me.*

When the bus came it was black, which seemed fitting but was a surprise nonetheless. It was the first all-black bus Declan had ever seen in London, and here it was, coming to take Beata away for the last time. It was too much for Beata. She sobbed loudly and pressed her forehead into Declan's chest.

'The bus is black,' she said. 'Like when you bury a dead person in the ground.'

Declan went home alone and for the first time in months, he went straight to bed without chanting.

The very next evening Beata phoned from Poland. Instead of going home and sleeping after the twenty-two hour bus trip, she had visited every ESL school in the centre of her town. Three different schools had offered Declan a job, and she gave him each school's contact details and advised which offered the best pay and conditions. She had also found cheap accommodation for him. If he wanted to he could stay with a young married couple who were friends from her old high-school.

'If you still want, everything is waiting for you here in Poland,' Beata said. 'I am waiting. I have your picture on my wall. It stays near my bed until you come.'

Declan hung up the phone. He knew he would never make a choice; he was afraid to. In his fear he knew he would remain passive, and in this passivity he knew the choice would be made for him. He would not move. He would remain rooted to the spot until the choice was no longer there to be made. In the future he might regret it, but his feelings of regret would be reduced because he had never consciously said "no".

That night Declan chanted for an hour and within the first five minutes of chanting his whole being was telling him calmly: *you must go.* When he finished, the idea of leaving London seemed crazy again. He was just running away, once again, to another anonymous life in a new city where pretty soon it would all fall apart like it always had before. Then he would have nowhere to run. He did not know how he could be in love with a woman he had only known for two months. It was nothing more than the old romanticism returning to trick his senses and trump his reason. But he would never know unless he gave it a chance.

That weekend Declan told the producer at *Massive* that he was leaving. Jeremy Larkin wanted to organise a goodbye party, but Declan said he had too many things to do. On the Monday he rang Francis, the editor of *Fluid* magazine, and asked if they could have lunch.

They met in the Admiral Duncan in Old Compton Street, the site of the nail bomb explosion in 1999 that had killed three people. Francis had sent Declan an email saying he would wear a

CANDY baseball cap. Declan saw him sitting by the open window sipping a Kir Royal and staring at the passing crowd.

'Francis?'

'Declan!' Francis stood up and kissed him on both cheeks. Declan ordered a beer and sat down, and Francis slapped his hands together like a schoolboy.

'It's so great to finally meet the real you in the flesh! It's funny, I feel I know you so well after reading your reviews every month. They're fabulous by the way, but you already know that because I tell you every month!' Francis reached over and touched Declan's hand for a moment to emphasise the point. 'I feel we have this kind of symbiotic connection. I know you know it, but I have to say it again, your stuff is amazing, it's simply amazing!'

'Thanks Francis. I wanted to see you because I'm quitting. I've decided I'm not going to be writing the reviews next month.'

Francis shook his head sarcastically and smiled. '*Hello*? What? Are you *serious*?'

'Yes, I'm sorry.'

'But ... is it the money? Look, we'll be reviewing the budget in a few weeks and I guarantee you, it's guaranteed, you'll have at least twenty-five per cent more. At least!'

'No, it's not the money.'

'So what is it?'

'I'm not gay.'

Francis took the words in and translated them into something he understood through experience. He gave a relieved sigh and took hold of Declan's hand again like a mother.

'Look, we all go through that, Dec. Well, not all of us, but some of us have moments when we wonder. It's only natural when the whole of our society is pushing heterosexuality down our throats, every day in every way. It's only natural when our choices make us outsiders, it's only natural when we experience prejudice again and again, and we know we'll be facing this all our lives. Honestly, Declan, I've questioned myself too. Five years ago I had a *girlfriend*!'

'It's not a phase,' Declan explained. 'I've never been gay. I've never had sex with a man. I don't have any problem with gay people; I'm just not gay myself.'

'So why have you been doing gay reviews? What was it, a joke?'

'I just needed the money. I thought ... I thought Jeremy would have told you.'

Francis stood up and marched out of the pub. Five seconds later he returned and consumed what was left of his Kir Royale. Then he slammed it down on the table.

'That was a bit dramatic of me, wasn't it?' he said.

He sat back down and Declan ordered another round of drinks. They sat and got drunk for several hours, and when they left Francis hugged Declan and wished him all the best.

Declan rang Beata the next morning and told her he had quit all his jobs. He was coming to Poland.

'You come to me?' Beata said, crying. 'You come to me, really?'

'Yes,' Declan said. 'I come to you.'

42

Sitting in his apartment in Poland in April 2008, Declan got a Facebook message from Juliet saying that she was returning to England. David was getting married, he was going to be a 'June Groom' and he wanted Declan to come to the wedding. David and Becca already had a young son, and David ran a small business producing hand-made cards. He had produced a popular series of postcards featuring the photographs of old shoes he had once kept under Bridget's bed.

Juliet and Declan tried to make small talk for a week, passing messages back and forth, and looking at the photographs each had posted in their Facebook albums.

I can't believe how many photos you've taken in the past five years! Juliet wrote. They each explained how much their lives had changed and in doing so, they both realised there was nothing much left to say. Juliet was married with three young children and lived in Portugal. She and her husband owned a small vineyard and winery and she looked after the marketing side of the business. They had wine-tasting events, summer concerts and a private hotel where guests visiting the winery could stay. She invited Declan and his family for a summer concert and he said it sounded great. He decided that he did not want to go to David's wedding and that he did not want to see Juliet again. Two days later he decided that he had changed his mind, and his desire oscillated like this for several weeks until he read about Tristan Russell's imminent release from prison in the *Guardian.* He had served a seven and a half year stretch.

Declan still had the phone number Tristan had given him at his parent's farmhouse. He went down to the basement and rummaged through boxes of things he had brought from London. It was mostly rubbish that he had been unable to throw away: the postcard paintings, cut-outs of his gay film reviews, the shoe boxes filled with old love letters that he had once kept under his bed, the catalogue he had written for Bridget's exhibition. He found the phone number and for a moment he considered throwing everything else into the skip outside. *Not yet,* he thought, *not yet.* He rummaged a little longer, and discovered a diary that he had written while living with the Posse in London. The diary began on the day he first met Bridget, and the last page detailed the day he learned Tristan was being charged with manslaughter. He kept it in hand, turned the basement light off and locked the door. He checked it a couple of times to make sure it was secure.

When he returned to his apartment he read over the diary entries that described his time in Turin Street. It contained such a confused mish-mash of thought, as if it had been written by several different people of different ages, maturity and experience. Most of all the writing was detached, it betrayed no feeling for the life he had lived. He phoned Beata at the hospital just to hear her voice and to ground himself in the present.

On the first weekend of June, Declan flew to London. Mr Russell was waiting outside the arrival gates at Stansted Airport.

'Mr Russell,' Declan said, embarrassed that this man, whom he had only met once, was here to greet him.

'I wanted to surprise you and I thought you might get lost. Come on, we can get the next train.'

'That's OK,' Declan said, 'I need to rent a car, we can drive.'

'Tristan told me you didn't drive.'

'I didn't.'

It was a beautiful morning. The sky was blue and the air was warm. Mr Russell and Declan enjoyed a pleasant conversation all the way to the farmhouse. Declan recognised the place when they turned off the main road, but it was hard to believe that he had ever been there before. It was hard to believe that the last time he had taxied up the driveway, he had feared for his life. Now the farmhouse looked like a scene from a Winnie-the-Pooh story. He parked the car, they got out and Mr Russell unlocked the front door to the house. Declan strode confidently through the door but when he saw Tristan he stopped still and tried to hide his shock. Tristan was sitting and smoking on the same sofa they had sat on eight years ago. The sofa looked much the same, but Tristan was barely recognisable. His eyes were two dark coal pits and his teeth were black. He was fat, and bald, and Declan would not have recognised him if they had passed each other on the street.

'How are you, Triz?'

'You wanna smoke, Dec'?'

'I gave up five years ago.'

'Right.'

Tristan did not seem pleased to see Declan. Mr Russell said he was going to the supermarket and asked if Tristan wanted something.

'Coke, please, Dad.'

'You want to try that Zero?'

'Fat Coke, Dad, please.'

'No calories in that other stuff.'

'No taste either,' Tristan smiled. He stood up quickly and took some money from a jacket that was hanging on the door. 'Here, take some money,' he said. Mr Russell said that he had enough money, but Tristan insisted and gently pressed a ten-pound note into his father's palm. 'Come on,' he said, smiling sadly, 'you can't pay for everything.'

Mr Russell nodded and left. As the front door closed, Tristan smiled sentimentally at the space that his father had just vacated. 'God that man is a twenty-four-carat pain in the arse,' he said with affection.

Declan told Tristan about David's wedding and asked if he was interested in coming.

'I'm sure David would love to see you there,' he added. He was not sure if David would love to see Tristan there, and it was silly to offer the invitation but he knew Tristan would say no.

'Yeah, OK,' Tristan said, then he wheezed and said he was joking. 'Wouldn't mind tagging along if Vivian was going. Hasn't she turned into a babe-o-rama!'

Vivian had been spotted at Cannes in 2004 by Hollywood director Roy Green. He married her and took her back to LA with him, and cast her in his 2004 summer blockbuster *Life Form Two,* a movie about aliens intent on destroying the world. The film made over four hundred million dollars and in December 2005 Vivian was voted #43 Sexiest Woman Alive in *Maxim* magazine's annual reader poll. The following year she rose to #38 and by 2008 she was sitting pretty at #27.

Tristan was keen to revive his career and was looking for representation. He had written hundreds of songs in prison, and wanted the Rods to reform and record an album, but none of the music producers he used to work with were interested. Tristan was sure that once people heard his new songs there would be massive interest. He was very keen to discuss his future with reality television programmes like *Celebrity Big Brother* and *I'm A*

Celebrity Get Me Out Of Here and he had already spoken to producers of the latter programme about appearing in the next instalment.

'Who knows,' he coughed. 'I could do a Peter Andre and walk away with some hottie-tottie glamour model wife!'

After talking about his future for some time the conversation inevitably wound back to those few months when they had all lived together in East London.

'I realised some things,' Tristan said. 'Locked up all those years ... you start to see things.' His eyes were smiling and Declan knew that he was going to be nasty in a genial way, which meant Declan could not show outwardly that he was offended. Tristan spoke in his most ethereal Essex voice, the words like tiny crystals of dust in a rainbow, 'Why was I always in the papers?' he asked. 'Why was my life so newsworthy?'

'You're asking me that?'

'Because everyone loved it, they loved me! Everyone wanted to be me ... but you were all too scared of being judged, and you all sat and watched me instead, and ... you all shook your heads.'

'I wasn't shaking my head,' Declan said, shaking his head.

'You all wanted it. All of you ... the desire was all over your faces.'

Declan continued to shake his head. 'There's a big gap between a thought and a desire, Triz, and there's an even bigger gap between a desire and an action. I used to think about killing myself. I always knew I never really wanted to kill myself. I just liked thinking about the idea.'

'You probably wanted to but you were too scared.'

'No,' Declan said firmly. 'I knew it would be a bad idea.'

Tristan was not listening.

'Everyone used me. Vivian and Bridget; they sat back and they rode the train to fame on my coat tails … and they were guilty … just as guilty as I ever was.'

The way Tristan delivered this speech it was clear that he was not making it up as he went along. He had probably sat in his prison cell night after night rehearsing different variations, after all those years of waiting the words were real now, and Declan could tell that they must have sounded different to what Tristan had imagined, for he stuttered and faltered at every step.

'I was an *artist*, you understand? I was living the … *artist's* life.' Tristan's lips parted as if he were blowing cigarette smoke into the air. His eyes were restless and he scratched his neck uncertainly. 'Everyone wants to be an artist,' he mumbled. 'Jesus, why do you think Jeffrey Archer writes books?'

'Because he can't lick his own balls like a dog?'

'Because only the artist is truly free. The artist is free to push the boundaries, to think outside the square, the circle, to transcend, to transgress, otherwise he is a slave to moral society, and his work becomes enslaved too. And society views artists differently; they might not accept what we do, not totally, not at first, but it's certainly expected that we misbehave, and then over time it's forgotten.' Tristan tolled off a list of names with the fingers of one hand. 'Woody Allen, John Lennon, Oscar Wilde, Jimi Hendrix, Roman Polanski, Charlie Chaplin, Jim Morrison, Lord Byron, Baudelaire, Nabokov, James Joyce … me … Artists who create scandals and transgress the morality of the era, they are attacked in their lifetime but in the end, when they die, the scandals die too, only our art remains, because *that* is the only thing an artist can be judged on. As soon as Michael Jackson dies he'll be a legend again. And I'm no different. You know what Oscar Wilde used to say? *Wickedness is just an invention of good people to account for the curious attractiveness of others.*' Tristan's eyes were electrified.

'I'm not really wicked, you see? I'm just … curiously attractive.' He lowered his head and scratched at the back of his neck with one hand. His eyes held a soft, pleading glow then his face creased up and his mouth, as if unsure of the shape it should form, bent in the middle to create a horizontal figure-eight. Then, just as it looked like he would cry, his muscles relaxed and he looked out with a blank stare.

'I just wanted someone to say, stop, stop you idiot. But you didn't, you all loved it. I just gave people what they loved and I got no love in return. Instead I was crucified like … like Jesus Christ.'

Tristan sniffled and his face quivered and twitched grotesquely again. Then everything was plain and clear once more. 'I'm not excusing what I did, but I was just as much a victim, the media crucified me, they hung me on a cross to die, and why? Because I never played the game by their rules. At least I can hold my head up high and know that I never sold out. Whatever people say, I never sold out. I was offered half a million pounds to do a campaign for Panadol. I was supposed to say something like, *whenever my head is sore, I know one sure way of pain relief, Panadol.* Five hundred thousand pounds they offered. You think I didn't want the money. I wanted the money. I owed Mo fifteen K and he wasn't a man you wanted to owe money to.'

Declan could have reminded Tristan that he owed him several hundred pounds but it would have sounded a bit twee in the circumstances.

'I said no to Panadol. I said that's not me. I'm not a brand. I'm not for sale.' Tristan's eyes glowed with a fierce pride but his voice remained soft as melting candle wax. 'You see, it doesn't matter how dirty I was in my private life, my art was always pure. I could have made millions – *millions.* Every other week I was offered something by someone. I took drugs, I shagged lots of girls, but they all knew what they were doing, I was doing everything, but I wasn't doing anything to anyone who didn't want it.'

A pigeon fluttered outside the window and landed on the ledge outside. It looked through the window pane with that permanent expression of round-eyed shock that pigeons tend to have.

'Each person's morality boils down to what they can live with, doesn't it?' Tristan sighed. 'I couldn't do gay film reviews. You probably wouldn't have a problem getting paid to advertise some tacky product on the TV."

This was true, and Declan could live with that. 'I guess I'm not an artist,' he said.

'*I* could never do that without feeling inauthentic, Dec. I hate the commercial world like some people hate drugs. I think the commercial world is destroying our culture more; it's the reason why people like me take so many drugs in the first place. All I was doing was destroying me. That was all I was trying to do, because I hated the world and I hated myself.'

Tristan's eyes were like two blue pools of lacquer. In all the months they lived together Declan had never noticed how blue his eyes were. They were blue with hatred for Declan. He hated himself, no doubt, but at that moment he hated Declan more and Declan could understand why. He had never been a friend. He had never respected Tristan.

'You know the irony?' Tristan said as a buzzer sounded somewhere like the end of a game show. 'I was the only one in that house living authentically. What you saw was what you got, the rest of you were all playing games and acting.'

He nodded his head and looked gravely into Declan's eyes, as if his words represented the most profound human insight since Pythagoras square rooted a number.

43

Juliet and Declan arranged to meet the next day at Random Bar in Shoreditch. When Declan arrived he saw Juliet smoking a cigarette and drinking soda water at a table near the bar. She hardly looked a day older.

How do women do that?

They kissed each other on either cheek and Declan sat down and ordered a beer. Bread had already been served and it lay on the table in a small wicker basket. Juliet broke some bread and ate it. She told Declan to order some food before her meal came out. Declan glanced at the menu and ordered some pasta. When the waiter left, Juliet complained that Declan had not taken more time to order something he wanted.

'My taste buds have never been fussy,' Declan said. 'You look great, by the way – out of the pharmaceutical game and looking ten years younger.'

Juliet winked and smiled, 'Recreational drugs don't suit motherhood. I don't even drink any more.'

In the first flurry of emails they had sent to each other, they had divulged most of the key details about their new lives; their jobs, their respective partners and children, so a lot of the conversation was simply repeating those same details. For the first half an hour they discussed their children, the standard joys and fears and affections that middle-class parents discuss when they first meet: literacy and other developmental issues, emotional intelligence, socialising and, of course, some cute anecdotes detailing their kids' behaviour.

'I can't believe we both ended up all right,' Juliet said. 'And you, a bloody teacher.'

'Can you believe it?' Declan laughed. 'How could anyone give me the responsibility of educating young adults? I'm in a small room full of teenage girls and I'm not even scared. None of them have any idea about my past, of course.'

'They're not the only ones,' Juliet smiled. 'We never knew much. You were always a mystery. When Bridget first told me about you she said you were emotionally retarded, that you had brain damage and you had lost the ability to feel anything. "We'll never fight with him", she said.'

'I think I was just scared. I wanted to feel but I was scared where my feelings might take me. After my brain injury I was devastated. I felt my life was over. So I took drugs just to feel *something*, however artificial and fleeting. Besides, everyone in that house was emotionally retarded. Even you.'

'Especially me,' Juliet conceded. 'So what do you teach?'

'Art,' Declan said.

'*Art*?' Juliet repeated, 'I thought you couldn't paint any more?'

'I thought I couldn't either. I do paint a bit now, just for pleasure, for myself, and the teaching's fun too.'

Juliet ate some more bread. Her eyes narrowed slightly, she smiled and Declan knew who she was. All of the old memories had lined up and he was right there beside her, happy and relieved that the memories were already eight years old.

'I used to regret so many things Juliet: why didn't I do this? Why did I do that? My whole adult life, I felt like I was carrying a sack of stones everywhere. But now, today, I don't have any regrets. I let go of the past.'

'When I heard you'd run off to Poland with some girl, I thought you were nuts.'

'It was probably the sanest choice I've ever made.'

'So you're still in love then?'

'God yes.' Declan shook his head. He knew the words that could accurately translate the depth of his feeling did not exist.

'You know Susan came and visited me last summer?'

'Yes, she told me.' Declan waited a moment. 'Of course I didn't know.'

'Ugh! It always was impossible to tell when you were lying.'

'*Me?*'

'Yes. You practised all the time, just like that. All the time you'd monologue these shocking lies, jokes to fool people for an instant, to scare them, mostly. I think you wanted us all to know that you could fool every one of us whenever you wanted to.'

'So how is Susan?'

'She's twenty-two, can you believe that? Finished university, went and worked in Berlin as a translator, then took off on some Yoga mission in India, lived on an ashram or something and now she's all "boom-shanka" New Age "come-join-us-little-one" yogastastic.'

'I did Buddhist chanting for a while after I left the flat. It changed my life. I think it gave me the courage to leave London.'

'Well,' Juliet said, 'Susan speaks very quietly now, very slowly, as if she's reading Sanskrit from the sky with diamonds, and if wrapping your legs around your neck counts as good, well, she's fine.' Juliet smiled warmly and changed her tone, 'God I love that girl, she's amazing.'

'Twenty-two?'

'She's all grown up. My little baby girl,' Juliet laughed. 'Look at us now; you, me, David: all married with kids and living stable middle-class, tofu lives. God, we were all so self-centred and … lost … back then. The funny thing is I miss it, too. It was fun, wasn't it, being so totally fucked up?'

'I don't think about it any more.'

'Never?'

'No.'

'Jesus, that sounds a bit ruthless coming from you.'

'But it's not. I like myself now. It's funny, the closest thing I've got to a social life these days is watching the *Guardian*'s "Over-By-Over" report during an Ashes series.'

Juliet's brow creased up.

'The *Guardian* posts live cricket updates online, but readers write in too, and their comments get posted. They even made a book out of the comments in 2005.'

'That's sad, Declan.'

Declan smiled. 'I know. Who else is coming to the wedding? Is Bridget coming?'

Juliet choked on her soda and slammed the glass down on the table with such force Declan thought it might shatter.

'Bridget? Are you kidding me?'

'I don't know, water under the Bridge. Where is she now?'

'She disappeared. Maybe she moved to Nepal or something. You do know she was fucking Tristan the whole time he was living with us?'

Declan shook his head and released a *pffft* sound. 'She was hardly his type. She was about three hundred years too old.'

'She was a very persuasive woman. That night on the balcony, Drake was trying to tell Vivian about it all.' Juliet paused so that Declan could digest all of this.

'So ... ' Declan waited until the question formed properly in his mind. 'So did someone push Drake off the balcony then?'

A waiter brought a glass of beer and Declan moved to pay, but Juliet said she was running up a tab. She looked at Declan with an expression that seemed to betray a sentimental sincerity.

'Of course he wasn't pushed. There was an argument, that's all. He staggered back and fell from the balcony all by himself. Drake never needed any encouragement from anyone to fuck things up.'

Declan didn't know whether to believe Juliet at first, then he realised she had nothing and no one to lie for any more.

'Did Vivian ever find out?' Declan asked. 'About Bridget and Tristan?'

'She already knew. Everybody knew.'

Declan sipped his beer and shook his head in disbelief. This news was more than a surprise, it was great disappointment.

'Nobody told me anything then. I thought everyone talked to me.'

'They only talked bullshit to you.'

'What do you mean?'

'You were the one who listened to people's bullshit. People could say anything to you and you never judged them, or criticised them, or made them feel bad about themselves. You seemed to accept anything anyone said as if it were the gospel truth. That's why you could never be trusted with the truth.'

'Are you kidding?'

'If you knew the truth you wouldn't let people forget it, like me with Susan.'

Declan sipped some more beer and looked enviously at Juliet's cigarette.

'Do you want one?' she asked.

He shook his head. 'No, no, I gave up years ago.'

Juliet smiled and shook the open pack in his direction so one cigarette fell out half way. Declan took it, lit it, and blew the smoke out the side of his mouth and smiled. He was happy.

'I don't know you at all,' he said. 'Do I?'

Index of Related Paintings

Certain images are discussed or mentioned in particular chapters. If readers wish to search for these images, they are listed below.

CHAPTER ONE
Jacques-Louis David, *The Death of Socrates*, 1787, Metropolitan Museum of Art, New York, USA

CHAPTER FIVE
Mark Rothko, *No. 61 (Rust and Blue)*, 1953, Museum of Contemporary Art, Los Angeles, USA

CHAPTER SEVEN
Laocoön and His Sons, 200 BC, Vatican Museums, Rome, Italy

CHAPTER NINE
Pompeii Lovers, 79 AD, from the 'A Day in Pompeii' exhibition

CHAPTER TEN
Hieronymus Bosch, *The Garden of Earthly Delights (or The Millennium)*, *c.*1503, Museo del Prado, Madrid, Spain

CHAPTER ELEVEN
William Blake, *The Garden of Love*, 1789, Tate Britain, London, England

CHAPTER TWELVE
Artemisia Gentileschi, *Judith Slaying Holofernes*, 1612–13, Museo di Capodimonte, Naples, Italy

CHAPTER FIFTEEN
Raphael, *Madonna and Child*, *c.*1503, Norton Simon Museum of Art, Pasadena, USA

CHAPTER 17
Cornelia Parker, *Cold Dark Matter: An Exploded View*, 1991, Tate Modern, London, England

CHAPTER 18
Damien Hirst, *Pharmacy*, 1992, Tate Modern, London, England

CHAPTER 19
Domenico Ghirlandaio, *Old Man with a Young Boy*, *c.*1490, Louvre, Paris, France

CHAPTER 22
Pablo Picasso, *Child with a Dove*, 1901, National Gallery, London, England

CHAPTER 26
Pieter Bruegel, *Landscape with the Fall of Icarus*, *c.*1558, Musées Royaux des Beaux-Arts de Belgique, Brussels

CHAPTER 27
Gian Lorenzo Bernini, *Apollo and Daphne*, 1621–3, Borghese Gallery, Rome, Italy

CHAPTER 30
Raphael, *Deposition*, 1507, Borghese Gallery, Rome, Italy

CHAPTER 32
Paolo Uccello, *The Battle of San Romano*, 1438–40, National Gallery, London, England

CHAPTER 40
Diego Rodriguez de Silva y Velázquez, *Venus at her Mirror (Rokeby Venus),* 1649–51, National Gallery, London, England

CHAPTER 43
Michelangelo Merisi da Caravaggio, *The Supper at Emmaus*, 1601, National Gallery, London, England